Luke Swanson

Curtains On
A Christmas Carol

Black Rose Writing | Texas

ISBN: 978-1-68513-330-6
PUBLISHED BY BLACK ROSE WRITING
www.blackrosewriting.com

Printed in the United States of America
Suggested Retail Price (SRP) $23.95

Curtains on A Christmas Carol is printed in Book Antiqua

*As a planet-friendly publisher, Black Rose Writing does its best to eliminate unnecessary waste to reduce paper usage and energy costs, while never compromising the reading experience. As a result, the final word count vs. page count may not meet common expectations.

Praise for
Curtains On
A Christmas Carol

"*The Muppet Christmas Carol* meets *Clue*. A beautifully wrapped holiday present for theatre kids and cozy mystery lovers alike."

  —B.A. McRae, author of *The World Ends Christmas Day* and *I've Never Danced*

"What a charming, delightful little book. I love how it's a tribute to the multitudes of theatre folks who work on professional and community productions alike year after year. The small-town setting radiates pure warmth. And it's a fun murder mystery?! I was sold from the beginning."

 —Michael Baron, director of *A Christmas Carol* at Ford's Theatre

"The well-drawn characters and intriguing mystery are both clever and delightful. *Curtains on A Christmas Carol* is a new classic that should be pulled off the shelf and enjoyed every December."

  —Mary Ellen Bramwell, author of *The Apple of My Eye*

"A love letter to theatre, Christmas, and Agatha Christie all wrapped in one."

   —Timothy Gene Sojka, author of *Payback Jack*

The City of Tennant Park proudly presents

The 35th Annual Production of

A Christmas Carol

From the Novel by Charles Dickens

Directed by Simeon Callahan

Cast Bios:

PERCIVAL JENNINGS (Scrooge) has been a part of Tennant Park's *Christmas Carol* for its entire thirty-five-year tradition, and he is honored that audiences have returned to see him time and time again. He previously appeared as Man #3 in the 1986 production of *Our Town*.

JAMES QUINN (Bob Cratchit) is thankful that the theatre has accepted him to be in the show once again! Though his experience is limited, he always enjoys his time as Bob Cratchit. Jimmy enjoys powerlifting, participating in triathlons, and crocheting. His most notable accomplishment was when he and his wife tried out for *American Ninja Warrior* together.

VICTOR STASSI (Fred / Ghost of Christmas Past) was last seen onstage as Raymond Butler in *The Butler Did It*. His previous credits include Inspector Williams in *Heaven Can Wait*, Director in *Last Dress Rehearsal*, and the self-created role of Jeff in *Hamlet (and Jeff)*. Victor is one of the most sought-after attorneys in the county, which keeps him quite busy, but he's never too busy to participate in the theatre.

TEENA FAKHOURY (Ghost of Christmas Present) has been in the ensemble of *A Christmas Carol* for 6 years, and she's excited to take the role of her favorite ghost this year! Teena has loved theatre for most of her life, and the idea of contributing to a performance in a significant way means the world to her. She is a teacher at Tennant Park Middle School and loves getting to know her students. If any are here tonight, be sure to say hi after the show!

DON SCHRADER (Ghost of Christmas Yet to Come / ensemble) is playing the Ghost of Christmas Yet to Come. <insert more later>

ROY JENNINGS (Marley's Ghost) is making his stage debut this year! The last time he spoke in front of a large group of people was when he gave an eighth-grade book report 60 years ago. He hopes he gets an A+ this time! He would like to thank his brother Percival for putting up with him for the last year.

EVELYN BARRIE (Mrs. Cratchit) is a 13-year veteran of this show, having brought Mrs. Cratchit to life for more than a decade! She has also directed, produced, written, and starred in the Tennant Park First Baptist Church's Christmas program for the past 10 years. She would like to thank her husband and 7 children for all their support.

MARKUS DANIELS (Young Scrooge / ensemble) is a senior at Tennant Park High School. He is proud to serve as president of the biology club, editor of the yearbook, and first-chair clarinet. This is his third year in *A Christmas Carol*, but his first speaking role. He's ready to make the most of it before heading off to college next year.

CORRINE TALLY (Belle / ensemble) is making her seventh appearance in *A Christmas Carol*, her first as Belle. She is a gym teacher at TPMS, and if any of her students are here tonight, forget you saw her. Or else. (Director's Note: She's kidding, I promise.)

COLTON MCCOWDREY (Tiny Tim Cratchit / ensemble) is already a budding young thespian. Some of the productions he has been a part of include *Willy Wonka and the Chocolate Factory, Velveteen Rabbit,* and *Fairy Tale Time.* He also appeared on a segment of the local news talking about the new baby otters at the zoo. Besides acting, Colton is involved in soccer and baseball and is learning the piano. He would like to thank his mom for writing his bio for him.

ANDY NGUYEN (Peter Cratchit / ensemble) is an eighth-grader who likes to play basketball, read, and walk around in the trees next to his house. He doesn't know what else to write here, so he'll write "pickles" to see if whoever makes these programs will really just put whatever he writes. Pickles.

HALEY SCHRADER (Belinda Cratchit / ensemble) is proud to make her onstage debut in this year's fantastic production of *A Christmas Carol.* Haley is in the eighth grade at Tennant Park Middle School, and she's already making a splash in the world of theatre. Her training consists of voice and musical theatre performance at Globe Academy, voice at CU Boulder's Performing Arts Academy, ballet and jazz at Tiana Dunnel's School of Dance, and acting at STAR Academy. She would like to thank her dad for driving her to all her practices and lessons, as well as God for her wonderful talent.

cont. -->

Curtains On
A Christmas Carol

Act 1:
Set Dressing

1.

Church bells rang as if announcing Christ's second coming. Pigeons cooed and flapped their wings in tandem. Carolers of all ages and statures stood along the cobblestoned streets, smiles stretching across their faces as they filled the air with their joyous notes.

"We wish you a merry Christmas, and a happy new year! Glad tidings we bring, to you and your kin…"

Townsfolk began to emerge from their homes and businesses. They smiled, laughed, and embraced one another. Moment by moment, the city awoke from its chilly slumber. Children ran to and fro, bakers distributed their goods, and lamplighters snuffed out the flaming posts. All the while, more and more pedestrians joined in with the carolers. The song grew louder, fuller, and bolder.

"And a happy new year! Oh bring us some figgy pudding…"

It was a festive Christmas morn indeed.

A large family rounded the corner and approached the carolers. There was a man and wife, both walking with all the boisterous cheer that the season provided. They beamed at one another, then at their many children. Two daughters walked arm in arm, while a boy ushered along two more younger siblings. In the center of this group was an elderly gentleman, wearing a nightgown. Stringy hair dangled from underneath his sleeping cap, and his wrinkles were deep enough to gather dust. But he walked with the vigor of a schoolboy, and he even carried a child on his shoulder. This boy was small, though his smile could be seen from the other side of town.

The family stopped in front of the carolers and basked in the music. The old man dropped a few coins in the singers' donation dish.

And at that moment, snow began to drift from the sky. Large white flakes dotted the pedestrians' coats and shawls. The children gazed upward in wonder, as did the adults. No one was immune from the magical feeling that only a Christmas snowfall could give.

The small boy on the man's shoulder looked around at his family. It was a truly perfect tableau, a storybook ending. Through his dazzling smile, he said, "God bless us."

The elderly man nodded. He addressed the entire city when he said, "God bless us, every—"

SPLAT.

"Crap on a cracker!"

The old man retched and recoiled suddenly, nearly dropping the little boy. The father and mother rushed to catch him before his small frame hit the ground. The man didn't notice—he just blustered around and shouted at no one in particular: "Dangshootcrapdarndangit!"

The father rolled his eyes. "What, Al? What happened?"

"One of the pigeons defecated on me!"

The children giggled, which the old man did not take well. The father leaned in to look at the old man's shoulder, and… Sure enough. One of the white globs on the nightgown was *not* a snowflake.

A voice called from outside the scene. "Okay, okay, okay. Let's reconvene, alright, guys?"

Just like that, the quaint Christmas tableau evaporated. Left in its place was a stage full of actors on a homemade set. The businesses and homes were plywood. The cobblestones were painted on. The London cityscape was a backdrop. The snowflakes were torn shreds of plastic that would be swept up at the end of the night and re-used tomorrow.

And, of course, the merry pedestrians and citizenry were really just cashiers, real estate agents, middle school students, stay-at-home moms, dads roped into this sort of thing, and other local stars-to-be. In short: community theatre actors.

Rehearsals for Tennant Park's thirty-fifth annual production of *A Christmas Carol* were well underway.

Without the momentum of the scene, things started to get chaotic onstage. The actors dropped their roles and started chatting with one another and tugging at their costumes. The "professional bird wranglers" — AKA the few stagehands who had been assigned that position — trotted out from backstage to try to coax the half-dozen-or-so pigeons into their cages. The elementary-aged actors let loose entirely, running around, playing tag, and cackling at the dripping doo-doo on the old man's gown.

Teena Fakhoury watched all this from her place among the ensemble. This sort of entropy happened every time a scene stopped, for any reason. It was like spinning plates on top of long poles — the slightest jolt could cause it all to come crashing down. Often, spinning through any wobbles was the best course of action.

"Come on, people!" The play's director, Simeon Callahan, scampered between the rows of empty seats, headed for the stage. He always watched rehearsals from the back of the theatre, armed with a clipboard and a headlamp so he could take notes in the dark. Most of the cast made fun of his silly headgear. He, of course, did not know that.

Corrine Tally, Teena's best friend, leaned over to whisper to her. "Hi-ho, hi-ho, here comes the miner." She snickered.

Teena exhaled sharply through her nose and sort of smiled at Corrine's joke, hoping it was convincing. She avoided making fun of people whenever possible. As a plus-sized woman with dark skin, she knew how much it hurt. But she also wanted Corrine to feel funny.

"Listen up, please!" Simeon had made it to the stage and was waving his arms to get everyone's attention…to no avail. No one paid him any mind. In fact, they got slightly louder.

The cast of the show could be divided into two camps: those who didn't take it very seriously, and those who took it *way* too seriously. Those two camps went to war, lobbing grenades of "Shut up!" and "No, *you* shut up!" at one another.

"Ahem!" Simeon literally said the word 'ahem.' "Everyone listen, please!"

After lots of shushing and cajoling, the stage quieted down person by person.

"Ah! Thank you." Simeon looked around at the actors on the stage. "Now, I know we—"

Someone called out, "Could you cut the flashlight? You're blinding us."

"Huh?" Simeon looked confused, then remembered the light strapped to his forehead. "Ah, yes." He clicked off the headlamp. "Okay then. We know what happens next, yeah? The scene ends, we do the curtain call, and you all wait in the green room for exactly five minutes. Right? Then you all file into the lobby to take photos with the patrons and sign autographs. Mmkay? And then you can enjoy some of the complimentary hot cocoa. Make sense?"

A few actors nodded in affirmation.

Simeon sucked on his front teeth as he consulted his clipboard, then he continued. "Now. I think we all know where that last scene went wrong."

"Obviously we know what went wrong," Percival Jennings, the elderly man playing Scrooge, growled. "Why do we need birds this year? I've been in more productions of this show than I can count—thirty-four!—and we've never felt the need for fancy gimmicks like live animals."

Simeon flashed a strained smile. "Like I've been emphasizing to everyone this year…including you, Percival…this is year thirty-five! A great milestone for our town!"

About half of the actors onstage sighed and shuffled their feet. They'd heard this spiel so many times, they could almost recite it.

Undeterred or unaware, Simeon speechified on. "When our curtains open at the end of the week, *A Christmas Carol* will have been performed in this theatre for three-and-a-half consecutive decades. Thirty-five years! And I am honored to be only the second director to have ever helmed this show. Every day, I wake up and remember how lucky I am to be here, doing this, with you all."

He paused, as if for a swell of applause. No one obliged, except for the preteen girl playing Belinda Cratchit. She clapped and whooped once, likely looking for brownie points with the director more than anything else.

"Hey, Simeon," one of the stagehands called out from behind the backdrop. "Can we start resetting?"

"Uhh…" Simeon checked his watch. "Yes, go on ahead."

Immediately, five stagehands in black t-shirts began rearranging the set, getting things back in order. High above the stage, ropes creaked and strained as backdrops were raised. Heavy sandbags acting as counterweights plummeted like fallen stars. Curtains swooped in from the wings, meeting in the middle and hiding the Dickensian scenery…and forcing the cast to hurry to the front of the stage to get out of the way. Clangs, scrapes, clanks, and bangs filled the air. The stagehands clearly wanted to get out of there as quickly as possible.

As a first-time director, Simeon sought to pull out all the stops for the finale. He wanted the audience to leave on a high note, feeling as though they had witnessed something truly spectacular. Hence the live pigeons, falling snow, and onstage carolers. But with great reward comes great risk. Hence the bird droppings.

"Okay. So." Simeon clicked on his headlamp and consulted his clipboard. He began to half-yell over the noise. "I have just a few teensy-weensy notes."

More sighs and shuffling from half of the group. More overly-enthusiastic claps from the other.

***

Teena walked out of the green room, slinging her bag over her shoulder. Her face was stiff and kind of itchy from all the stage makeup, but at least she was out of her elaborate robe. While it was pretty comfortable, it took forever to put on and take off, and she was always glad to hang it up in the green room at the end of each rehearsal. Some of the actors took selfies while in their costumes and even wanted to buy them to keep, but Teena was just fine leaving her character on the stage.

Since she played the Ghost of Christmas Present, her costume consisted of a crown of holly and a velvet green robe with white trim. She and the other spirits got to wear some interesting costumes, while everyone else was trapped in bonnets, corsets, and impossibly uncomfortable shoes. She had no idea how people stayed sane wearing all those Elizabethan clothes. Or was it

Victorian? She could never remember — she taught biology, not history or literature.

Corrine was waiting for her in the hallway outside the green room, also in her normal clothes. "Hey. Let's get out of here before we have to make pointless small talk with Bernie."

"Um. Yeah, definitely." Again, Teena forced a smile and an airy laugh. She didn't really mind chatting with Bernie, who was the theatre's usher/box office manager/security/sometimes-custodian. He was nice. But she didn't want to ruffle Corrine's feathers, so she went along with it.

Teena and Corrine exited the theatre's front door, and they were smacked in the face by Colorado winter. Corrine shoved her hands in her pockets and walked briskly across the parking lot. Teena had to scurry to keep up.

"Good grief," Corrine hissed. "Lemme tell you, tonight, I'm getting some hot apple cider and going into the bath for a few hours."

Teena laughed — genuinely this time. "Sweetie, it's already ten p.m."

"And? It's winter break for us too."

A mass exodus was underway as the actors all moved across the parking lot toward their cars. There went Evelyn Barrie, getting into a minivan that usually carted her brood of children to church on Sunday. The insanely muscular Jimmy Quinn lowered himself into a compact smartcar that looked like it weighed half as much as he did.

Various ensemble members and stagehands dispersed, once part of a whole, now scattering back to their real lives.

As usual, the two elderly Jennings brothers went to separate vehicles. Teena always found that odd, since it was common knowledge that they lived together. Percival, who played Ebenezer Scrooge, got into a boxy, vintage car that looked extraordinarily expensive. Roy Jennings, the younger of the two, headed for a nondescript sedan. Roy played the ghost of Jacob Marley, so he always left rehearsals with his face painted white with black rings around his eyes.

Simeon the director was at the back of the pack, wandering around the parking lot, clicking his key fob again and again. He seemed to have forgotten where he'd parked…which was weird, since only a few cars were left. Finally, a purple sedan beeped and flashed its lights as it unlocked. Simeon scampered through the cold, got in his car, and fired up the engine. It slowly rolled away, down the road, and out of sight.

Teena and Corrine passed a cluster of younger actors who were waiting for their parents to pick them up. The kids had found a patch of ice on the concrete, and a few were taking turns sliding across. More than a few phones recorded the action.

One of the younger teens caught sight of the two women: It was Andy Nguyen, who played a

Cratchit boy. He swept his arm over his head in a big wave. "See you tomorrow, Miss F!" The rest of the kids turned and, seeing Teena, called good-bye to her. This was enough of a distraction for an ice-surfing guy to slip and land on his keister. A fall like that would've put Teena out of commission until opening night, but he just laughed it off.

Teena chuckled and waved back at the kids.

Corrine muttered, "I'm here too. No love for the gym teacher, I guess."

"Wanna get breakfast for lunch tomorrow?" Teena tried to steer Corrine back to a conversation that would put her in a good mood.

"Ooh, sounds nice. We could do the twenty-four-hour place on Main Street. And then we could do a movie."

"I have rehearsal tomorrow night. We're running through the Cratchit scene of the Christmas Present section a few times."

Corrine clicked her tongue. "Bummer."

Teena rushed to offer a solution. "We could do a movie before lunch?"

"Nah, too early. I'm sleeping in and no one can stop me. It's okay. This stinkin' play just takes up so much of our winter break each year."

Teena somewhat agreed. *A Christmas Carol* did, in fact, dominate Tennant Park's winter season, and it got stressful teaching during the day and working on the show at night. But she loved it all.

She had moved from Detroit to Tennant Park, Colorado, seven years ago and gotten a job at the middle school, teaching eighth grade biology. On her first day, she'd stood in front of a sea of glassy-eyed teenagers and written her name on the whiteboard: "Ms. Fakhoury." No matter how many times she'd enunciated it for her students, no one had been able to nail it. So, finally, she'd wiped her hand across most of the letters and shortened it to "Miss F." Easy enough.

On her second day, she'd met Coach Corrine, one of the gym teachers, and they'd become fast friends. Corrine had a big heart and truly loved kids, but her social capacity was extremely small. She could only take so much *people* at a time. During her first period gym class, she was the nicest, most encouraging mentor imaginable. By the end of the day, she could make a drill sergeant wet his pants.

But she never seemed to tire of Teena's company. They had lunch in the teachers' lounge every day, went to the movies on the weekend, and tried different hobbies together.

"I swear," Corrine said, "I'm not doing this next year."

"You said that last year."

"Well, I mean it now. Rehearsals start while school's still in session, then cut into our winter break. Performances run for a weekend right in the middle of the break… Geez Louise, why do I do this?"

They reached their side-by-side cars. Teena pulled her car keys from her pocket and hit the unlock button. Her sedan beeped and flashed. "Don't pretend you don't like it, Coach. You don't do something for seven years without loving it a little."

"I… I mean…" Corrine shrugged and leaned against her own car. "It's not… I mean, you know."

"I do know." Teena smiled. "Rehearsals can suck. They're stressful and annoying and long. But performing the actual show… You get that feeling in your stomach. Sort of a thrill, sort of contentment. I can't really describe it. Like you're doing something beyond yourself. It's something else."

Corrine couldn't argue. She smiled pensively.

"Besides," Teena said, "during my first winter after I moved here, *you're* the one who suggested we both audition. You said it'd be fun to hang out together outside of school."

"Oh yeah." Corrine squinted at the memory. "Can only blame myself, I guess."

They both laughed, creating big puffs of mist in the cold air.

"Okay, Miss F.," Corrine said, unlocking her own car. "I'll see ya."

"Be safe driving down Mountain. And enjoy your cider and bath."

"I always am. And I definitely will!"

With that, Corrine slid into her car, cranked the engine, and rolled out of the parking lot. Teena watched the taillights turn down the road, then took a deep breath through her nose. She loved the feeling of frigid air, the way it scraped against the inside of her skull like sandpaper. It had been cold in Detroit too, and that was how she liked it. When Corrine complained about the bitter weather, Teena went along with it, but now that she was alone, she didn't mind lingering outside.

She sat on the edge of her sedan's hood and looked around. Perhaps the locals who'd lived here all their lives were simply desensitized to it, but she was always taken aback by the beauty of Tennant Park's theatre.

Well, not the building itself. The leaning pile of brick and mortar was hardly remarkable. Its windows were cloudy, the sidewalks and concrete steps were cracked, and the roof was going bald shingle by shingle. The equipment inside was nothing to write home about either. The seats in the auditorium were seemingly stolen from a passenger jet from the '70s, and the air conditioning was distractingly loud. The lights and toilets worked, but only most of the time.

But *where* it was. That was special.

On the northern edge of Tennant Park, a small mountain kept watch over the town. It wasn't monstrous or intimidating. It didn't block the sun or cast a looming shadow. It was comforting, like an older sibling. Its official name, according to the atlas, was Mt. Tennant, from which the town got its name, but residents simply called it "Mountain."

The town's community theatre rested snugly at the top of Mountain. Lush coniferous trees surrounded the building, as if the construction had happened centuries ago and a forest had grown around it. The whole area smelled of pine and fresh air, and pinecones and needles constantly dotted the parking lot.

For the holiday season, the theatre's staff—AKA Bernie—had hung white lights and ornaments from many tree branches. Tinsel wrapped around the trunks like candy canes. Standing there, breathing the deliciously cold air and basking in the décor, Teena wouldn't have been surprised if it started snowing, just like at the end of the show. It was a winter wonderland.

Only a single road led to the theatre, weaving back and forth up Mountain like a loose thread dangling from a sweater. Trees and boulders lined the road, and whenever Teena drove up or down it, she felt like she was going on a journey.

Having grown up in Detroit, she'd been constantly surrounded by noise and concrete. But on top of Mountain, she was transported into a fairy tale.

She peered through the trees and caught sight of the twinkling lights far below. The town sported

Christmas decorations of its own. From the top of Mountain, Tennant Park looked like a toy set Santa would have in his workshop. Tiny cars, tiny roads, tiny houses, tiny people. And tiny lights of red, green, and white.

Tennant Park didn't have state-champion sports teams or celebrity citizens. It didn't have huge concert venues, casinos, or a national park. It had this theatre, and this theatre had *A Christmas Carol*.

Every year, an influx of people from neighboring towns came into Tennant Park to see the show: school trips, retirement homes, and church groups, not to mention families. Lots and lots of families. *A Christmas Carol* gave the local economy a healthy boost each and every year.

But it was more than that.

It was the hot cocoa that Bernie passed out to patrons after the show.

It was the wreaths and garlands strung throughout the lobby.

It was the way the lights seemed to glow brighter in the cold December air.

Standing in the parking lot, Teena knew. It was magical. Now, she would never say that out loud. Especially not to Corrine, who would laugh her into oblivion. But this centuries-old story performed in a rickety theatre on top of a smaller-than-would-usually-be-considered-impressive mountain was special.

Teena loved being a part of *A Christmas Carol*. She took one final pull of night air, enough to make her lungs shrivel even as they expanded, then finally slid into her car. As she drove down Mountain's winding road, she took it slower than she needed to.

Admiring the trees in the moonlight.

Watching the town's lights get closer and closer.

Feeling as though she was turning from a human into a figurine, then taking her place in the toy set that was Tennant Park.

2.

The next day, Teena and Corrine met at Crawful o' Waffles, the all-day breakfast joint on Main Street. It was always open twenty-four hours a day, which made it a popular spot for post-rehearsal hangouts and late-night snacks. The place was decked with festive décor, from lights and ornaments to cotton-snow and paper-cut flakes. Mariah Carey played in the background. The bell over the door chimed as they entered, and they continued the conversation they'd started outside.

"*Die Hard* is definitely a Christmas movie," Teena said with more conviction than she'd ever felt in her life.

Corrine was aghast. "No. No way!"

Teena was prepared to meet this challenge. "It has Christmas music, Christmas decorations, a Christmas party. At the end, Christmas wrapping even saves the day!"

They both waved at the hostess, who gestured that they could sit wherever they wanted. They chose a booth, sat, and ignored the waiting menus. They'd been before and knew what they wanted.

Corrine continued. "That doesn't mean it's a Christmas movie."

"Huh? Of course it does."

"Not necessarily." Corrine shrugged as she looked down at the table.

Teena knew she had her on the ropes. She pressed, "Then what defines a Christmas movie?"

"It can't just be set at Christmas. It has to be, I dunno, *about* Christmas."

Teena grinned slyly. "Okay then. So be it." She had a trump card she'd been waiting to play her entire life.

Corrine looked at her in fear. "I don't like that smile."

"If *Die Hard* isn't a Christmas movie..." Teena paused for dramatic effect. "...then neither is *It's a Wonderful Life*."

Corrine gaped in shock, as well as a little disgust. "What! How dare you."

"*It's a Wonderful Life* has nothing to do with Christmas until the last third, and even then, it's all just setting. Sure, there's a tree, and people say 'Merry Christmas,' but I wouldn't say it's *about* Christmas. It's more about angels and banking than Christmas!"

Corrine was speechless. Her mouth moved up and down as if she wanted to argue, but her eyes flicked back and forth as she thought through the movie, and she had nothing to say.

Teena came in with the knock-out punch. "And what song do they all sing at the end? Not 'Joy to the World' or 'Deck the Halls.' It's that weird New Year's song no one likes."

Corrine sat for a moment, shellshocked. Then her face lit up in a big smile as she cackled. Her laugh petered into a long sigh, and she said, "Well I'll be. I guess so. I concede."

Teena pulled back her shoulders, feeling quite proud of herself.

"You aren't usually so argumentative like that," Corrine said, still smiling.

But Teena deflated as a pit formed in her stomach. She'd forgotten herself—she hadn't been accommodating. She shrunk into the booth seat.

"No no no!" Corrine held out her hands. "It was fun! We should debate stuff more often."

Their server approached, carrying two cups of water. He appeared to be the only server in the restaurant. "Morning, Coach Tally, Miss F.!" He set the waters down and checked his watch. "Or afternoon, I guess." He wore a syrup-stained apron and a permanent grin. Teena had literally never seen him without that shiny smile affixed to his face—she halfway believed his muscles were physically locked in that position.

Teena beamed up at him. "Hey, Markus!"

Corrine shot finger-guns at him. "There he is, my favorite Scrooge."

"I'm honored." Markus dipped his head.

"Eh," Corrine continued, "don't be. The competition is nada."

Markus smiled as he took out his notepad. "No comment. What sounds good for you two?"

Teena ordered a scramble with ham and cheese, and Corrine got the waffles. Markus jotted down the orders then began to walk away, but he lingered.

"Hey, Miss F…"

Teena waved off the name. "Please. I'm Teena to you now."

He shook his head. "I don't think that'll ever happen. I was going to tell you next time I saw you at rehearsal. But I settled on my major for when I apply to college."

Teena widened her eyes. "Biology?"

Markus spread his arms grandly. "That's the plan. And I'm gonna shoot for the stars: CU Boulder!"

Corrine whistled lowly. "Big school…"

Teena clapped in delight. "That's what I like to hear. Thank you for sharing!"

"No, thank *you*. Best teacher I ever had. Anyway." He tapped the notepad. "I'll get your orders going." He jogged away from their booth.

"Nice guy," Corrine said. "Wish I had him in gym class."

Teena nodded. Markus Daniels was playing young Ebenezer Scrooge in the Christmas Past section of the play, but he couldn't have been further from the type. He was polite, kind, and well-liked by pretty much everyone he met. He had been a student in Teena's eighth-grade biology class four years ago, and they'd gotten along well. Now that he was a senior in high school, she was going to be sad to see him leave Tennant Park, although she knew he had a bright future ahead.

Corrine went on: "It's so weird that I have to play his love interest, though."

"I…" Teena searched for a positive spin but found none. "I can't argue with you there."

No age-appropriate girls had auditioned for the role of Belle, the apple of young Scrooge's eye. So they had to settle for Corrine, the high school gym teacher. She and Markus only "courted" for a couple of scenes, and they didn't even touch each other. But still. It was awkward. Oh the joys of community theatre.

The restaurant was getting surprisingly full—the people of Tennant Park liked their breakfast-for-lunch. Markus had a lot of tables to serve, so Teena and Corrine wouldn't get their food for a while. But that was okay by Teena. She enjoyed the feel of the place and didn't mind basking in the ambiance.

Mariah Carey had transitioned to Andy Williams. The December breeze whistled by the windows, blowing leaves here and there. Eggs and sausages sizzled on the griddle. Coffee pots bubbled and sputtered. People jostled the decorative lights as they entered the restaurant, setting them swinging and twinkling. The bell above the door sounded festive every time someone entered.

"Ugh," Corrine groaned as she looked out the front window. "I had a feeling this jolly atmosphere wouldn't last long."

Teena craned her neck to see what Corrine was looking at. A vintage car had pulled into the joint's parking lot. Of course, she recognized it too.

Percival Jennings unfolded his frame from within the car and lumbered toward the entrance. Teena had to look closely to see if he was still in his Scrooge costume, but no—he simply wore a long black coat, shined shoes, and some sort of fancy cravat around his neck.

When he pulled open the door and entered, his presence made the whole room ripple. Even the bell chimed uncomfortably, as if stammering. He walked toward an empty table, looking out of place among all the Christmas décor: a thin, gray man with thin, gray hair and thin, gray eyes.

"Y'know," Corrine said in her quiet making-fun-of-people-while-they're-in-the-room voice, "he really deserves an Oscar. He's been method-acting as Scrooge for a long time. Being a jerk to everyone, living alone in a big empty house, being the richest D-bag in town…"

Teena didn't exactly want to defend Percival Jennings, but the sight of him sitting at a table by himself stirred her heart. "Well, it was only empty for a couple of days. And even you have to admit the whole situation was sad."

"Okay, yes." Corrine mock-surrendered. "It's sad his wife died last year."

"She died *on Christmas*. That makes it extra sad."

"*Fine*. Extra sad. But everyone's been walking on eggshells around him for the whole year. The truth is he's an arrogant jerk, and being old and rich doesn't give you a pass. Neither does being a widower."

Teena added, "I feel bad for his little brother Roy."

Corrine chortled. "*Little* is relative. They're both old as dirt."

"They always drive separately, even when going to rehearsal. Not very hospitable."

Roy Jennings was new in town. As far as Teena could tell, he was Percival's only living relative. He'd moved in with his older brother a few days after Percival's wife had passed the previous year. This season, seemingly on a whim, Roy had auditioned to be in *A Christmas Carol* and gotten the role of Marley's ghost. Teena liked to think it was to be closer to his brother. Corrine often said it was because he wanted to drive his brother crazy by desecrating the art of acting.

No one could deny that Roy was the worst actor in the cast. His line-reading was stilted and jerky, but the director Simeon said it was the perfect delivery for a ghost. Whether Simeon really believed this or was simply trying to make do with a bad actor was anyone's guess.

Corrine speculated, "I bet Percival doesn't want anyone other than himself in that fancy old car of his."

"Or," Teena shrugged, "they just don't want to argue more than they already do." Percival constantly derided his brother for his bad acting, and Roy responded by yelling about how everyone hated his guts—many a rehearsal had been sidetracked by a Jennings civil war. "It's a sad situation all around."

As Teena and Corrine watched Percival at his table, Markus approached with a water glass. Percival saw this, grunted, and looked around for another server. This act made Teena regret even her half-hearted defense of him a moment ago.

It was no secret that Percival disliked working with Markus in the play. But the reasoning was a mystery. Maybe it was general disdain from the elderly to the youthful. Perhaps it was jealousy, since they both played the same character at different ages and Percival didn't want to share the spotlight. Or maybe Percival was simply, in Corrine's words, a D-bag.

From her seat across the dining room, Teena couldn't hear what Percival said to Markus, but she could tell it wasn't warm and fuzzy. He spoke derisively to his young co-star, using every muscle in his face to sneer as deeply as possible. As always, Markus didn't give Percival the reaction he wanted. Instead of cowering or getting upset, Markus just smiled. He nodded like a good active listener, even as the old man no doubt insulted him.

After a minute or so, Percival gave up on trying to break Markus's smile…for the time being. He placed his order and waved Markus away. Teena gave her former student a small nod as he passed.

Corrine said to Teena, "If you had Jennings levels of money, what would you do?" She asked this question every so often, and she always had a funny answer for herself.

Teena set a fist under her chin in faux fascination. "You first. Do tell."

"It's a multitiered masterplan. First, I would buy up every football team in the country. All of them. Then I'd abolish the game altogether and start a campaign to rename 'soccer' as 'football,' the way it should be. I would then be named a saint for ridding the world of such a garbage sport."

Teena laughed. "I don't think even Percival has that much money."

"Not alone," Corrine said, tapping her temple. "But I said 'Jennings money.' That includes Roy. I bet with their stacks of cash combined, I could finally take out football once and for all."

"Roy doesn't seem as rich as Percival." Teena thought for a moment, then shrugged. "At least not as flashy."

"Whatever." Corrine beckoned for Teena to speak. "Okay, your turn."

"Ditto. The football thing." Teena smirked — she always seconded her friend's outlandish schemes when it came to this game.

Corrine rolled her eyes enough to see her own brain. "You're no fun. Humor me! Imagine you have Percival's bank account. For real, what would you do?"

Teena took a breath and thought it through. For the first time, she answered Corrine's silly question. "I would fund my classroom fully. Go nuts with labs and experiments for the kids. Take them on lots of field trips into the mountains and national parks."

She smiled and nodded to herself. That truly sounded wonderful to her.

Corrine did the same, acknowledging her friend's thoughtful answer…but after a few requisite moments, she re-donned her sarcastic persona. "*Psshhhh.* Of course you give the sweet, goodie-goodie answer and make me look bad."

"And then," Teena held up a finger, "Caribbean cruise. Scuba diving. Bottomless Mai Tai's."

Corrine clapped once. "*That's* what I like to hear!"

They both laughed.

"Wanna hear something else?" Corrine went on, "I was talking with Evelyn at rehearsal last night. She heard a rumor that he…" She paused, shot a glance at the old man, then lowered her voice further. "He didn't have to audition for Scrooge. He hasn't auditioned for a few years now."

Teena didn't like to peddle in rumors. But all the same, she leaned in, fascinated. "Shoot. Well, kinda makes sense. I guess that's what happens when you've played the same role for decades."

"What? No!" Corrine's voice shot up a few octaves and decibels. "I worked my tukus off to get out of the ensemble. I memorized a whole scene from *Streetcar*, and all I got was Belle."

"Belle's a good role!" Teena was trying to soothe her friend, but she also meant it.

"No one's dream role is Belle. Maybe in *Beauty and the Beast*, but not friggin' *Christmas Carol*. And Belle is only in two scenes, so I'm still stuck in the ensemble the rest of the time."

Teena nodded, because that's what Corrine wanted her to do, then offered some advice. "Well, it's all a stepladder. We've both been in the show seven years, and each year, it's like we climb a little bit higher, yeah? You can use Belle this year to get a role you want next year."

"Yeah." Corrine already looked more encouraged. "I just hate the politicky-ness of it all. But you're right." She chuckled as she realized something. "Hey, we both made it to characters with actual names this year."

"Progress!" They both laughed.

Auditions for this year's show had been more dramatic for Teena than expected. She had been in the production the past six years, spending four in the ensemble and two as Mrs. Fezziwig, who had neither a first name nor any lines. Over the years, Teena had tried to get the role of one of the spirits, but the stalwart director hadn't been open to the idea. Roger Marius was nearly ninety years old, and he had directed Tennant Park's *Christmas Carol* since its very beginning. He liked his plays traditional and his spirits male.

But last year, all of a sudden, Roger had retired and moved to Florida. According to the rumor mill, he'd left town to live out the rest of his life on the beach with a secret mistress. Teena doubted that was true, but if it was, she was mainly impressed he could pull a mistress at all.

The new director who had stepped in this year, Simeon Callahan, was younger and eager, especially since this was the show's thirty-fifth anniversary. He wanted to shake things up while simultaneously being stylish. So Teena had taken a chance and auditioned for the role of the Ghost of Christmas Present.

Simeon had loved it. By the end of the day, it was official: She'd gotten the part!

When Teena had told Corrine the news, her friend had scoffed. "Of course. They cast the plus-sized, *exotic* woman in the role usually played by a big, fat, bearded guy. That's ridiculous."

Teena had nodded quietly, not mentioning that she'd actually auditioned for the part of her own volition. As a little girl, the Ghost of Christmas Present had always been her favorite character in the Muppet version of the story.

As rehearsals went by, Corrine had stopped her grumbling after seeing that Teena fit the role perfectly and was having the time of her life.

Teena thought of something. She said, "How did Evelyn know Percival didn't have to audition for Scrooge?"

"Beats me." Corrine's gaze was, again, elsewhere. This time, she had the look of a wild beast about to pounce on her prey. That could only mean one thing…

Markus arrived at their booth with their dishes of glorious breakfast food. The aromas nearly knocked them both flat. His smile was a tad more stressed than it had been a few minutes earlier, but the combination of the lunch rush and an interaction with Percival Jennings will do that to a person. He said, "Enjoy!" and bustled away.

Teena and Corrine dove headfirst into their food without another word. The mark of true friendship, after all, is not forcing someone to chat while their waffles are getting cold.

In the background, Darlene Love began to sing about the snow coming down. It was perfect.

3.

"I see a vacant seat at the table, as well as a crutch without an owner, carefully preserved. If these shadows remain unchanged, the child will die."

Teena delivered the line with all the power she could muster. It was one of the show's most famous lines, and while she was supposed to be somber when saying it, she always felt a trill of excitement. When speaking as the Ghost of Christmas Present, she tried to sound enormous yet intimate, youthful yet wise. The ghost was a larger-than-life character, and she did her best to capture that feeling.

She stood onstage during that night's rehearsal, positioned on stage-right, next to Percival. The Cratchit home dominated the stage, featuring an oven, cabinets, a few beds, and a large dinner table. Six children and two adults sat at the table: the Cratchits themselves.

The Cratchits were dressed in ratty, stained clothes, some too big, some too small. Teena suspected this was mainly because the theatre couldn't afford to rent enough costumes that fit all the kids perfectly, but it worked for a family that was supposed to be dirt-poor. Percival wore Scrooge's iconic nightgown and cap—the same costume he had worn for eighteen consecutive years, or so he proudly announced at every opportunity. Teena wore her green robe with white trimming and the holly-wreath crown, and she carried a foam torch filled with sheets of colored paper that looked like flames.

After Teena's line, it was Percival's turn. He faced the audience and projected all the way to the back row. "No, no, that cannot be. Say he will be spared!"

"Umm." Simeon's voice interrupted the flow of the scene. His headlamp bobbed in the darkness as he jogged from the back of the audience toward the stage. "Hey, Percival, just a little bitty note. Remember we discussed this before? This moment is a turning point for Scrooge. All his anger for the world is turning inward, upon himself. Try saying the line more dejected, mmkay? Less big and showy."

"Big and showy?!" Percival squared his bony shoulders.

Teena winced. Simeon had chosen the exact wrong words.

"I have been in this show," Percival barreled on, "for thirty-five years. Longer than you've been alive!"

"I'm actually forty-two." Simeon smiled at the perceived compliment. "But I *do* moisturize each night."

"No, I mean…" Percival shook his head and dove back into his tirade. "I have delivered this line this exact way for decades."

As this conversation on stage-right was underway, the table full of kids began to get unruly. The law of entropy was merciless. Without the momentum of the scene, the children got wiggly and giggly. Mr. and Mrs. Cratchit did their best to keep them quiet and on-task, but it was an uphill battle. Even Tiny Tim seemed to want to jump up and run around, despite his crutch and illness. Andy Nguyen, who was one of Teena's current students, was the oldest boy at the table, so he put in some surface-level effort to hold things together. But he was an eighth-grade boy, and he could only resist his nature for so long. In a matter of moments, he was wiggling and giggling too.

"Well," Simeon said to Percival, donning the voice of a principal trying to discipline a kid while still being their pal. "Maybe it's time to change things up. It's the thirty-fifth anniversary, after all!"

"Thirty-fifth anniversary," Percival scoffed. "The former director, Roger Marius, never had an issue with my performance. He was a brilliant man. Understood the value of letting actors think for themselves!"

Simeon took a calming breath. "I can see your frustration. But Roger isn't here anymore. I'm just saying maybe we can evolve your performance a bit."

"Evolve?!" Percival was an expert at repeating words in an incredulous tone. "I *am* evolved! I-I-I'm a professional. I've done th-this for thirty-four years." His stutter began to surface, which only did so when he was particularly flustered.

Teena felt for the man. She softly stepped in. "Hey, it's okay. We all need direction sometimes."

Percival huffed. "I d-d-don't need advice from a piece of stunt casting!"

All the adults gasped and went quiet. The theatre was still except for the boisterous children. In that moment, Teena felt every inch of her body. Both its weight and its color. She felt so...visible. She wanted to rush offstage, but she bit the inside of her cheek and stood her ground.

"Holy crap." Jimmy Quinn, who was playing Mr. Cratchit, stood up from the table and took off his wire-rim glasses. "Al, that was insanely out of line."

"I-I-I am not *Al*." Percival got slightly quieter, as if he knew he'd gone out of bounds. But he didn't apologize and tried to move on as though nothing had happened. "So, on with the scene, yes?"

"What? No!" Jimmy began to round the table, approaching Percival. "You just insulted a really nice lady! That really sucked of you."

Teena said, "It's okay, Jimmy." Even though she didn't feel okay.

"Nuh-uh, it's not." Jimmy snorted, glaring at Percival. "Y'know, Evelyn and I have been in this show a long time too, Al, and we're not twerps about it. A lot of people in town are scared of you, but I'm not!"

Mrs. Cratchit, played by Evelyn Barrie, stood and grabbed Jimmy's arm. "Now, now, now. Let's all just…" She bugged her eyes out at the director, desperately hoping for him to intervene.

Simeon stood frozen among the audience seats, mouth agape. From the perspective of the actors onstage, he seemed miles away. He looked like the textbook definition of "a deer in the headlights" — AKA "a first-time director."

Finally, he snapped back into the present moment but still fumbled for a course of action. "Uhh, let's, uhh, let's all of us now… We could… Let's take a break? Yeah! Let's all take a little break." He turned off his headlamp and gestured for everyone to come offstage. "Just take a break, everyone."

The kids didn't need to be told twice. They bolted offstage and immediately started a game of tag. Jimmy blustered away, followed closely by

Evelyn. Percival walked off without looking at Teena.

For a heartbeat or two, she stood alone on the stage. She took it all in—the set, the costumes, the décor—and for the first time, she didn't want to be there.

She stepped off the stage, feeling all eyes on her. They were like burrs tugging at her flesh. She wanted to shake them off.

"Screw you, Al!" Jimmy's voice filled the theatre as he stomped down the aisle. He shoved open the doors leading to the lobby and exited, likely going to get some air.

Percival ignored this final jab and took a seat in the front row, on the far right side, by himself.

Teena knew Jimmy meant well, but he was only intensifying the situation and drawing more attention to herself, which she hated.

Despite being in his mid-fifties, Jimmy looked like he could bench-press an elephant without needing to warm up. He was one of Tennant Park's premier accountants, but he was also a fitness freak. The local protein shake business had him to thank for keeping it afloat. Teena had always known he was a hot-headed guy, but she'd never seen him get so aggressive. It was scary.

Simeon sidled up next to her and spoke in a low voice. "I'm so so so sorry about that. Are you okay?"

Teena didn't trust herself to speak more than a few words. Even though she wanted to rip off her green robe, throw her holly crown across the room, and quit the production, she said, "I'm fine."

"Okay. Okay, good." Simeon took several breaths, as if calming himself down. "Whew! That was something, huh?"

Frustration boiled in Teena's gut. Simeon was speaking to her like a bystander, not like the leader he was supposed to be. Not like a director. He'd had the power to defuse the situation earlier, but he hadn't used it. She clenched her jaw. "Yeah. Something."

Simeon rubbed the bridge of his nose and muttered, "That Percival. He's a disruptor. Bad for cast unity. I mean, he's picked fights with his brother Roy, and Markus, and now you and Jimmy? Yikes. I don't know how the former director put up with him for so long. Next year, I may have to find a new Scrooge."

Teena widened her eyes. A new person playing Ebenezer Scrooge would be unprecedented in Tennant Park. "Really?"

Simeon smiled at Teena's reaction. "I don't think anyone would be sorry to see him go. In fact, I have a…" His words screeched to a halt. He suddenly gulped. "I shouldn't be telling you this. Forget all that." He waved his hands as if erasing a chalkboard and hurried away.

Teena needed to get off her feet. She chose a random seat in the middle of the auditorium, plopped down, and tossed her foam torch next to her. A monster headache was forming between her eyes.

She wished Corrine was there. Her friend would've ripped Percival to shreds. No one was cruel to Coach Corrine — at least, no one who had lived to tell the tale. Meanwhile, Teena was polite and accommodating to everyone, including Percival, and she got publicly humiliated. What was the point of it? She should start acting more like Corrine.

Even as Teena thought it, she knew it wasn't possible. Politeness was baked into her DNA.

The kids were done running around the auditorium. They'd moved on from their haphazard game of tag to the snacks their parents had packed for them. They sat in rows on the right side of the audience, chittering and panting as they opened their bags. Some had candy bars, some had fruit. Trades were made, smiles shared.

Andy Nguyen withdrew a king-size Butterfinger, which prompted many *ooh*'s and *aww*'s. A girl named Haley Schrader, who played Belinda Cratchit, was particularly enamored with the candy. And Andy was particularly enamored with Haley — as a teacher, Teena was good at picking up on those sorts of things. Andy began to unwrap the Butterfinger to share with Haley.

The nearby Percival eyed the candy bar. He began to bellyache and bemoan loud enough for Andy to overhear.

"Oh, I think I forgot to bring something to eat. Ever since my darling dear Rebecca *moved on* last year…on Christmas Day, no less…I haven't quite gotten into the habit of packing snacks for myself."

Andy paused. He looked at his candy, then Haley, then Percival, then back at his candy. He leaned over to the old man. "You can take half of my Butterfinger if you want."

Teena nearly teared up. She couldn't have been prouder of her student.

Percival's woe-is-me performance disappeared. He scoffed. "Half? You think I can perform to my full potential on only half a candy bar?"

Tears gone. She wanted to stand up and yell at Percival. But she didn't. Couldn't. That wasn't part of her DNA.

Andy looked at Percival for a moment, then tossed the whole Butterfinger onto the old man's lap. "Here," he said. "Just take it." He led the swarm of young actors to the opposite side of the auditorium, leaving Percival more alone than ever.

The old man slowly picked up the candy. Unwrapped it. Took a bite. His shoulders sagged as if he had put on an invisible backpack. He sighed and—for a moment, only a brief flash—looked lonely. Sad. Regretful. He then wolfed down the rest of the Butterfinger.

Footsteps approached Teena from her other side. She turned her head to see Evelyn Barrie tip-toeing over. She waved with a few fingers and sat next to her…right on her prop torch. Paper and foam crunched, echoing throughout the auditorium like an avalanche.

Evelyn frowned. "Oh bother." She pulled the ruined torch out from under her bottom. It was flattened beyond recognition. She gingerly set the mangled corpse on the floor and said, "That was my fault."

Despite herself, Teena laughed. When Evelyn saw Teena wasn't mad, she joined in.

As much as the muscle-bound Jimmy Quinn didn't fit the picture of Bob Cratchit, Evelyn embodied Mrs. Cratchit to a T. She was in her late fifties, wore her graying hair in a bun, and volunteered as the choir director at First Baptist, the local church. A whimsical smile rarely left her face.

Evelyn asked, "Are you alright, dear?"

Teena nodded once, her eyes on the seatback in front of her. "Yep. I'm fine." She liked Evelyn enough, but she didn't feel very chatty.

Evelyn smiled sadly. Understandingly. It was the smile of a woman who'd been hurt a few times over the years. She sighed, "Percy, Percy, Percy."

If the old man hated being called "Al," Teena doubted he would like "Percy" any better. The thought made her smirk.

"I've tried to get him to come to church." Evelyn shook her head. "I've invited him so many times, but he always says no. That reminds me…" She gave Teena a big Sunday-morning smile. "Are you planning on coming to our cast party on Thursday night? It's right after our final rehearsal, the night before we open on Friday. It'll be in the church recreation room. I mainly ask so I can make sure we have enough brownies and finger sandwiches for everyone."

"I don't know, Evelyn." Teena couldn't imagine herself wanting to socialize, even in a few days.

Evelyn gave her words some space. They simply sat in the quiet for a few beats. Finally, she spoke.

"Teena, dear, this show would not be half as good without you in it. You are a wonderful Ghost of Christmas Present. You are not *stunt casting*, and don't let that ogre of a man convince you otherwise."

Teena lifted her chin and felt a flicker of light in her chest.

Evelyn went on. "When I heard you had auditioned for the role, I was thrilled! I thought, 'Finally, another woman is going for it, trying to get a traditionally male role.' Simply auditioning was enough. But then you got it, and I was over the moon!" She giggled and shook her hands like pom-poms. But then her smile faded, and she gazed at the stage. She sighed, "And here I am. Stuck as Mrs. Cratchit."

Teena arched a brow. "You don't like Mrs. Cratchit? You've been her for longer than I've lived in Tennant Park."

Evelyn seemed surprised she'd spoken her inner thought aloud. She startled and caught herself. "Oh, me? Yes yes yes, I do love being in that family onstage."

"But...?" Teena prompted.

"But." Evelyn grimaced, as though she were about to spill a secret she'd sworn never to tell. "But she doesn't even have a first name. Hardly ten lines. It's just..." She spoke meekly, almost embarrassed. "Oh, I shouldn't be complaining."

After a pause, Teena nodded encouragingly. "It's okay, Evelyn. Feel what you feel."

Evelyn took a breath, as if about to jump in a cold pond. "It's just... I can do more. For goodness sake, I do more every week at the church! I sing and lead and perform all the time. I could do better than Percy."

That last sentence piqued Teena's curiosity. She remembered how Evelyn had said "another woman" a moment ago.

She asked, "Better than Percival at playing Scrooge?"

Evelyn smiled mischievously. "Mhmm." She looked around to make sure no one was listening, then leaned in. "I auditioned for Scrooge this year."

"Really?" Teena raised her eyebrows and grinned. "That's so cool!"

"Well," Evelyn bobbed her shoulders, "clearly, I didn't get it. But Simeon told me privately, he loved my audition. He said as soon as Percy retires, I'm the next Scrooge."

Simeon's previous comment to Teena a few minutes ago made much more sense. He already had another Scrooge lined up.

Speaking of which: Simeon jogged over to their seats. He said to them, "Hey, you two. We're gonna run through the Cratchit family conversation a few more times tonight. We open soon, and…" He looked around and, seeing the children were on the far side of the auditorium, whispered, "I want the kids to get their wiggles out." He returned to a normal volume. "Anyway, Teena, that means you're free for the evening!"

Teena smiled up at Simeon, although she wondered if this was just him trying to curry favor from her so she wouldn't complain about her experience to anyone. Regardless, she was excited to go home and unwind.

"Alright." Evelyn set her hands on her knees and pushed herself to her feet. "Duty calls! I'll go get Jimmy from outside." She gave Teena one last kind smile, then shuffled out of the auditorium. Simeon went to round up the Cratchit kids, who were now hopped up on sugar with infinitely more wiggles to get out.

Percival wasn't in his seat on the front row anymore. He must have slipped away in the past few minutes. Good. Teena didn't want to see him again tonight.

She stood and made her way to the green room. Yes, a relaxing evening sounded great. Maybe she would watch *Muppet Christmas Carol*. At least the scenes with the jolly, friendly, endlessly lovable Ghost of Christmas Present.

She touched the holly on her head. The notion of throwing it across the room seemed blasphemous now. If she could make an audience member feel half as joyful as the Ghost of Christmas Present made her feel, then it was all worth it.

As she changed out of her costume and put it in its proper place, she thought about all that Simeon and Evelyn had said. Teena was often amazed at how much people opened up to her. Just in the last few minutes, two people had complained to her about Percival Jennings and even shared juicy secrets. She wondered why. Maybe she just had one of those trustworthy faces. Or maybe it was her accommodating nature — she didn't talk much and let other people pour themselves into her.

She exited the green room just as she did yesterday: bag slung over shoulder, face stiff and itchy from makeup, body weary and ready to lie down. But as she walked toward the theatre's front door, she heard a large *CRASH* in the lobby. Then another. And another.

CRASH CRASH CRASH.

She hurried toward the lobby, hoping no one was hurt. When she got there, she saw only one person: Bernie, the theatre's jack-of-most-trades. Fallen on the floor all around him were three big folding tables.

Bernie rubbed his bald head as he assessed the damage. He muttered, "No harm done, looks like, no harm done." As his gaze swept across the floor, he noticed Teena and jolted in his boots. "Oh!"

His sudden yelp made Teena jump, which made Bernie squeal again, and so on and so on. Eventually, their tennis match of scaring each other devolved into big belly laughs as they realized how ridiculous they looked.

Bernie set a hand on his chest and spoke through his chuckles. "Whew! I didn' know people were leavin' yet. Thought you were a ghost!"

"Well, kind of." Teena struck a pose. "Christmas Present!"

Bernie let loose another rich, cavernous laugh, the sort that could make you feel warm in the middle of a blizzard. He wiped a tear from the corner of his eye. "Aw man, we should put a bell on you. You walk pretty quiet."

"I heard some crashes. Are you okay?"

"Yes, ma'am, I'm all good. I was jus' setting up these tables for cocoa on show night, and I thought

I could carry all three at once. I was wrong. My body doesn' always cooperate with me, y'know." Even as he shrugged, he couldn't seem to stop smiling.

Teena's eyes automatically went to the thick scar that bisected his bare scalp. She didn't know the story behind it. Asking him directly felt rude, but it seemed ruder to ask someone else about it. Regardless, Bernie's movements were jerky, and his words always came out a bit sideways, and she assumed the scar had something to do with that.

She asked, "Could I give you a hand?"

Bernie shook his head before she had finished asking her question. "No no no, you're on your way home. I don't wanna bother ya."

Teena set down her bag. "I insist."

"Then I 'ppreciate ya." He walked up to the first fallen table. "You grab one side, I'll get the other."

While they set up the first table, Teena smiled as she pictured what the lobby would look like in just a few days' time. Families and patrons bustling back and forth, clutching their tickets, taking pictures, sipping cocoa… She couldn't wait.

"This is one of my favorite parts of the whole year," she said. "Especially all the decorations outside. The trees and lights and everything."

Bernie beamed ear to ear. "You like that?"

They set the table's legs in place with four metallic CLANGs.

"Oh yeah! I love how the theatre goes all-out. Of course, the show is great on its own. But the décor really takes it a step above. It's like you've stepped into a Dickens book."

"Well, I'm honored." He dragged the table against the wall. "It's not easy payin' for all that myself, but I get a kick outta it too."

Teena was taken aback. "You pay for it? It's not the theatre?"

Bernie pursed his lips, as if he'd said something he wasn't supposed to. Again, Teena had extracted a secret from someone.

"Yeah," he mumbled, "keep that b'tween us, okay?" He lit back up. "But people seem to enjoy it, so I'm happy to keep doin' it. Design and plannin' aren't my specialties, so I pretty much just throw out pretty stuff wherever I can. Branches, trunks, walls…"

"It looks perfect every year," she smiled.

"Thank you greatly. Next one?" He gestured to the second table on the floor, and they got to work.

"But," Teena pressed, "I *do* think the theatre board should pay for it."

Bernie sighed. "Eh, I'm not great at askin' for stuff. Rockin' the boat."

Teena knew exactly what he meant. She wasn't exactly Miss Assertive.

He changed the subject. "Can I ask you somethin'?"

She helped him position the table next to the other one. "Of course."

"I heard summa the kids call you 'Miss F.' Is that…?" He gestured with his hands, like he didn't want to say something awkward.

"Is that what?"

He pulled the rest of his question out of his mouth. "Is that cuzza something dirty? Like the F-word? Are they bein' mean to you?"

Teena laughed so hard she had to lean against the wall. Bernie stared at her, unsure how to respond. Finally, she answered, "No, not at all. I'm a teacher at the middle school, and I tell the kids to call me that. My last name is hard to say."

"Huh. What is it?"

She spelled it out: "F-A-K-H-O-U-R-Y."

"Fakhoury?" He pronounced it perfectly.

She paused, speechless. She hadn't heard her surname come out of someone else's mouth correctly in the past seven years.

He went on. "That's a nice name. Last table?" They bent to pick up the final fallen table. "You got family in town, Ms. Fakhoury?"

Teena chuckled. Corrine would call this "pointless small talk," but she found Bernie very easy to talk to. "Nope. I moved here a handful of years ago. On my own. How about you?"

"I got a brother. His name's Tanner. He's a cop with the Tennant Park PD. I applied to join the force a few years back, 'fore I worked here. Didn' get in."

"Sorry to hear that."

"Naw, naw, it's okay. I like this job. And I couldn't be prouder of my lil brother. If we had the same job, that would kinda diminish how good he is, knowwhatimean?"

Teena didn't agree with the last thing he said, but she understood the need to explain one's own shortcomings. "Well, we're certainly lucky to have you here." A question bubbled in her mind, and before she could think it through, she blurted it out. "Are you coming to the cast party Thursday night at the church?"

Bernie hesitated. He clearly didn't know about the party and, therefore, wasn't invited. "I mean, it's jus' for the cast, right? That's not me."

"Yeah, but you're more than welcome. I'm sure everyone would be thrilled to see you."

He gulped, suddenly reticent. "I, y'know, I… People don't seem to wanna talk with me. I kinda put people off, I think."

She knew this was true. Bernie always spoke a little too loudly. His hygiene wasn't impeccable.

His manner of moving and talking could make people uncomfortable.

But he was a good guy. And good guys deserve to be invited to Christmas parties.

"Well then, *I'd* be thrilled to see you."

He was still cautious to commit. His eyes flitted from the floor to the ceiling, back and forth, as if searching for the answer she wanted to hear.

Once again, she knew exactly how he felt.

She said, "It's at First Baptist, after our last rehearsal. Stop by if you're up for it."

He sighed in relief, now that he didn't have to give an answer immediately. "I 'ppreciate the offer."

The voices inside the auditorium grew slightly louder as people began to dismount the stage and mill about. Rehearsal must be over for the night. Chatting with Bernie had somehow caused her to forget about her dust-up with Percival.

She gathered her bag and inched toward the theatre's exit — as encouraging as Evelyn had been, she didn't want to run into her or Simeon again tonight. She said to Bernie, "I'm gonna head out for the evening. It's been a day."

"I hear that. Drive safe down Mountain, Ms. Fakhoury!"

She headed for the door and waved over her shoulder. "Until next time!"

The night air was gloriously brisk. Lights danced in her vision as she made her way across the parking lot. The decorations outside were even more special, now that she knew they weren't the corporate strategy of some faceless theatre board. Bernie had placed each ornament with purpose, wrapped the tinsel with his own two hands.

Effort. Intention. Care. Now *that* was Christmas spirit.

4.

The remainder of the week passed in a blur. Rehearsals were as Teena had described them to Corrine: stressful and annoying and long. Yet, she could feel the show coming together, which was one of the biggest thrills she could imagine. Each day, her excitement mounted. Show night couldn't arrive soon enough.

During rehearsals, Percival steered clear of Teena unless they shared a scene. Teena knew she should make some sort of effort to bridge the gap between them…but at the same time, she didn't really want to. If Percival was determined to be a crotchety, prideful old man, so be it. Her life was easier with him keeping his distance.

When Teena left rehearsals with Corrine, she clandestinely waved at Bernie. Corrine had no interest in chatting with the theatre's employee, and Teena didn't want to rock the boat too much, so she settled for a wave here and there. Teena hoped she'd get to see Bernie at the cast party on Thursday. That would be a good opportunity for him to hang out with the others, and they could see what a nice guy he was.

Eventually, the show ran like clockwork. After all, many of the performers were *Christmas Carol* veterans, and they were able to guide the newbies along fairly easily. Andy, Haley, and the rest of the Cratchit children fell into a rhythm. Jimmy and Evelyn were believable as a longtime married couple. Simeon, the first-time director, steadily improved his rapport with the actors. Roy Jennings's makeup was by far the most intensive, since he played Marley, and he got the hang of doing it himself, rather than getting help from some of the ladies. The stagehands consistently nailed their cues for lowering the backdrops, closing the curtains, and dropping the snow during the finale. And the pigeons didn't poop on anyone else.

Teena didn't want to jinx anything, but she felt the production was coming along as well as possible. She didn't dare say this aloud, for fear of the community theatre gods striking her with pink eye for her arrogance.

Finally, the week was nearly over. Thursday night was a run-through of the entire show, and it went well. After the performance, Simeon gave a standing ovation for a full minute, yelling things like "Encore!" and "Sensational!" He whipped off his lit headlamp and twirled it over his head, prompting hearty laughs from the whole cast—even the half who didn't take him very seriously.

After rehearsal, as they put away their costumes in the green room, Teena suggested to Corrine that they stop by the cast party at First Baptist. "It sounds fun and low-pressure."

Corrine grimaced. "Mmmmmnah. My people meter is way past its limit. I may rip someone's head off if I don't go home right now."

Teena would typically acquiesce and head home too...but her *"Die Hard* is a Christmas movie" instincts kicked in. She knew the single sentence that would result in Corrine sprinting to the party as quickly as possible. "Y'know," Teena said faux-casually, "I heard that Victor Stassi will be there."

Just as Teena had predicted, Corrine's eyebrows shot up. "Then what are we waiting for? We need to get there before he does, so there isn't a moment where his memory of the party isn't associated with me."

Teena chuckled. She drove down Mountain in front of Corrine to force her friend to obey the speed limit. Once they got into town, Corrine's car zoomed around hers and peeled off in the direction of the church.

Victor Stassi, the county's most popular estate-planning attorney, pulled double duty as both the Ghost of Christmas Past and Scrooge's nephew Fred in this year's production. It was common knowledge that his real name was Terrence Stansley, and he had changed it to sound more "glamorous" and "lawyerly," but none of the women in town seemed to mind. Including Coach Corrine Tally, who had quite the crush on him.

If there were two things Tennant Park was famous for, they were *A Christmas Carol* and Victor's glorious mustache. It was thick and dark, reaching all the way down to his chin. His billboards were plastered all over the surrounding area of Colorado, advertising his services as well as his trademark facial hair.

This had caused some trouble at the start of the show's production. Since Victor was to play two very different roles in the same show, Simeon had asked Victor to shave…which was tantamount to Tennant Park blasphemy. Victor's professional nickname was "The Stache Stassi," so it was safe to say he was very protective of his lip-warmer. He'd refused Simeon's request, which then turned into an insistence, then a demand. When the rest of the cast caught wind of this, Simeon almost had a violent revolt on his hands. *A Christmas Carol* nearly fell apart over The Stache's mustache. Simeon quietly dropped the issue. Peace was restored, and Victor's facial hair remained.

When Teena pulled into the church's parking lot a few minutes later, Corrine's car was nowhere to be seen. She stepped out and leaned on her sedan's hood, enjoying the cold night air as she waited. One by one, cars of her fellow castmates arrived—including Victor's snazzy Lexus. She waved at each of them as they entered a smaller building next to the towering sanctuary. She assumed this was where the rec room would be.

She pulled in a breath through her nostrils, let it out her mouth. In, out. In, out. December air had a unique aroma. Sort of like the winter equivalent of that wonderful post-rain smell.

The outside of the church was decked out for the holiday: twinkling lights, wooden snowflakes, and a nativity scene on the front lawn. It was all very picturesque, pulled straight from a postcard.

Tires squealed as Corrine's car zoomed into the lot. She parked and leapt out of the driver's door, looking harried. "I got lost. That's what I get for thinking I know where friggin' churches are. Is Victor here?"

Teena flicked a glance at the Lexus, then politely lied. "I don't know."

"Well, let's get in there. What're you waiting for?" She hurried toward the church in such a rush, she didn't even close her car door. Teena bumped it shut with her hip and followed.

The rec room was a wide, open space with couches, foosball tables, and a few classic arcade game cabinets. The carpet had likely been in style when the second Bush entered office, and the walls were discolored from years of fluorescent abuse, but the place was cozy enough. Cotton snow and festive lights brightened it up, along with the Michael Bublé Christmas album playing on the speakers. The George C. Scott version of *A Christmas Carol* played on a TV in the background. And don't forget the huge painting of the Magi visiting baby Jesus. Mustn't forget that.

The cast members sat around eating snacks, laughing, trading stories, and having a good time. The stress of rehearsal was behind them. Next came the joy and excitement of actually performing. They had earned a night to unwind.

There was Markus Daniels, looking somewhat uncomfortable as he snacked on cookies—there weren't many other cast members his own age. Hanging by the TV were Roy Jennings and Jimmy Quinn, deep in conversation. The sight was pretty funny: the massively muscular Jimmy next to the wiry, older Roy. Truth be told, Teena was glad to see Roy—if he was there, his brother Percival likely wouldn't be.

She then spotted Victor Stassi in a circle of chairs, chatting with a few other castmates. She elbowed Corrine and subtly gestured toward him. "I spy with my little eye…"

"Gah, he *is* here." Corrine sighed like a middle school girl watching her crush from afar. Teena would've laughed if she wasn't positive Corrine would punt her into outer space.

"Now's the perfect opportunity for small talk. You know, your favorite thing."

Corrine rolled her eyes. "Small talk is the worst. If you talk, it should be *about* something." She bounced on her heels, full of nervous energy. "It's a bummer he's in all my scenes but I never get to interact with him. While I'm supposed to be gaga over a high school senior, all I can think about is running my fingers through the Ghost of Christmas Past's mustache."

Teena chuckled, doing her best to keep that image from settling in her mind. "Not all small talk has to be small. It can just be fun and nice."

"I know, I know." Corrine exhaled. "Wish me luck." With that, she sauntered over and commenced her infiltration into Victor's conversation circle.

Teena made a pit stop at the snacks table. Evelyn had promised brownies and finger sandwiches, and she had overdelivered. There was also eggnog, hot cider, and cocoa on the drink side, as well as pretzels, sugar cookies, and gingerbread men—all decorated in their Christmas best, of course.

"Oh helloooooo, dear!" A syrupy voice came from behind Teena. She turned to find the woman herself, Evelyn Barrie, wearing a sweater complete with jingle bells and holly sprigs. Her stage makeup was gone, replaced with holiday colors and glitter. She must've driven even faster than Corrine to get here with enough time to put it all on. "I'm delighted you made it!"

"Thank you for all this." Teena gestured to the spread.

"The church ladies really outdid themselves, didn't they? So festive of them!" Evelyn clutched her heart warmly. "All of us here at First Baptist are big supporters of the show each year."

Teena began to compile a plate of one of each snack. "How do you feel about the show?"

"Oh goodness, I'm very excited! Always am." Evelyn's sweater jingled with excitement too.

"How many years have you done this again?"

Evelyn thought through it. "If memory serves, this is my fourteenth year. My thirteenth as Mrs. Cratchit. I started in the ensemble."

Teena whistled. "Wow. Do you still get nervous? I mean, you're an old pro."

Evelyn laughed cheerily. "I get nervous every time. Heck, I'm nervous every Sunday when I lead the choir. Even when you enjoy performing in front of a lot of people, it's not something you get used to. Not me, at least."

The door to the rec room swung open, letting in a whoosh of cold air as well as the chatter of a half-dozen children. The Cratchit kids barreled in, laughing and hollering, no doubt relishing the fact that their days of rehearsals were behind them. The kids' parents followed, similarly thankful to hang up their chauffers' hats, at least for the year.

At the sight of energetic children, a look of panic crossed Evelyn's face. She said to Teena,

"Excuse me. I need to…check something." She scurried away and began putting "DO NOT TOUCH" signs on the old, expensive arcade games.

Andy Nguyen sized the place up, particularly the food and foosball. "Whoa, this place is cool!" He had evidently never been to First Baptist before. Teena was somewhat thankful Evelyn hadn't been around to hear that, or else she would have undoubtedly swooped in to convince him to become a lifetime member then and there.

Led by Andy, the kids rushed to a foosball table. He caught sight of Teena and waved like a windshield wiper. "Hiya again, Miss F.!"

She replied, "Hey, Cratchits!" The six kids giggled at the idea that they were actual relatives. Andy blushed, giving Haley Schrader a covert glance.

It was cute to see all the kids who comprised the Cratchit brood hanging out outside of rehearsal. They made up a little family unit, from Andy and Haley, the eldest "siblings," all the way down to the boy who played Tiny Tim, who was, indeed, very tiny. His name was Colton McCowdrey, a third grader who barely came up to Teena's waist. And he was so stinkin' adorable—every time she saw him, she wanted to pinch his little cheeks, but she imagined he got enough of that, so she did her best to treat him respectfully, as a fellow castmate.

"Ooh, what's down here?" Andy began crawling under the foosball table. Then under the snack buffet. Then under each of the couches, on a journey only he understood.

As his teacher, she knew how adventurous and distractible he was, which could be challenging. But she was up to the challenge. During biology class, she framed assignments as "missions," and she incorporated scientific experiments into the agenda as much as possible, which everyone loved. Ultimately, he made her a better teacher, and he held a special place in her heart.

An unusual sound arced across the room. Something Teena had never heard before, like a tractor that had inhaled helium. She spun around to find its source, and when she did, she gasped.

Corrine was sitting next to Victor in a circle of chairs, laughing at something he'd said. But it wasn't her normal, friendly laugh. It was artificially high, flirtatious, and, for lack of a better term, girly. She was trying way too hard.

Teena couldn't stand by and watch this happen. It looked like Corrine needed a wingwoman when it came to casual small talk. After restocking her plate—what was a Christmas party without eating too many cookies?—she crossed the rec room to join.

"Hey, all," she said. "Mind if I sit?"

Victor smiled up at her. "Hey, Teen! Pull up a chair. Join the spirit circle."

As Teena did so, she realized what Victor meant: Once she sat down, the group would consist of Corrine, herself, and Victor, as well as Roy Jennings, who played Marley, and a man named Don Schrader, who played the Ghost of Christmas Yet to Come.

All four of the show's ghosts in one circle. And Corrine, whom Teena had unwittingly made a fifth wheel. Oops.

But it was too late to back out. Teena sat and sized up the group.

Roy Jennings had extricated himself from the chat with Jimmy and had joined this conversation circle. Over the few weeks of rehearsals, she hadn't spent much face-to-face time with the man, but she knew him to be a nice guy. He was only a few years Percival's junior, but he seemed at least twenty years younger. Even now, with the remnants of death makeup lingering in his wrinkles, his eyes sparkled. He spoke with vigor and radiated likability…at least, when among friends. Onstage, all his charm evaporated. But he was doing his best, which earned him points in Teena's book.

Don Schrader was the person in the cast Teena knew the least. This was his first year in the show, and he'd only joined because his daughter Haley had roped him in. He was tall and wide, stoic and imposing. In other words, he was born to play the terrifying, silent Ghost of Christmas Yet to Come. He clearly didn't want to be a part of the production, so luckily for him, a stick puppet could play his part. He only had to attend a handful of rehearsals, wear a hooded cloak, and ominously point at things.

"Oooooooh." Teena shivered and wiggled her fingers. "Spoooooky."

Victor and Roy laughed, while Don continued to down eggnog and brownies like there was no tomorrow. Corrine gave her a pleading side-eye.

"So Victor," Teena said, "how's work?"

"People are always making and amending wills, even in small towns." He shrugged with a grin. "So business is pretty good. You're a teacher, right?"

"Yep! Eighth grade biology. And *Corrine*," she said, dragging her friend into the conversation, "works at my same school. She's the gym teacher."

"*A* gym teacher. Just one of many," Corrine uncharacteristically downplayed herself.

"Huh! How about that." Victor's mustache curved with his smile. "Roy here was just talking about how he teaches too."

"Is that so?" Teena turned to Roy Jennings, genuinely intrigued. "I didn't know that."

Roy nodded. "I'm an instructor at the vo-tech school a few towns over. Construction and mechanics."

"I was just saying, when you joined us..." Victor held up his hands, which were slender and tactile, like a pianist's. He laughed, "These are hands that've never done a hard day's work. I went to law school, then right into a firm as an intern, then worked up to where I am now. I wouldn't know a screwdriver from a soldering iron. You, my good sir," he said as he slapped Roy's shoulder, "are a genius."

"Just good at tinkering, is all." The younger Jennings brushed off the compliment good-naturedly. He examined his own hands: gnarled, wrinkled, worn. A lifetime of labor was etched on each knuckle. "I mean, everyone's good at something, and I'm not really an artsy guy."

Everyone in the circle looked at the floor and pretended they had no idea what he was talking about.

Roy cackled and went on. "It's okay! I'm no Brando or Day-Lewis. So it's a good thing I can work with my hands."

Teena asked, "Then why did you audition?"

He paused. Thought. Considered, seemingly for the first time. Finally, he shrugged. "Wanted to get out there, meet some folks. I'm new in town, after all. Been here less than a year. The school I work at isn't in town, so if I wasn't in the show, I wouldn't have met anyone here."

Corrine said, "So in addition to the spirit circle, this is kinda the school circle too."

Victor waggled his fingers and donned an eerie voice. "Oooooooh. Spoooooky."

They all laughed—Roy until he rocked back and forth in his chair—and Teena marveled at how easily inside jokes could be made, yet how they could be the bedrock of friendship and memories.

Don Schrader, whom they had all forgotten was there, awkwardly interjected, "I'm a cook at Denny's." He petered off. Shifted in his seat. Shotgunned another brownie.

The others in the circle waited for Don to continue. But he seemed content to simply be a part of the conversation.

Roy went on. "Speaking of spooky. I really like how Simeon is steering into the ghost aspect of *A Christmas Carol*. I've always wanted to see a film version that's full-tilt horror. I mean, it's a *ghost* story!"

Teena agreed. For all the flak the cast gave Simeon about his headlamp, he was a director with a vision. If his debut went down in flames, it wasn't for lack of trying. He had the idea to use lights and fog machines to accentuate the terror of Marley's appearance in Scrooge's bedchamber. He wanted the climactic graveyard scene to be truly bone-chilling, so that the happy ending would feel even more uplifting.

His best idea, in Teena's opinion, involved Marley's ghost. She said, "I love how Marley stalks Scrooge in the background of the first couple of scenes. Like a slasher."

"Mhmm." Corrine nodded. "Simeon can get on my nerves, but that was a really good idea. In the opening scene on the streets, and then in Scrooge's office, Marley is just *there*. Looming. Waiting for Scrooge to be alone." She shuddered.

Roy said, "Waiting to strike. Yeah, it gives the whole thing a real horror flavor."

Victor added, "I think that's a Simeon original, as far as I can tell."

"And," Teena said, happy to keep complimenting someone instead of tearing them down, "I really like how we're on the stage during the final scene." She gestured to herself, Don, and Victor: the three spirits. "How we're just kind of in the background, among the pedestrians and regular people. Like we're there to see if Scrooge has learned his lesson. And he has!" She smiled. "It's a sweet moment."

Roy said, "But then, during that final scene, I'm all alone backstage. I'm truly the only person not in that scene. Even people like Markus and you, Corrine, get to be townspeople too once their roles are done." He laughed self-deprecatingly. "I don't get it! Do I smell bad or something?"

"Well, the way I see it..." Teena gesticulated with her hands as she talked, on a roll. "Marley is the harbinger of doom and gloom. The three spirits are Scrooge's salvation. You loom over him at the beginning, when he's cruel and nasty. And at the end, when he's saved, we're there to celebrate with him."

When she finished her thought, she realized everyone in the circle was staring at her. She gulped and tried to sink into her chair. She hated sounding pretentious and know-it-all-ish.

But Corrine slapped her shoulder. "Nicely put, Shakespeare."

Victor beamed. "Y'know, I've always wondered why the three spirits are onstage in that last scene. And you summed it up perfectly! Now I don't mind the quick-change I have to do between Fred and my ghost costume at the end." He laughed again.

Roy rubbed his chin, as if lost in thought. "The harbinger of doom and gloom…" His eyes lit up, and he raised a cup of cider like a toast. "Sure sounds like me!"

More laughter from all in the group.

A chill swept into the rec room as the door opened again. Conversations sputtered as everyone looked to see who had entered.

It was Bernie, wearing a puffy winter coat and carrying a brown paper bag from a grocery store. His smile faltered as he realized dozens of eyes were on him — he wasn't used to being onstage. He waved. "Hey, ev'ryone. I brought ice cream." He lifted the bag.

Teena knew she had to join him in the spotlight so he wouldn't flounder. She hustled out of her seat toward him, smiling. "Hi, Bernie! Glad you came."

When she was close enough to hear him, he said quietly, "It's all the cast. I shouldn' be here."

"No no no," Teena said, patting his arm. "We're happy to see you." Even as she said that, she saw Corrine rolling her eyes, distinctly unhappy to see him.

He took a few shuffling steps forward. His bald head gleamed in the fluorescents. "So, uhh, how's it goin'?"

"Better now that you're here. And you brought ice cream? Great idea." She led him to the snack table, where she prompted him to set the paper bag.

His gaze landed on something across the room. He smiled. "Whoa! They have an old *TMNT* game?!"

Teena saw he was eyeing one of the vintage arcade games. The games Evelyn had specifically marked off-limits.

"Umm..." She made a snap decision. "Yeah! C'mon, let's play." She strode across the room to the brightly colored *Teenage Mutant Ninja Turtles* game cabinet, ignoring her castmates' silent stares. Before Bernie could catch up, she brushed off the "DO NOT TOUCH" sign.

"Oh, baby." Bernie giggled as he sized up the gaming cabinet. "Haven't done this in a while..."

Teena gulped. All at once, she pictured Bernie's clumsy hands breaking the joysticks, or short-circuiting the machinery, or causing the whole thing to spontaneously combust. She would be on the hook to pay for it. This may have been a bad idea.

But Bernie expertly turned on the machine…and began to work magic. The game had built-in controls for each of the four Turtles, and he chose Raphael's red buttons and joystick. His hands flew between the buttons as if he had been training for this moment his whole life.

"Shoooooooot." A small voice came from below. Teena looked down and saw little Colton McCowdrey staring at the game screen in awe. "You're killing it!"

Bernie shot Colton a smile without missing a beat in the game. "I'm a mere mortal, like ya'self." He laughed his big, rumbling laugh. Just like that, the room thawed.

Conversations continued. Music played. The Cratchit kids gathered around Bernie and cheered him on. He offered to let them join in, but they insisted he keep going by himself. As the night went on, several adults came to watch Bernie progress through the whole game. Evelyn even brought him brownies and cocoa to refuel, once she saw that he was treating the expensive cabinet with respect.

When Bernie beat the game, the rec room erupted in cheers. The kids pretended to lift Bernie on their shoulders and parade him around.

Finally, it was time to go home. They all pitched in to help clean up the room and put things back in order. When the trash was disposed of and everyone had plates of goodies to-go, they trickled into the cold night.

As they dispersed across the parking lot, Evelyn called out, "See everyone tomorrow!"

Victor trilled, "Showtime!"

More cheers.

The kids waved good-bye to Bernie as they piled into their respective parents' cars. They had declared him an honorary Ninja Turtle named "Bernardo."

Bernie gave Teena a big high-five. Corrine gave him a quick side-hug—which, for Corrine, was a huge deal.

It was a great night.

5.

When Teena first opened her eyes the next morning, she stared at the ceiling for a few minutes. She always felt this way on a show's opening day: a churning in her gut she could only summarize as "nervous thrills." Like clicking up the first hill of a roller coaster that she wasn't sure she wanted to be on.

Her experience with theatre was limited, all things considered. Each Saturday growing up in Detroit, she and her mom had walked to the local library to spend the afternoon reading or just relaxing—it was a free public space, so they spent a lot of time there. One day, Teena had stumbled upon a CD of the original cast recording of *The Pirates of Penzance*. The music transfixed her, and she began to gobble up all the theatre the library had to offer. She listened to CDs, read scripts, and watched VHSs of filmed productions. *Dreamgirls,*

Annie, Into the Woods, You're a Good Man Charlie Brown, Candide, Anything Goes, and on and on.

She was in love. No doubt about it. She wanted to be a part of that world, but she didn't see a way in.

Her parents were immigrants who made their livings with odd jobs. They weren't able to afford acting camps or lessons. Even if she was good enough to get a role in a local production, they couldn't spare the gas to drive her to practices.

Then, her freshman year of high school, she heard about open auditions for the school's musical. *The Wizard of Oz.* Teena knew all the lyrics from watching the movie over and over on TV. Without telling her parents, she signed up, memorized a song and monologue, auditioned…

…and got a part. She was in the ensemble: a talking tree, a flying monkey, and an Ozian. She was over the moon. When she told her parents this amazing news, they smiled, but then immediately looked concerned. Teena rushed in with her plan: She would take the late bus home after rehearsals. Or catch rides with a castmate's parents. Or walk. Whatever it took. Her parents tentatively approved.

Rehearsals were, as they always are, stressful and annoying and long. She got along well with most of the other kids, but a few were less than welcoming to the rookie daughter of immigrants. They were the stars-to-be, the divas, the kids whose parents could afford acting lessons and extra gasoline.

It wasn't easy for a freshman girl. At every turn, she was different. She didn't have money to go to the movies or McDonald's with friends after rehearsal. Her base foundation makeup was darker than that of most other Ozians. At that point in Teena's life, she was already on the plus-sized side, and seeing her larger costumes hanging on the rack next to dainty tutus and glitzy gowns took a toll.

So she started playing along. She laughed at everyone's jokes. She backed down in disagreements. She became accommodating. And she got by.

Opening night was a dream. It was all worth it. Her hard work paid off, and she nailed all her parts. The curtain call made her feel something new. When she took her bow, an entire audience clapped for her.

Including her parents. They'd made it and were on the front row.

In the ensuing years, she auditioned for other school plays and community theatre productions. No matter how experienced she became, she always felt the nervous thrills of opening day.

As she entered college, her parents passed. It had been sad but not unexpected. She still missed them, but she knew they had lived wonderful lives. More than anything, she was thankful for the opportunities they had gifted her.

In college, she stopped participating in theatre so she could focus on her studies. She graduated, became a biology teacher, and moved to Tennant Park…where she met a feisty gym teacher named Corrine who suggested they both try out for the town's annual production of *A Christmas Carol*.

Seven years later, there she was, staring at the ceiling. The nervous thrills were in full swing. She couldn't wait for the show to start.

The thought struck her as funny: She had truly just woken up, was still in bed, and was excited for nighttime.

She hoisted herself out from her warm cocoon of blankets and wandered to the living room. Her home was standard for a single public-school teacher in a small Colorado town: one bedroom, one bath, a couch she'd bought on clearance, a few bookcases, a tank with a betta fish, and a modest kitchen.

She ate cereal. Took a shower and got dressed. Read some of her current book. Worked on her lesson plan for next semester.

All the while, she knew she was just killing time. Treading water. Running out the clock until she could drive to the theatre and get to the day's main attraction.

Her lines swam in her head. To exorcise her anxious energy, she decided to run through a scene on her own.

There, in her own living room, she took center-stage. She donned her boisterous, booming Ghost of Christmas Present voice, and declared, "Come forth and know me better, man!" She then unleashed her best jolly laugh, one that would put Santa to shame. If there was one thing the Ghost of Christmas Present was known for, it was his lively laugh.

She wanted it to be perfect, so she paced backward and forward, letting "ho-ho-ho"s and "ha-ha-ha"s fly with abandon. The Ghost was older than time, and this laugh should reflect a sense of jovial eternity.

A noise rattled behind her. In the middle of a "hee-hee-hee," she spun around to see the mailman leaving a package on her doorstep. He locked eyes with her through the door's glass window, then nodded and awkwardly slunk away.

Heat rose from Teena's gut to her face. How utterly embarrassing. She began to mentally map out a way to be gone during mail delivery every day for the rest of her life. She hoped the mailman was going to attend tonight's show, so he would understand that when she was cackling at different pitches alone in her living room, she was really practicing for a play…but then she would have to face him, and she didn't really want to do that either.

But a minute later, the whole situation already felt silly and objectively hilarious. She couldn't help but laugh at herself…after checking that no one could see through a window.

***

It was still a while until call time, when the actors were instructed to arrive to get ready before showtime, but Teena wanted to get there before the crowd. She enjoyed moments of quiet before a busy night, so she knew she should be headed that direction. As she did before every rehearsal, she checked the inventory of her bag and restocked as needed: face wipes, Q-tips, tissues, pens and highlighters, a sturdy water bottle, and, of course, her script.

She stepped out her front door and locked up. In an instant, her fingers were numb and red. This was probably the coldest day of the season so far. She held her fists to her mouth and exhaled, booking it to her car in the driveway.

The sky was already inching toward darkness, even though it was barely evening. Early winter nights could be rough. Getting home from school at what felt like the middle of the night but the clock told her was five p.m. always made her feel extra tired. During winter break, however, she took guilty pleasure in the early darkness. It made everything feel more Christmas-y, with the lighted décor and an excuse to light a warm fire.

Her car breathed steam from its exhaust pipe as she started it. She sat in the driver's seat for a minute and stuffed her hands in her armpits, letting the engine warm up. When she was confident her hands wouldn't fuse to the cold steering wheel, she started to drive to the theatre.

Cruising through town, she couldn't help but feel a warm ember in her chest. It was just so charming. Windows provided views into little coffeeshops and stores. Bundled-up pedestrians walked their dogs, and a group of kids played soccer on a side-street. A city worker wrapped garland around lampposts, waving to passersby.

Oddly, it felt like a scene out of *A Christmas Carol*, specifically the happy finale. Carolers, pigeons, peace on Earth, all that jazz.

As she turned north, the small mountain that lent Tennant Park its name came into view. It peeked over the shops, trees, and houses like a curious child standing on its tiptoes to peer into a window. While some may look at its modest size and wonder why the town put so much pride in it, Teena would say its modest size was part of why Tennant Park loved it. It was a lot like community theatre: It may not be the biggest and the best, but it was homey, endearing, and not too full of itself.

She drove up the side of Mountain, the last leg of her journey to the theatre. The trees and boulders that lined the road had a few visitors: bright orange work cones, placed periodically all the way up. That was an unusual sight—she hoped everything was okay.

Otherwise, the drive was uneventful. As always. Just how she liked it.

When she pulled into the theatre's parking lot, the sky was dark enough for the surrounding lights to have kicked on. She parked and got out quickly so she could stand in the delightfully cold night. She felt like she was in a storybook world: a theatre hidden amongst a pine forest, with lights and ribbons adorning the trees. The nervous thrills in her gut spread all over her body, and for a fleeting second, she thought she might levitate off the ground.

She stood in the parking lot until the tips of her ears started to sting. With her bag slung over her shoulder, she made her way into the theatre.

The lobby was breathtaking. It had been transformed from a typical small-town community theatre into a snapshot of Christmas perfection. Wreaths, poinsettias, electric candles, evergreen garlands, cut-out snowflakes... She had no doubt Bernie was responsible for it all.

Speaking of which, only one person was in the lobby: good ole Bernie. Tonight, he wore a wool cap over his bald head, concealing his scar. He was carrying a large drink dispenser to one of the tables she had helped set up.

As she walked past, Teena said loudly but calmly, "I'm here, Bernie! Just making my presence known, so I don't startle you again."

Bernie laughed but thankfully made it to the table. He set down the dispenser and turned to her. "Evening, Ms. Fakhoury! Happy showtime!"

"Please, call me Teena. Is that for the hot cocoa?"

"You know it! I love cocoa. Migh' be my favorite drink." His smile turned slightly bashful. "Thanks for invitin' me to the party las' night. I had a lotta fun."

"You made it fun for us. Andy Nguyen nearly had a heart attack watching you play that game. And you're pretty much Colton McCowdrey's hero."

"Yeah." He glowed while thinking of the memories. "All those kids are great. I'll miss 'em when this show's over. I hope they come back next year and get parts."

A bittersweet melancholy settled over Teena. She'd been excited all day long, thinking that the show was just beginning. But in reality, the whole process was nearly over. One show tonight, two tomorrow. And that would be the end of it. She would see Corrine at school each day, but she had grown close with some of her other castmates this year. She would miss talking with Evelyn and

Victor. And Markus and Roy, despite their respective age gaps. Even, to Bernie's point, the young children had grown on her.

And Bernie. After seven years of being in *A Christmas Carol*, Teena had only just now started to get to know him.

Without the binding experience of the show, she likely wouldn't see these new friends again until next year. Unless she was intentional.

"Hey," she said, "tonight, if some friends and I hang out after the performance, would you want to join us?"

He scratched at his hat. "Doin' what?"

She chuckled. "I don't know yet. Just being friends, I guess."

Bernie gulped, seemingly taken aback. "Really?"

"Of course!"

A dozen emotions crossed his face. He finally settled on joy, and he let a huge smile bloom. "Well, jus' let me know! I'll be around." He spread his arms to encompass the whole theatre. "This is my office!"

Teena snickered. "Sounds good. I'm gonna head back to the green room..." She struck a diva pose. "...and begin my ghostly transformation."

"Shouldn' be too hard!"

"Hey!" She feigned offense, but Bernie's thunderous laugh was too infectious.

"I kid, I kid!" He checked his watch. "Speakin' of, I should get the box office opened pretty soon. An' make sure the bathrooms have enough TP. An' hang some tinsel in here…" He wandered away, counting his to-do list on his shaky fingers.

Teena smiled, thinking that he should get a massive raise from the theatre board. Whoever they were. She wound her way behind the stage to the green room.

A handful of actors were already there, milling about somewhat leisurely. Markus Daniels sat on one of the communal couches, reading a thick novel that Teena assumed was assigned from school. A couple of ensemble members chitchatted as they helped each other get their Dickensian hairstyles just right. Evelyn Barrie was, true to form, setting out some home-baked goodies for everyone, humming a hymn to herself. Teena wondered if they really weren't nervous about the upcoming performance, or if they were forcing themselves to relax.

She was a few minutes early, and she knew the calm atmosphere would balloon into frantic chaos soon enough. It would be a good idea to soak in the quiet while it lasted. Taking a deep breath through the nose, she willed the butterflies in her stomach to get it together.

"You okay, Miss F.?" Markus glanced up from his book.

Teena realized she'd been lingering just inside the door for about twenty seconds. She stepped fully into the green room and chittered, "Yes! Yes, I'm all good. Thanks."

Despite its name, the green room was a dull brown. Its carpet was stiff and slightly crunchy. A few ceiling tiles were missing. On the list of the theatre's priorities, beautifying this room was near the bottom.

But it had its own charm as well. Many props from past shows were scattered around as décor. Encouraging graffiti like "You got this!" and "Enjoy the moment" dotted the walls here and there — messages sent through time between actors.

The four walls of the room each had their own stations, so to speak. At the back of the room — which was closest to the lobby, next to the door Teena had just walked through — were the racks of costumes and changing booths. The performers could grab their costumes, hop into a booth, whip the curtain shut, and, like Superman, emerge as a new person. Early in rehearsals, one of the Cratchit boys had tried to do a costume change as fast as possible, but he'd only ended up shoving his foot through the bottom of his trousers. The boy's mom had had to sew the pants herself, since Simeon didn't have the budget to get new ones. As a result, quick-changes were heavily discouraged.

Counterclockwise from there was a line of desks with lighted vanity mirrors, where the performers did their makeup. Both the mirrors and the desks were covered in old, chalky makeup. An archeological dig would likely find prehistoric fossils preserved in the layers of blush, powder, and foundation.

Next was the prop table, which could more aptly be called the prop pile. Plastic food items, baskets, candlesticks, quills and ink wells, money pouches... Everything the actors carried throughout the show was on this table. Teena kept the Ghost of Christmas Present's flaming torch there. Or she *did*, until Evelyn sat on it.

Finally, the most barren quarter of the green room. The place everyone steered clear of, even the rowdiest of the Cratchit kids.

The door leading backstage. Once someone stepped through there, they had to be ready to go on. Two huge, rumbly vents were built into the walls on either side of the door, covering some of the noise made in the green room.

The place was designed so that an actor could make a big circle on their way to perform: Get in costume, put on makeup, grab their props, and head backstage. In the middle of the circle were various tables, couches, and chairs picked up from thrift shops years ago. Teena didn't want to even begin to imagine the amount of crumbs and gum hidden under those couch cushions, and in her seven years of *Christmas Carol*ing, she had never sat on one.

Resting on one of the tables was a copy of that day's *Tennant Telegraph*, the town's newspaper. The front-page, above-the-fold, color photo caught her eye: Percival Jennings, Jimmy Quinn, and Colton McCowdrey, dressed as their onstage characters, were posed on the set of London. It was a good photo, with Percival snarling his best Scrooge sneer and the two Cratchits cowering away from him. How life imitates art. Teena picked up the paper and thumbed through it.

As with most small-town papers, a majority of the stories were more like advertisements for local goings-on. Since the annual production of *A Christmas Carol* was by far the town's biggest event, no less than ten stories were devoted to various aspects of the show: features on a few of the actors, stats about the anticipated tourism, a photo gallery of the light display at the theatre, and so on.

The front-page story was all about the show's thirty-fifth anniversary in town. Teena nearly skimmed past it, but the first line made her screech to a halt:

"This Friday and Saturday, Tennant Park will once again be home to Ebenezer Scrooge as *A Christmas Carol*, directed by Roger Marius, will be performed at…"

Teena grimaced. The local journalist who'd written this story clearly hadn't done any interviews or research. According to the *Telegraph*, Roger Marius—the geriatric Florida retiree who had directed the show for the past thirty-four years—was still at the wheel. Simeon Callahan's name was nowhere to be found. What had likely happened was the writer assumed nothing about this year's production would be any different from its past thirty-four iterations. Copy, paste, boom, done.

Teena hoped Simeon hadn't seen this story, though that was unlikely. Simeon seemed like the kind of guy who would make a scrapbook of every piece of media about his directorial debut. Still, Teena crumpled up the paper and stuffed it under a couch cushion.

It was time to get moving. She pulled her costume from the rack and hung her bag in its place. As she held the emerald robe and holly crown in her hands, it struck her that she would only get to wear them three more times.

For this year, at least. Maybe next year, she would get to don it again. Or perhaps she might audition for a different role? Who knew.

Shaking her head like an Etch-a-Sketch, she cleared away the cobwebby thoughts. She still had a show to do tonight. She stepped into a vacant booth and slid the curtain shut to change.

When she emerged a few minutes later, the green room was much more populated. Many of the children had arrived, so the small space felt much smaller. People bustled in all directions, grabbing props or shoes or hairbrushes or eyeliner or script pages or makeup sponges or any other number of things. The calm before the storm had passed, and Hurricane Dickens had arrived.

"Eyy, there's that jolly green ghost." Corrine, still in her everyday clothes, spotted Teena from her seat on a couch. It took her a few attempts to get up from the sinkhole between the cushions. "How're you feeling?"

Teena thought it over, then answered, "Good." She smiled. "Ready, I think."

"Hey, I want to say…" Corrine looked her friend in the eye. "I'm really excited for you tonight. Auditioning for and taking this role was no small thing. I know it means a lot to you."

Teena's heart swelled. "You do?"

"Duh." Corrine rolled her eyes. "You talk about that Muppet movie ten times a day." They both laughed. "Anyway," she went on, "I'm proud of you. You're gonna crush it."

Amid the noise and disarray of the green room, they smiled at each other and shared a quick hug.

"Okay." Corrine clapped and moved toward the costume racks. "I gotta get in my bonnet and boots."

Teena followed her on the circle, headed for the makeup desks. "Hey, you have two roles tonight. I just have one. I'm proud of *you*, missy."

Corrine grabbed her hanger off the rack. "Oh yeah, I can't wait to accept my Oscar for the role of

Townswoman Number Four." She stepped into a changing booth and swished the curtain shut.

"Oscars are for movies. For a stage role, you'd be getting a Tony."

From behind the curtain, Corrine yelled out, "My sarcasm stands!"

Teena chuckled as she sat at one of the makeup desks. She scooted forward, leaned in…and felt something scurry over her feet. She yelped and jerked backward, flailing and kicking. The image of a mouse filled her mind, and she nearly let out a full-throated scream.

But no. Andy Nguyen scampered out from under the desk. "Sorry sorry sorry sorry." He darted across the green room.

Teena set her hand on her chest to steady her heart rate. She called after him, "Mind people's space, Andy!"

He replied over his shoulder, "Okay, Miss F.!" But within two seconds, he had crawled under a table, then made a beeline for the space behind the costume racks.

She sighed but couldn't hold back a small smile. He wasn't hurting anyone. And besides, she wasn't his teacher here. If he wanted to explore every nook and cranny of this extremely cluttered and un-vacuumed room, more power to him.

Jimmy walked by Teena's desk, wearing his Cratchit costume. She was always struck by how silly his massive biceps looked in Dickensian clothing. But of course, she would never breathe a word of that to him.

"Hey, Teena," he asked, "have you seen Simeon around?"

She thought, then said, "No, sorry. Everything okay?"

"Yeah yeah. Just wanted to ask him something." He moved to walk away, then muttered, "Did you see the *Telegraph*? About…Roger?"

Teena bit her lip and nodded. "Mhmm. That has to hurt. Simeon has put in a lot of work, and for him to not even be recognized…"

"No kidding. Anyway," he patted her shoulder affably, "break a leg. See ya onstage." He continued on his way.

Victor Stassi came up and sat at the makeup desk next to Teena's. He was dressed in his Fred costume—coat, kerchief, pantaloons, the whole nine yards. He smiled cordially at Teena, then leaned toward his mirror and got to work grooming his mustache.

Teena checked the time on a clock on the wall. Her early arrival had been eaten away minute by minute. The house would open soon, meaning the audience members would be allowed to enter the auditorium to find their seats. When that happened, showtime was just around the corner. The butterflies in her stomach fluttered again. Even though she didn't show up onstage until midway through the story, she wanted to be fully ready. So she got to work on her makeup.

Foundation. Blush. Eyeliner. Lipstick. Some sparkles and glitter to add that ghostly-yet-jolly look. It had to be subtle for the effect to work, yet strong enough for those in the back row to feel it as well. It was a tricky balance, but Teena felt she'd homed in on it during rehearsals. At least, no one had told her otherwise.

In the crusty mirror, she could see the opposite side of the room. Next to the door leading back-stage, Percival and Roy Jennings stood talking. They were both dressed and ready for the show, minus Roy's Marley makeup. The contrast be-tween the two brothers couldn't have been greater. Percival was slight and scowling, while Roy was lanky and charming. She couldn't hear their con-versation over the hum of the vents.

Finally, Percival threw up his hands and walked away. His words rose above the general commotion of the green room. "Have fun ruining the show, Roy Boy. Everyone knows you're the worst actor here."

The people in the vicinity awkwardly quieted down and looked at Roy with sympathy. The younger Jennings rubbed his eyes and walked to-ward the desks. He sat a few places away from Teena and began setting out his numerous jars of white and black makeup. His movements were slow and solemn, which was unusual for him.

"Hey," Teena said before she could convince herself it was none of her business. "You're going to do great tonight."

Roy gave a mirthless laugh. "Thanks."

"And…" This was *definitely* outside the realm of her business, but she said it anyway. "Everyone thinks you're a good guy for moving in with him. Even if he doesn't appreciate you, we all see it. The past year couldn't have been easy. After, you know…his wife's death."

His mouth curved into a smile, and he chuckled harshly. Like she had just told a dirty joke. Teena was caught off-guard—that was the exact opposite of what she'd thought his reaction would be. He opened his mouth to speak…then paused, then finally said, "I think I'm going to have some quiet time now." He turned to the mirror and didn't say another word.

Teena gaped, feeling absolutely rotten. She'd stepped over the line, far beyond accommodating, and she'd gone out of bounds. She felt terrible—not for herself, but for having hurt Roy. She wanted to say something more, but she got up and gave him space. Should she circle back later and check in to see if he was okay? Or should she just let things lie? She didn't know. Now the butterflies in her stomach felt seasick too.

"Oof." Victor hissed as if he'd just seen someone wipe out on a skateboard. "That was rough."

Corrine approached the makeup desks in full Dickensian regalia, strutting for Victor's benefit. She posed like a runway model and said, "I'm ready to be a star." But when she saw Teena's drawn face, she dropped the schtick and blocked out Victor almost entirely. "You okay?"

"Just nervous," she quickly answered.

Her friend entered coach-mode. "You need to visualize it, Teena. Total domination. Goal. Hole in one. Home run. Touchdown."

"I know some of those words," Teena said with a laugh.

"How about standing ovation? Curtain call? Umm, whaddya call it…" She snapped until the words came to her. "Tony Award! That's it. Winning a Tony."

Victor tried to interject himself into the intimate conversation, not used to being left out. "My brother's name is Tony. Believe me, you don't want one of him!"

Teena politely laughed at Victor's joke, but Corrine didn't even look at him. Her focus and affection were focused entirely on her friend. Teena knew how much Corrine was into Victor, and this small gesture made her well up with happy tears.

"Oh no!" Corrine began to wave her hands, as if trying to calm a bucking horse. She'd seen the tears and started panicking. "Uhh, you can—I mean, how about we… Shoot, I'm no good at this."

Teena dabbed away the tears before they messed up her makeup. "No, it's a good thing, Corrine. Thanks for the pep talk."

Giggles streaked across the green room as the Cratchit kids stampeded from the prop table to the costume racks. They flew by the booths, kicking up the curtains and revealing anyone unfortune enough to be changing at that moment. Out the door they went, headed for the lobby.

"Hey!" Teena seemed to be the only one who noticed the gale-force hurricane that had just blown through. She looked around, searching for an adult who was in charge of corralling the kids… And she realized *she* was the adult. She headed across the room, toward the exit.

"Where're you going?" Corrine instinctively followed.

"Can't have the kids bursting out into the lobby. Not in their costumes and makeup. Simeon would have a conniption." Teena and Corrine left the green room and walked quickly through the hallway that led to the theatre's lobby.

They found the six kids, shockingly quiet and all leaned against the door that opened into the lobby. They each had an eye pressed to the slit where the door was ajar ever so slightly.

Now that she knew they weren't running rampant throughout the theatre, Teena let out a breath. "What're you all up to?"

Haley Schrader looked up at her. "Oh, hey, Miss F. The home is open, and we're looking at all the people who came." An expression of awe painted her face, as if she had just seen the Sistine Ceiling in-person.

Teena smiled. "I think you mean the 'house' is open."

Andy vibrated in his buckled shoes. "Come check it out, Miss F.!"

Corrine spread out her arms and put on a "fun-loving aunt" grin. "I'm here too, kids! Coach Tally!"

The Cratchits didn't react, just kept gazing through the small opening. The light from the lobby illuminated their faces in the dark hallway, like they had opened a treasure chest full of gold.

Corrine lowered her arms. She muttered, "Just no love for the gym teacher."

Teena whispered to her friend, "These are theatre kids, Corrine." She chuckled and looked around. Seeing no harm, she stepped up to the door and joined the kids in peering into the lobby.

She instantly understood why the children were so enchanted — the sight was magical. In her six previous years in the show, she had never snuck a peek like this.

Dozens of people loitered in the theatre lobby. Maybe hundreds. It felt like thousands. They wore heavy coats, earmuffs, and sweaters like figurines inside a snow globe. The air crackled with their conversations and…something else. Something intangible. Some special ingredient that filled the entire room. The peeping Cratchit kids didn't seem to know what it was.

But Teena did. It was the excitement you feel before seeing a live show. Even a community theatre production of a tired old story you've seen a million times can inspire that feeling. There's something special about the idea of sitting in a dark room and having real human people weave a tale before your very eyes. It's tactile, yet fantastical. Reality becomes fiction, and fiction becomes reality.

"There's my dad!" one of the Cratchit boys burst with joy. Teena set a hand on his shoulder to remind him to keep it down.

The other kids began identifying their own family members, friends, and random acquaintances from around town. Indeed, Teena recognized a lot of people herself. It appeared most of Tennant Park had come to see the show.

There was one of her fellow teachers. And there was her favorite grocery store cashier with his wife. And there was a man she didn't quite recognize but certainly knew…

Aha! She remembered. That was the head of the theatre's board. The man she wanted to talk to about giving Bernie a raise. Made sense—he was wearing a suit and tie, which didn't fit the vibe of the rest of the room.

Teena pulled back from the door. She saw that the kids weren't going to do any damage, so she quietly stepped away, letting them enjoy their moment. She beckoned Corrine back to the green room.

As soon as she and Corrine stepped back into the green room, Simeon stormed in from the backstage area. To call him frazzled would be an understatement: The buttons on his shirt were misaligned, a coffee stain decorated his left pec, and his brows were knit together in consternation. He loudly said to the room, "Places in fifteen minutes!" His voice was strained, like a screechy violin note.

As they went about their business, the actors automatically responded, "Thank you, fifteen," acknowledging that they understood the announcement.

Simeon began to tromp right toward the green room's exit—right toward Teena. She panicked, thinking he knew that the kids were hanging by the lobby. It was his debut night as a director, and he was wound so tight, the smallest indiscretion could set him off.

She hissed to Corrine, "C'mon, he's gonna rip them to pieces."

Corrine nodded in understanding, and they rushed back to the kids on tiptoes. They pulled the children away from the door, much to their surprise and frustration.

When they began to whine, Teena whispered to them, "Go back to the green room. Now. Simeon's coming, and he's mad."

Andy got the message loud and clear. He buttoned his lip and quickly ushered the rest of the kids back down the hallway to the green room. The littler kids thankfully mirrored his tone and tenor.

Corrine smiled. "Andy's a nice kid. Why don't I ever have nice kids in my classes?" Before Teena could respond, she lamented, "I know, I know. Theatre kids."

Footsteps rumbled from the hallway. Simeon marched into their line of sight. He must've passed the children on their way back to the green room. His mouth was turned downward as if he was trying to eat his own chin.

Teena launched into protective mode right away. "Simeon, we sent the kids back. They weren't causing a disturbance in any way, I promise. Besides, it's their opening night too—"

But Simeon wasn't listening. He apparently hadn't even noticed the children. As he paced in the dark hallway, he passed back and forth across the sliver of light from the ajar door.

"It's all going wrong," he moaned. "It's all going wrong."

Teena and Corrine traded glances. Directing a show was no easy feat, and despite his good ideas and conceptual innovations, Simeon had never quite seemed up to the task. Now, on opening night, the cracks were showing.

Corrine cleared her throat. "What can we do to help?"

He kept pacing as he listed off his woes. "Our Ghost of Christmas Yet to Come has pink eye. No one even knows my name or cares about how much I've poured into this show. And *I can't find my headlamp!*"

Teena threw on her teachery persona and stepped into his path. "Simeon, it'll be okay…"

But Corrine wasn't as confident. "Don Schrader has pink eye?!"

"Roger Marius!" Simeon spat the name. "He did the same exact show for thirty-four years. I step in and inject new life into it, and what do I get? Nothing! Literally nothing!"

Teena interjected, "Does Haley have it too?"

"Huh? Who?" Simeon was barely listening as he carved a rut in the ground with his frantic feet.

"Haley Schrader. Don's daughter. Does she have pink eye too?"

But Simeon was back on his tirade. "I've brought live pigeons to this show. Falling snow. Freakin' ghosts!"

Corrine answered Teena's question: "I think I saw Haley's mom drop her off this evening. Doesn't seem like she's sick."

"Okay." Teena exhaled. "Good. I'm glad she's okay."

Simeon wailed on. "And they say *Roger Marius* is still the director. Nothing I've done matters. This show will be just the same as all the others…"

"Simeon!" Teena sharpened her voice. "Snap out of it!"

Simeon screeched to a stop, seemingly noticing the two women for the first time. He rubbed his hands over his face, then let out the deepest sigh in recorded human history. "Okay. Don can't make it tonight. Corrine, you'll sub in as Yet to Come."

"Wait." Corrine reeled a bit. "What? I'm the new ghost?"

"Yep. Have Percival teach you the blocking for that section." With that, Simeon spun on his heels and headed back to the green room.

The two friends stood in the dark hallway, still absorbing what had just happened.

Corrine shook her head and sputtered. "Let me get this straight. *Percival* is going to teach *me* my new role."

Teena smiled shakily, putting a positive spin on it. "Hey, look at you. Triple billing! Belle, ensemble, and the Ghost of Christmas Yet to Come!"

"Yeah yeah yeah." Corrine started to powerwalk back down the hallway. "I need to see if Don's robes even fit me." She mumbled to herself, "Okay, I can do this. I just have to point at a gravestone, point at some people, act all spooky…"

They trotted into the green room, and Corrine darted for the costume racks. Teena rarely saw her anxious, but this was definitely one of those times.

The room was full. Percival, Markus, Roy, Evelyn, Jimmy, Victor, all the children and members of the ensemble… They were all there. In costume. Ready for the curtains to part.

Simeon planted himself in front of the door leading backstage. "Okay, everybody!" He raised his voice over the hubbub of the room and waved to get everyone's attention. Since most of the actors had ensemble roles in the opening scene, a sea of old-timey Londoners turned to face him.

Mostly, they tuned him out. They were all certain they were about to hear a variation of the same spiel they'd heard before: *When the curtains open, this show will have been performed thirty-five years! I'm lucky to be here, doing this with you all. And so on and so on, blah blah blah.*

But instead, Simeon merely said, "Places. Break a leg tonight."

The cast stood frozen for a moment, surprised by Simeon's brevity. But then, like a dam bursting, they all rushed forward. Headed backstage. To their rehearsed spots. A quiet energy pulsed from person to person, as if they were all part of a single organism.

Teena saw a frantic look in Corrine's eyes. She said, "I'll come with you. To see you off." She softly elbowed Corrine's ribs.

Corrine nodded, still fairly off-kilter, and moved with the current of actors. Teena kept a comforting hand on her forearm as they walked.

Something caught Teena's attention. As Markus was about to step backstage, Percival pulled him aside. Just like at the restaurant earlier in the week, she couldn't hear their conversation, but she certainly picked up on its tone. The old man said something to Markus, then paused, a look of slimy arrogance on his face. Par for the course, Markus's kind smile didn't flicker. He simply shook his head and slipped backstage. Percival was left glowering as the actors flowed past him.

Teena was curious what Percival had felt was so important just a few moments before the show began. But she didn't have time to wonder for long.

The migration quickly and quietly moved backstage. A few kids whispered to one another, but for the most part, the actors didn't speak. They were like soldiers marching to the frontlines, wholly focused on what was about to transpire. Hours of rehearsal had led to this, and they were ready to execute. They positioned themselves in the wings backstage, and after a moment, even the kids stopped talking. Only a few low lights illuminated the backstage area, giving everything a dreamlike texture. Everyone took a breath, gave each other encouraging glances, and looked outward, toward the empty stage.

And just like that, the cast had taken their places.

The lights in the auditorium dimmed.

The audience quieted.

And Tennant Park's thirty-fifth annual production of *A Christmas Carol* began.

Act 2:
Showtime

6.

The entire cast was crammed into the wings on both sides of the stage, shoulder-to-shoulder. Bonnets were shoved in people's faces, buckled shoes stepped on dresses, and the layers of period clothing made for layers of sweat. The five black-clad stagehands were packed in with them, unaccustomed to being so up close and personal with the actors.

Simeon elbowed his way through the crowd to one of the stagehands. His clipboard was clutched to his chest: a life preserver in the middle of the ocean. He hissed to the stagehand, "Open curtains."

The stagehand yanked on a rope that looped up to the ceiling. Pull by pull, the curtains opened and revealed a cobblestoned London street to the audience. The stage's lights slowly brightened, evoking the sense of a foggy December morning.

From backstage-right, one of the stagehands released two pigeons from their cage. The birds
fluttered across the London skyline, and the audience gasped with glee. They'd never seen live
animals in this theatre before. Miracle of miracles,
the rest of the stunt went just as planned: The pigeons were lured by a pile of food into an empty
cage on backstage-left, where a stagehand locked
them in. A smattering of applause sounded from
the audience, and Simeon allowed himself a small
fist-pump in victory.

Bells chimed from the theatre's sound system.
One by one, the ensemble members trickled onstage. Bakers, lamplighters, carolers, children...
The streets of London came alive. They called to
one another, laughed, and embraced. An occasional greeting of "Merry Christmas Eve!"
informed the audience of this first scene's setting.

Teena took it all in from her place in the wings
of backstage-right. The nervous thrills of opening
night had been transformed into manic energy. All
the actors moved and spoke like cartoon characters. Their expressions were big, their gestures
bigger. Teena could tell all the actors were having
the time of their lives. From her angle, she could
only see the first few rows of the far-left side of the
audience, but they were all smiling too.

Corrine hadn't joined the pedestrians onstage
yet. She bounced on her heels, mouthing her Belle
lines silently to herself. It was clear that her sudden

casting as the Ghost of Christmas Yet to Come was weighing on her mind.

Teena squeezed her forearm and leaned in to whisper to her friend. "Have fun, sweetie, and relax. Break a leg."

Corrine swallowed her nerves and gave Teena one last smile. With that, she slipped into character and strode onstage, where she began quibbling with a poulter for a lower price for the prized turkey hanging in a window.

With most of the actors out of the wings, Simeon took a breath. He wheezed, "Okay okay okay…" He looked to his clipboard to see what should stress him out next. But without his headlamp, he couldn't read his notes backstage. A faint red light glowed from an EXIT sign over a door on the back wall, which was right next to the mechanisms that controlled the curtains and backdrops. The door led to the outside world behind the theatre, meaning the air around it was arctic and shiver-inducing, but it seemed to be his best option, so he planted himself within the red glow. He looked a bit silly, squinting at his clipboard while lurking among the ropes, pulleys, and sandbags…but not as silly as he looked with his headlamp, so it was technically an improvement.

Teena crept away from the stage, headed back towards the green room. She had a lot of time to kill before she needed to make her grand entrance as the Ghost of Christmas Present. There were the scenes with Scrooge and the townsfolk, then Scrooge and Marley, as well as the entire Christmas Past section—all told, about thirty minutes. The green room would be empty for the opening scenes, so Teena could relax, unwind, and actually have some quiet alone time.

But a metallic creaking sound came from the green room. She picked up the pace and opened the door to find…

"Andy?!" Teena gasped.

The grate of one of the huge vents near the door was open, and Andy's pantalooned legs were sticking out of it. He tried to curl up in a ball to hide himself.

She bent and started dragging Andy out of the duct. "What are you doing? You're supposed to be in the scene *right now*!"

Andy gave up and shimmied out of the vent on his own. Dust was smudged on his face. He lowered his head in embarrassment. "I never get to be alone in here, and I wanted to see what was in these big metal holes."

Teena nudged him toward backstage as she explained. "They're air ducts, Andy. You're not supposed to be in them normally, but especially not now. You have to be onstage."

He planted his feet stubbornly. "But I'm not even Peter Cratchit right now. I'm just some kid. I'm not important in this scene."

She stopped trying to push him. Instead, she stooped to his level and gave him a "mission," as she often did for him in the classroom. "Are you kidding? First impressions are everything. If the audience doesn't like what they see right when the curtains open, they won't like anything. This is the most important scene in the whole show, and you're in it! You need to make sure the audience is primed to enjoy the rest of the show!"

"I do?" Andy wiped dust off his cheek.

"You do! Whether or not people like my scenes later on—or *your* scenes—is being decided right now." She hooked a thumb over her shoulder, pointing to the door leading backstage.

Andy jostled as he tried to run around her. "I gotta get out there!" He sped out of the green room.

"Walk quietly," she said to him, but he was already gone. Oh well. He still had dust on his face too, but people would likely assume he was supposed to be a chimneysweep.

She chuckled as she lurched to her feet—as comfy as her lush robe was, it could be cumbersome to move around in. She adjusted the holly wreath on her head and turned a scrutinizing eye to the vent. She'd never seen it open before. How had Andy managed to wriggle inside? His curiosity rivaled the Mars rover's, but even he couldn't open a sealed vent with his bare hands.

When she leaned in to investigate, she saw that two of the screws holding the vent grate in place were gone. It swung open freely on a hinge. That was odd. Had a maintenance worker unscrewed the vent and left it open?

She went to swing the grate shut, but at that moment, the air conditioning kicked in. Warm air blasted her in the face and blew the holly right off her head. It toppled like a tumbleweed a few paces away. She chased it down and replaced it on top of her hair.

But then, she heard a sound. Paper, flapping against a breeze.

It was coming from inside the vent.

Once again, she stooped to investigate. There, an arm's length inside the duct, was a sheet of paper, held down by a paperweight of some kind. Its edges fluttered in the air conditioning. Teena squinted against the hot air as she reached in and grabbed the paper with one hand, the weight with the other.

She pulled them out of the duct, into the room's light. Yes, in one hand, she held a piece of paper. A diagram of some sort was drawn on it, but she didn't examine it right away.

Because in her other hand, she held a knife.

Her blood froze in her veins, rendering her as still and cold as a marble statue. She'd never seen a knife like this one before, much less held one herself. Its blade was short and serrated, with a slight curve at its end like it was smirking. It looked downright wicked.

Immediately, her brain tried to rationalize its presence in the green room air duct. Maybe it was some sort of technician's tool that had been lost? Or it might be an antique, long forgotten. Surely it hadn't been hidden here by someone intending to use it as a weapon. Besides, even if it was, the person who'd hidden it wasn't necessarily a member of this cast. This theatre was old—the knife could've been left in the duct at any time in the past several decades.

But once she looked at the sheet of paper the knife had been holding down, all reasonable explanations disappeared.

Drawn on the page were many small circles, scattered around seemingly at random. At first, she couldn't really tell what it was supposed to be. An abstract picture of some kind? As she looked, however, it came together.

Each circle was labeled with a name. *Evelyn. Jimmy. Victor. Don. Teena.*

She gulped. Seeing her own name was surreal. Like finding yourself mentioned in a ransom note.

After scouring the page, she realized that most everyone in the cast was accounted for. But Percival's circle was unique: A big X was scratched over it. Like a treasure map. Or a target.

She hissed and let go of the page, as if it had burned her. As the paper slowly drifted to the ground and she saw the drawing from a bit of a distance, she realized what she was looking at.

It was a chart. A bird's-eye-view of the stage, marking where every actor was supposed to be standing.

What...?

Why...?

Who...?

Teena realized she was still holding the serrated knife. Although no crime had been committed and, technically speaking, nothing untoward had happened, she didn't want to be caught with it. She tossed it onto one of the couches in the middle of the green room, its blade gleaming as it arced through the air. It landed on the cushion, bounced once, and stared at her. Even when she turned her back on it, she could feel its sharp gaze.

She picked up the page again. It was a sheet of notebook paper, its left-hand side torn and three-hole-punched. Could've come from anywhere. The diagram and names were drawn and written with a thick black Sharpie. The handwriting was neat and blocky — she didn't recognize it off the top of her head.

Why would someone make a diagram of the actors' positions onstage? And why would Percival be X'd out?

But she knew the answer to that question. Even as she thought it, she shook her head. It was too ridiculous. Too fantastical. Too insane to consider.

Still, she thought it all the same.

Percival was a target. Someone was planning to stab him.

That was a huge leap to make, she told herself. All she had to go on was a knife and a random diagram. Those two things hardly qualified as a murder plot. The knife could be a tool, for all she knew, and the diagram was likely just a random doodle. And Percival had been X'd out—so what? Someone was mad at Percival. If that was a crime, all of Tennant Park would be locked up. The old man had a ton of enemies.

No. Teena began to laugh at herself. No, she hadn't stumbled across some nefarious scheme. No, this wasn't a plan to murder someone. It was silly she had even considered that. This knife was just a knife. And this diagram was just a doodle. Random circles with random names assigned at random. Nothing more—

But then she saw it. And her blood ran cold again.

She recognized the positions of the actors on the paper. It was the final scene of the show. The joyous finale, with carolers and live pigeons and falling snow. Someone had precisely charted the locations of every actor onstage during the last scene. Teena scanned the page two, three, four times to make sure it was accurate.

Yep. It was.

This diagram wasn't random at all. It was premeditated. Schemed. Plotted. Not good words.

The X on Percival's name grew bigger and bolder the longer she looked at it.

And the longer she looked at it, the more convinced she became.

Someone was going to stab Percival Jennings during the final scene of the show.

Applause drifted into the green room. A scene change was occurring. Most of the ensemble characters were coming offstage. They would be back in a matter of seconds.

A million thoughts flooded Teena's mind. Different courses of action to take. Scenarios. Possibilities. Theories. There were so many paths she could take, she ended up frozen with indecision.

Should she tell anyone what she'd found? Should she tell *every*one? Exposing the would-be killer, bringing the dark plot into the light, seemed like the right move. No one would die.

But. But but but.

She didn't know who the would-be killer was. If everyone found out about the scheme but not the schemer, that person would still be anonymous. They would retreat into the shadows. They'd run. Or go on with their lives. Or try to kill Percival another day, this time being more careful where they hid their weapon and diagram.

Teena couldn't reveal what she knew. She had to carry on as if nothing was awry. She couldn't let the killer think anyone was onto them.

So she snatched the curved, serrated knife from the couch, then placed it and the paper back in the air duct. She positioned the objects exactly how she'd found them, swung the grate shut, and power-walked to the other side of the room.

Just as a gaggle of excited actors entered the green room from backstage, Teena slipped out the other door, headed for the lobby.

She needed to talk to someone. Someone she knew beyond a shadow of a doubt wasn't a potential killer. Normally, this person would be Corrine, but Teena wasn't sure that was a good idea. If Corrine caught whiff of the notion that a murderer was in their midst, she would go into full-on drill sergeant mode. She would get in everyone's face, hurling accusations every which way and making a huge scene. That would cause the would-be killer to clam up and get away scot-free.

And if Teena explained all of this to Corrine, Corrine would likely do it all anyway.

No, as much as she loved Corrine, Teena needed an ally who wouldn't bulldoze her.

She sped through the dark hallway and arrived where she'd been a lifetime ago: the door leading to the lobby, peeking out alongside the Cratchit kids. In reality, that had only been about twenty minutes ago. Time sure flies when you're uncovering murder plots.

The door was still slightly ajar, and she leaned her eye against the sliver of light. The lobby was empty except for the folding tables holding dispensers of hot cocoa, rumpled playbills lying on the floor, and the man she was looking for.

She slipped out the door and stage-whispered, "Bernie! Hey, Bernie!"

Bernie perked up from his current task of sweeping up litter around the bathrooms. He looked around — and up, for some reason — for the voice that was calling his name.

Teena crept across the lobby and jostled his shoulder. "Bernie, can I talk with you?"

Bernie smiled at her. "Oh, hi, Teena!" He furrowed his forehead. "I'm not in charge, but I betcha aren't s'pposed to be out here in your costume. In case some people see you while they're walkin' to the bathroom or something."

Teena shot a glance at the closed doors that led into the auditorium. Big, booming voices came from within: Percival harrumphing as Scrooge, Jimmy groveling as Bob Cratchit, and Victor galivanting as Scrooge's nephew Fred. It was hard for Teena to wrap her mind around the fact that *A Christmas Carol* was still underway, even after she had uncovered something so earthshattering. From her perspective, at least.

Just as Bernie had said, if anyone exited the auditorium through those doors, they would see Teena. She wanted to draw as little attention to herself as possible, so she beckoned Bernie toward the far corner of the lobby. "Come on over here, so we can talk a little."

"Well, I gotta get all this trash gone 'fore people see it." When he held up the broom and dustpan, they quivered in his shaky hands.

"Just… Please, Bernie." Her voice sounded alien in her own throat. Tense. Apprehensive. Right on the edge of afraid.

Bernie heard this too. He leaned his cleaning utensils against a wall and followed her across the room. She huddled him under a huge wreath dotted with strikingly red poinsettias. It was a perfect spot: She could keep an eye on the doors to the auditorium, the door leading to the green room, and, for good measure, the front door leading outside the entire theatre. Suddenly, she knew exactly what paranoia felt like.

"Bernie…" She didn't know how to say what she was thinking.

He looked at her with concern. Not a drop of cynicism could be found in his eyes.

So she just blurted it out. "I think someone is going to kill Percival Jennings tonight."

Bernie rocked back on his heels as if she'd shoved him. He pushed aside his wool cap and scratched his scalp. "Percival…?"

Teena explained, "The old man who plays Scrooge. In this show. Here."

His mouth formed a perfect O. "Shoooooooot. Really?"

"I… I think so. I found a knife and a perfect diagram of all the actors' positions during the final scene of the show. Hidden in the green room. In one of the air ducts. On the diagram, Percival was X'd out."

Saying all of her evidence out loud, she realized it wasn't really evidence at all. It was fishy, sure, but hardly damning.

But Bernie gasped as if she'd produced a smoking gun. "Oh no! That's not good!"

She stumbled over her words in surprise. "Y-You believe me?"

He, in turn, was surprised by what she'd said. "I mean, well, why wouldn't I? You're a good, trustworthy person. If you think something's goin' on, and you think it enough to tell someone, then I betcha something's goin' on."

Teena felt a plume of warmth in her chest. She hadn't realized she was worried about not being believed. But he believed her intrinsically and without hesitation, and it felt good.

A wave of laughter crested in the auditorium and swept into the lobby. If Teena's memory was right, the Fred character had just delivered the line, "What reason have you to be dismal? You're rich enough!" That usually got a good chuckle from the audience.

Percival's voice, muffled by the doors, followed with, "Away with merry Christmas! What's Christmas to you, but a time for paying bills without money…"

The play continued with no regard for Percival's life. Indeed, Percival himself continued delivering his lines without knowing his life could be in jeopardy.

Bernie got the conversation back on track. "We should call the cops, yeah?"

That was Teena's instinct too. Even if she was completely wrong about this whole thing, and Percival wasn't in danger at all and there was no killer among them, having the police show up wouldn't hurt. They would question some people, look around, see it was a big misunderstanding, and go about their business. The show would be interrupted and Simeon would be more than a little upset, but on the whole, no harm no foul.

But if she wasn't wrong…

"If the killer realizes someone is onto them, they would go quiet and blend in with the rest of us. Or they'd run and try to kill Percival on another day."

"Or," Bernie said, nodding, "they might try to kill 'im right away. If they're cornered, y'know, go out in a blaze of glory."

Teena hadn't thought of that. "You're right. Both not great options."

"Mhmm. So…" He paused and raised an eyebrow, slowly realizing her plan. "You're wantin' to catch the killer before they do the killin'."

"I… I think so."

She expected Bernie to label her a lunatic, or laugh in her face, or call the police right then and there. But instead, he looked at her like she was a superhero. It made her stand up a little straighter and be a bit more confident. If Bernie believed in her, why couldn't she believe in herself?

"Well," he said, rubbing his hands like a surgeon before a procedure, "what can I help you with, detective?"

Teena chuckled dryly. She wouldn't go that far. "I need to talk things through. All we have to go on are the knife and the diagram drawn on a sheet of paper."

"By the way, where are those?"

"I left them where I found them. In the air duct. I didn't want the killer to know they'd been found."

"Smart move." He set his hands on his hips as he tried to think through the situation.

Teena took a breath. Her background was more in science than crime-solving, but one thing scientists and detectives have in common is asking questions. She tried to think logically. "Most obvious thing first: access. Do you know of anyone who was working on that air duct after hours? Maintenance, a technician, someone like that?"

Bernie shook his head right away. "Nah, no one I know 'bout. And I would know. I'm pretty much the keeper a' the keys 'round here." A thought struck him. "Could it be a stagehand? One of the guys who pulls the ropes with all the sandbags and stuff? They have pretty good knowledge of where everyone stands during scenes, y'know?"

"That's a good idea, but the green room would be a terrible hiding place for their knife. Stagehands never go in there, and when they go to retrieve the knife to kill Percival in the last scene, they'd stick out like a sore thumb. No, it's probably a cast member. Someone who can wander around the green room without looking shady."

From inside the auditorium came a resounding "*Bah humbug!*" from Scrooge. Or, rather, Percival. His Scrooge-y persona was so good, Teena had started thinking of him as such.

Bernie asked her, "On the paper, was it boy or girl handwriting?"

Teena closed her eyes to visualize the page. "It looked like a guy's writing." She sighed and threw up her hands. "But I mean… Anyone's handwriting can look like anything. I'm not confident enough to rule anyone out based on that."

It was a hopeless situation. Teena suddenly felt so small, overwhelmed, drowning.

"Mhmm, that's true." Bernie thought for a few beats. "A knife is up close an' personal. Whoever's usin' it probably wouldn't wanna reveal themselves 'til the moment of the stabbing. They'll be standing right next to him."

Teena nodded along. That made sense. With each moment, she became increasingly glad she had Bernie on her team.

He went on. "So, you're the actress here. Who's close to Scrooge during that scene?"

She could visualize the moment perfectly, both from the bird's-eye-view of the diagram, and from her perspective as the ghost in the ensemble.

"Pretty much the entire cast is onstage then. Victor Stassi and Don Schrader are right beside me. Well, tonight it'll be Corrine instead of Don. But almost everyone is within striking distance, really."

"Almost everyone?" Bernie asked.

"If I remember right, Roy Jennings is the only cast member not in that scene. Percival's brother. So he can't be the one who's trying to stab him."

"Unless he's a real good knife thrower." Bernie stroked his chin like Sherlock Holmes pondering a piece of evidence.

Teena couldn't tell if he was joking or not. "Umm. It seemed too big to be a throwing knife."

He mentally filed away the information. "Gotcha gotcha. Alright, so then who's *closest* to Scrooge on th' stage?"

"The Cratchits. The whole family is around him. Mr. and Mrs. Cratchit and the six children. Tiny Tim is even sitting on his shoulder."

A chuckle rumbled from Bernie's chest. "Well, we can count out the kids." His laugh suddenly stopped, and he looked deathly serious. "Right?"

Teena began to say "Of course"…but her mind was racing. She had become paranoid, looking for killers around every corner. Could Andy be planning a murder? Haley? Any of the other kids? Perhaps they were unwitting accomplices, tricked into doing the deed for someone else. Could little Colton McCowdrey be convinced stabbing Ebenezer Scrooge was just part of the show? Teena found that idea stupidly improbable. Then again, she was playing detective backstage at *A Christmas Carol*—ten minutes ago, she would have found this whole situation stupidly improbable.

She went with her gut and said, "Right. We can count out the kids." But she kept the Colton theory in the back of her mind. Just in case.

"So then. Mr. and Miss Cratchit." Bernie searched for their real names, but he came up empty.

"Jimmy Quinn and Evelyn Barrie."

"Our prime suspects."

Teena reeled him back in. "The two people I'll want to talk to first. See if they've heard anything suspicious."

"Or if *they're* suspicious." Bernie bugged out his eyes.

Yeah. That too. Teena hadn't fully grasped what she was doing until that moment. If she was truly determined to get to the bottom of this, that meant she would be interacting with a person who intended to commit murder. Someone in the cast—a person she knew—was dangerous.

"Okay." Teena formulated a plan of action. "Right now, Jimmy is onstage playing Bob Cratchit. In the meantime, I'll talk to Evelyn. Then Jimmy, once he's available. Bernie, I know this is a big favor, but—"

Bernie was one step ahead of her. "I'll call my brother in the Tennant Park PD. He likes me, we're good. I'll see if he can come up here without making a lotta noise."

She smiled, feeling a flutter in her stomach. More nervous thrills, but of a totally different breed. Instead of playing a part onstage, she was taking part in a real-life adventure. She'd never done anything remotely like this, and it was exhilarating.

"We'll reconvene when we have new information." She held out a fist.

Bernie bumped it with his own. "Pleasure t' be on the case with you, Detective Fakhoury."

"And you, Detective..." She paused, horrifically embarrassed. "Bernie, I'm so sorry. What's your last name?"

He rumbled a warm chuckle. "Bernard. But I like to go by Bernie."

She hadn't realized "Bernie" was a nickname for his *last* name. Now she felt too awkward to ask for his *first* name, so she just said, "Well then, best of luck to you, Detective Bernie." They parted ways, each on their own mission.

As the original author of *A Christmas Carol* would say, the game was afoot.

Wait, no. That wasn't Dickens. That was the Sherlock Holmes author. Teena clearly wasn't an English teacher. What was his name? Damon? Dahl? She knew it was a three-part name, but she was totally blanking.

Oh well. It would come to her.

Regardless, they were on the case.

7.

Teena slid back through the door and headed for the green room, her mind racing. Sprinting. Galloping.

What was she doing? She wasn't a sleuth. She didn't even watch murder shows on TV — *Planet Earth* and *New Girl* were more her thing. There was no sane scenario in which she should be the one solving a murder…even one that hadn't happened yet.

But she knew her gut was right. If she told anyone, they would make a big hullaballoo and put the quaint little theatre on lockdown. The killer would simply try again another day, learn from this trial run, and likely succeed in turning Percival Jennings into a memory.

Whether she was the right person for the job or not, she was stuck with it. Percival's life was in her hands.

That thought made her knees buckle a little. She shook her head to banish the idea—putting that kind of pressure on herself wouldn't help.

When she reentered the green room, she was briefly taken aback. She had dashed out of an empty, quiet room only a few minutes ago, frenzied and on the verge of panic. Now, it was full and bustling with activity. The children were entertaining themselves with their phones or one another, while the adult actors couldn't stop smiling and chattering. With the opening scene done, they were on top of the world. It didn't matter that they were amateur thespians in a community theatre show. Tonight, they were Broadway bigshots.

Teena spotted Corrine at the costume racks, grabbing her dress and bonnet for the Christmas Past section. She hadn't seen Teena walk in—good. As quickly as she could while still looking moderately well-balanced, Teena began to slink across the green room.

She desperately wanted to talk with Corrine. To wish her a broken leg in her upcoming scenes as Belle. To ask her how the opening scene had gone. To share the adrenaline of theatre with her, like this was an ordinary performance on an ordinary night.

But all of a sudden, this night had become far from ordinary. Teena didn't have time to get sucked into a black hole of conversation. With every scene, every line, every moment, Percival's murder drew closer. She had to get moving.

So she did something she'd never done before: She slipped past her friend without saying hi. Fortunately, the green room was busy enough that she could walk through without drawing too much attention.

As she crept through the door backstage, she forced herself not the look at the vent that concealed a potential murder weapon. It practically screamed at her, causing the ground beneath her feet to rumble and the ceiling above to crack open…but she walked right by. If the killer was watching her, they couldn't know that she knew something was hidden in that duct.

When she closed the door behind her, she exhaled. At least backstage, it was dark enough for her to show some emotion without tipping her hand. In just the past few minutes, everything had changed. She was confused by the mystery she found herself in. She was weirdly tired from the gears constantly turning in her mind. She was scared of the fact that she may have just been in a crowded room with a would-be killer.

And she was excited to be in the lead role of her own story. The star. The hero. Coming to save the day.

It was a lot to take in.

She walked backstage to the wing of stage-left. The scene in Scrooge's office was winding to a close. Percival, wearing a long black coat and top hat, stood in front of a heavy desk. Two ensemble members who played charity-seekers stood near the edge of the stage, backing up slowly as they were lambasted by Scrooge. Bob Cratchit, played by Jimmy, sat at his own small desk, sporting tiny eyeglasses and a dirty waistcoat.

And there, leering through a window, was the white-faced ghost of Marley, played by Roy. Teena got chills just seeing him. Marley stood in the background, not drawing attention to himself, stalking his prey. It was genuinely chilling and a great addition to the story.

Teena zeroed in on the muscular clerk trying to look small and sheepish. He was her first point of investigation: the hotheaded Jimmy Quinn, who had gotten into a number of shouting matches with Percival Jennings during rehearsals. And he stood right next to Scrooge in the final scene—the perfect place for a stabbing.

"I wish to be left alone!" Percival swept his hands through the air, gnashing his teeth at the well-meaning charity-seekers. "I don't make myself merry at Christmas, and I can't afford to make idle people merry either. I am taxed for prisons and poorhouses, and they cost enough. Those who are badly off must go there."

Teena had to admit it: Though Percival tended to go "big and showy" when acting, he was effective. He inspired fear in others. Even now, the charity-seekers recoiled at his tirade, despite the fact that they had rehearsed this scene many times. How much of that was due to Percival's talent as an actor, and how much was due to his real-life D-baggery, who's to say.

One of the charity-seekers stammered, "But many can't go there. And many would rather die!"

Next came one of Scrooge's most famous lines: "If they'd rather die, perhaps they should go ahead and do it and decrease the surplus population."

That always got a reaction from the audience. They rippled in their seats with hatred for Ebenezer Scrooge.

Even though Teena was mainly focused on her investigation, she couldn't help but get caught up in the rush of performing. The audience reacting exactly how they were supposed to, the actors feeding off each other's energies… It was good stuff.

Something rustled next to Teena. Paranoia flashed an image of a knife-wielding killer through her mind, and she jerked back in alarm.

But it was only a young girl. Haley Schrader stood there next to Teena, already dressed in her ensemble costume for the Christmas Past section. She was watching the scene onstage, smiling, transfixed, soaking in the magic of theatre.

When Teena reacted in panic, so did Haley. She backed up frantically and apologized with a yelp. "I'm sorry!" She remembered her volume and brought her voice down to a jumpy whisper. "I'm sorry if I'm not supposed to be here! I was just... Just..."

"Just watching?" Teena forced her heart to slow down. She gave Haley a soft smile. "Me too. It's a good show, isn't it?"

Haley inched back to Teena's side, then returned her attention to the scene onstage. She nodded, almost in a trance.

Teena asked, "Do you want to do this more when you grow up? Act, I mean?"

Haley said, "Yeah." But she was distant, focused on the show.

Chuckling, Teena stepped away and let the girl have a private showing.

The scene drew to a close. Percival and Jimmy, who were the only actors left onstage, hustled off to the side. A few stagehands dragged away the desks and props, as well as the walls that comprised the set of Scrooge's office. All that was left was the London street. A few ensemble members populated the city, going about their Christmas Eve business. Scrooge reentered, walking home. Marley's ghost trailed eerily behind him.

The scene continued on the stage, but Teena stopped watching. She stood backstage-left, while Jimmy had exited stage-right. She rushed behind the London backdrop to get to the other side of the stage before Jimmy could vanish elsewhere. Cords and cables lay tangled on the floor behind the set, and Teena had to hoist up her robe to lift her feet high enough to step over them—tripping backstage and making a huge crashing sound was every actor's nightmare. Dust bunnies and abandoned flakes of plastic snow also cluttered the thin space behind the backdrop. She wasn't looking forward to the day after the final performance, when the whole cast helped clean up the theatre.

She popped out the other side of the backdrop and leaned casually against the wall, hoping Jimmy wouldn't notice her heavy breathing. She was doing way more hurrying and running tonight than she usually did.

Jimmy walked in her direction, taking off his prop eyeglasses. Perfect—he hadn't noticed her sudden appearance.

What she was about to do ran completely against her nature. She'd spent most of her life being accommodating, not rocking the boat, and letting people talk to and question her, not vice versa. Now, she was about to start interrogating people right on the spot. Her friends, peers, and castmates. Who did she think she was? Why did she think she had the right to do this?

She pinched her side to snap herself out of her downward spiral. There was no time for doubt. Just doing. She tried to still her rocketing heart by taking a slow breath. It was time to make her detective debut.

"Hey, Jimmy?" She stepped away from the wall, pretending to cross paths with him coincidentally.

Jimmy stopped and looked around, searching for the source of the mysterious voice in the dark backstage. He slipped the tiny glasses back on his face, then quickly spotted her. "Oh, hey, Teena."

She beckoned him a little further away from the stage, so they could talk louder without disturbing the ongoing scene. Before she dove into her investigation, her curiosity won the first question. "Are those glasses real?"

Jimmy shrugged in mild embarrassment. "Yeah. I wear contacts, but Simeon wanted me to wear these instead. Something about authenticity, he said."

"I had no idea." She chuckled.

"Good. That's the idea." He subconsciously flexed his arms, seeming to think that glasses somehow undermined his daily trips to the gym.

Teena quickly cut off her laugh. She didn't want to give Jimmy a reason to get angry. Not before possibly accusing him of planning a murder, at least.

She wondered why Jimmy had played Bob Cratchit for multiple years. It wasn't exactly a He-Man-type role.

That wasn't important. She shoved away her curiosity and got back to the matter at hand.

She said, "The other night, at rehearsal… Thanks for sticking up for me. With Percival."

Jimmy looked at the floor. "Oh yeah, well… You're welcome." He lifted his head back up and smiled. "Sure thing, y'know?"

In truth, Teena didn't care for the way Jimmy had stood up to Percival the night the old man had called her "stunt casting." His outburst had drawn more attention to her, which she hated. And besides, it had felt less like he was actually defending Teena and more like an excuse for Jimmy to yell at someone he didn't like. But she wanted to get Jimmy talking about Percival and maybe see if his dislike leaned toward violence.

She went on. "I just hope he hasn't been giving you a hard time since then."

He snorted a laugh. "When *hasn't* he been giving me a hard time? I've lived in Tennant Park for a long time, and I've been Cratchit for a while too, and Al Jennings has always been a blackberry seed in my molar."

"Oh yeah?"

"Oh *yeah*." Jimmy scoffed, more than willing to rail against Percival. "Just yesterday at rehearsal, he wouldn't stop badgering me. He was asking me all kinds of questions, but not really looking for answers, you know what I mean? Like, he asked if there were any loopholes around taxes on vintage cars from Germany. And if he could write-off any construction on his house as a business expense.

And if he could will all his money to himself when he dies."

"Huh." Teena thought for a moment. "Can he?"

"No! Of course not." Jimmy threw his hands up in the air. "The answers to all those questions are no, but they're ridiculous questions. He was only asking them to rub his obscene wealth in my face. And whenever I would call him out on it, he would get all defensive and say, 'Can I not just ask questions?' But he had this nasty smirk on his face. He knows he has enough money to pay me to count it." He clenched his jaw, tamping down his boiling anger.

In the background of their conversation, Percival derided and insulted Londoners with relish. Teena was reminded of Corrine's earlier comment: With his money and demeanor, Percival Jennings has been method-acting as Ebenezer Scrooge for his entire life.

"Sorry about that, Jimmy." She swallowed. "And, uhh… I'm sorry if I've ever asked you for advice on my taxes or anything. I promise I didn't mean to insult you."

He puffed out a breath, like a tea kettle releasing steam. "Nah, it's all good. I'm used to it. That's the life of an accountant, right? Everyone's always asking you for free advice. Just the other day, Don Schrader had some questions about property management. That kid Markus asked me if large gifts were taxable — the answer is depends, by the way. And just last night, at the church party, Roy Jennings was telling me about this huge African safari vacation he's planning to take next year, and he had a few money questions too." He paused and whistled. "Rich people, man. Can you imagine jetting off on a big trip like that? Or buying cars from Europe just *because*?"

Teena chuckled. "Not even a little. I'm a middle school teacher, remember?"

"Oh, right." He laughed with her.

On the stage, Percival reached for the handle of his residence's door. At that moment, the ever-present ghost made himself known. Roy screamed in the old man's ear, "*SCROOOOOGE!*" Eerie fog filled the air, and the ghost's banshee-like wail echoed throughout the auditorium.

Roy may have been a lousy actor who couldn't deliver a line to save his life, but the atmosphere more than made up for it. The fog machines, the sound mixing, the theatre's acoustics… It all worked together to make for a really effective horror scene. The audience responded in kind, gasping and flinching in their seats.

Scrooge backed away from the door in terror…but once the fog cleared, the ghost was gone. He shook his head, giving the people in the audience permission to snicker at themselves. It was a classic haunted house scare: screams, followed by laughs.

Teena said quietly, "Simeon really is doing a great job. He deserves more recognition than he gets."

"Hmm?" Jimmy wasn't paying attention to the goings-on of *A Christmas Carol*. He was lost in thought. "I wonder just how much cash Al has weaseled away for himself. Probably more than I'll ever see. Pretty much only Victor knows for sure."

Teena pressed, "Victor Stassi? Why would he know?"

"He's Percival's estate-planning attorney. Handles his will and inheritance and stuff like that. And with Al's wife dying last Christmas, I'd bet Victor has seen a lot of him in the past year."

Made sense. Victor was the most popular estate lawyer in the county. Teena was sure he was very good at his job, but even if he wasn't, it felt right that Percival would hire the person with the most billboards.

Before they could continue talking, the backstage area grew frenzied again. Stagehands zipped every which way. The time had come for the London street to disappear and Scrooge's bedchamber to come into being. All of the scene transitions throughout the show had been painstakingly rehearsed again and again, but each one involved many moving parts, meaning there were infinite opportunities for something to go wrong.

Backstage was a flurry of activity. Stagehands carried props and furniture. Simeon, who had set up shop in the EXIT sign's red glow, was extremely in the way, and he bobbed back and forth, trying to get out of the traffic. Along the back wall, a stagehand pulled on a thick rope, hand over hand—in response, a sandbag lowered from the ceiling, and the London cityscape backdrop rose up and up and up, out of sight. A wall was wheeled onto the stage, acting as the interior of Scrooge's bedroom. The stagehands set an easy chair, a fireplace, and a bed on the stage, then scurried off.

Voila! In less than thirty seconds, the scene had changed entirely. Not a hiccup in sight. Simeon looked like he might pass out from relief. He leaned against the ropes on the wall and went back to scrutinizing his clipboard.

A thought suddenly struck Teena, flooding her veins with panic.

This moment—this scene change, these thirty seconds—was the only time in the entire play when Percival would be backstage. Right now, he was quickly changing out of his street clothes and into the iconic nightgown and cap. There was no intermission, and Scrooge would be onstage for the rest of the story. If Teena wanted to warn him about the threat on his life, this was her one and only opportunity.

But it was too late. At that moment, Percival waddled onto the bedchamber set, dressed for sleep. His costume change was done, and he wouldn't be alone again. She had missed her shot.

Her heart sank. Some detective she was. She'd taken her eye off the prize: Finding out the identity of the would-be killer was important, but keeping Percival safe was paramount.

If she was honest with herself, Percival likely would have ignored or laughed at any sort of warning she gave him, no matter how cautiously she'd phrased it. But still, she felt like a failure.

"You okay, Teena?" Jimmy leaned into her line of sight.

Teena startled herself back to awareness—she'd gotten lost in a haze of self-doubt. She may have missed her chance to possibly warn Percival, but she could still get to the bottom of the mystery. She didn't have a choice. No one else was going to.

"Umm…" She put on a smile. "Yeah, sorry. Just thinking about all that money Percival must have."

He chortled and bit the inside of his cheek. "I do that too sometimes. Rich chump."

Teena didn't know what to say next. She'd reached the end of her admittedly half-baked game plan. Jimmy definitely had a bone to pick with Percival, but he didn't seem like a murderer. Of course, that's exactly what a murderer would want her to think. But she liked Jimmy, so she decided she was done covertly interrogating him. Plus, she didn't want him to get suspicious.

"Okay, Jimmy. Again, thanks for your help." She turned to walk away, but she had one more question. A personal one. Ten minutes ago, she wouldn't have asked it, but she and Jimmy had fallen into a rhythm of conversation, and he seemed comfortable with her. So she asked, "Why do you keep auditioning for Bob Cratchit?"

He seemed surprised by the question but not offended. He shrugged. "I like the role, and I like being in the show. Don't fix what isn't broken, right?"

"Right. But you don't even like wearing glasses. And Bob is…" She searched for the right word.

Jimmy supplied it. "Shrimpy?" He laughed and nodded. "I see what you're asking. Yeah, I like acting in the show. *Acting*. Cratchit is an underling. Timid. Small. I'm not. And I *know* I'm not, so I don't mind playing a character who is. I'm confident in myself." Again, he held up his python-like arm. "But… But my eyes don't just belong to Cratchit. They're mine. I can't change those."

He pushed the tiny glasses up his nose and looked at the floor again.

They stood there for a moment, the ongoing scene acting as their only ambience. Teena said, "I know the feeling." She cleared her throat. "Sorry to steal some of your break time between scenes. I won't take any more."

He smiled. "It's not a problem. But I'll go sit in the green room for a bit before Christmas Present. Good talking to you." He ducked behind the set, headed for the green room.

As soon as she was alone, Teena released a low, silent whistle. She clenched her eyes until she saw stars. Her first session as a detective hadn't gone very well.

Or maybe it had gone great and she was absolutely crushing it. That was the problem with being an amateur sleuth: no benchmarks. Her success or failure would only be judged at the end of the night, when Percival Jennings was either alive or dead.

8.

So. What next?

Teena tapped a finger against her temple, as if giving her brain a kick-start would get things moving. She again brought to mind the bird's-eye-view diagram of the final scene, with Percival's position X'd out. Who was within striking distance of the old man?

Jimmy, definitely. Also Evelyn. There were also the six Cratchit kids, but Teena dismissed them. As paranoid as she was getting, she refused to cultivate the idea that a child would plan a murder. Plus, as a teacher, she knew kids. Even beyond the moral and ethical objections, an eighth-grade boy could hardly sit still long enough to write his name, much less draw an accurate diagram for the purpose of plotting an assassination. No, she was definitely looking for an adult.

Which left Jimmy and Evelyn.

But the more she thought about it, the more uncertain she became. The final scene involved nearly the whole cast, including the three ghosts. If someone wanted to stab Percival onstage, they likely weren't too concerned with being caught. Thus, the killer didn't need to be sneaky. The stage wasn't all that big—it could be sprinted across in less than ten seconds. If someone in the ensemble wanted to stab Percival, they could simply bum-rush him and do so. They didn't need to be right next to him.

As she thought about this, her shoulders slumped. In a matter of moments, her list of potential suspects had jumped from the two Cratchit adults to the entire cast.

Well… Not the *entire* cast. There was one character not onstage in the final scene: the ghost of Marley.

Roy Jennings was someone Teena could comfortably eliminate from her investigation, since he would be as far as possible from the would-be murder scene. Teena decided he was the next person she should talk to. Maybe he could provide the names of castmates who had beef with Percival. More specifically, *serious* beef that could result in murder—it seemed Percival got under everyone's skin.

But Marley's big scene was coming up. Teena wondered if she'd have time to talk with Roy before he had to go on.

Speaking of which…

The action onstage was picking back up. Scrooge, now in his Dickensian pajamas, sat in the easy chair. He began "eating" his dinner of plastic meat and beanbag potatoes.

Teena inched to the very edge of backstage-right, as if she was standing on a high diving board. She stopped so that the people in the audience couldn't see her.

She was too late to catch Roy. The scene was underway.

Across the stage, Roy stood in the wing on backstage-left, ready to walk onstage. He caught her eye and gave a small smile.

Teena still felt bad for pestering him at the makeup desks earlier, but he seemed to have moved on. Even from dozens of feet away, she could see he was nervous. It only made sense — his brother told him he was an awful actor at every single rehearsal. While opening night was fun for most people, it was likely a nightmare for him.

She gave him two big thumbs up.

The stage lights flickered. Fog rolled in. A theremin hummed in the background. This was Roy's cue. Even though he had been looming in the background during the beginning of the show, he wasn't fully visible to the audience. Now, it was time for Marley to make a grand entrance in all his ghostly glory.

Percival said, "Humbug! What hogwash is this?"

At that, Roy lurched out of the wing, moaning and groaning like a zombie. His face was painted completely white, except for the thick black rings around his eyes. His clothes were ragged, and his iconic chains hung from his body. The prop budget clearly hadn't gone toward the chains—they were plastic, and only three or four were draped around his shoulders—but the rest of the stagecraft made up for it. The lights, the sound effects, the makeup… It all came together to make for an unsettling atmosphere.

And then he opened his mouth.

"Ebenezer Scrooge, I come for your soul's salvation."

As harsh as the constant criticism of Roy's acting was, it wasn't exactly unfounded. He spoke jerkily and with zero confidence, as if he was reading his lines from a teleprompter for the first time. But he always did his best, and Teena was rooting for him.

Percival sputtered in fear, then quickly switched to annoyed hostility. How very Scrooge-like. "Who are you?"

"In life," Roy waved his arms, making the small chains clink, "I was your partner, Jacob Marley."

"I don't believe it." Percival crossed his arms.

"Why do you doubt your senses?"

Teena couldn't help but smile. This was one of her favorite lines in the show.

Percival stood and paced as he delivered his argument. "Because a little thing affects them. A slight disorder of the stomach can make them cheat. You might be a bit of undigested beef, a blot of mustard, a fragment of an underdone potato. Yes, there's more of *gravy* than of *grave* about you!"

The audience began to laugh, but Roy cut them off way too early with a monstrous wail. Undoubtedly, Simeon was chewing through his clipboard — he had run through the pacing of this scene with Roy a hundred times.

Percival cowered against the wail, but he did not fall to his knees. In previous years, Teena had seen him cry, shake, and grovel before Marley. Not this year, though. He stared Roy right in the eye.

Even in a fictional story on a stage, Percival refused to lower himself beneath his brother.

"Why do you come to me?" he said.

"If a man does not walk among his fellow beings in life, he is condemned to do so after death." Roy buckled under the supposed weight of his chains. Of course, he wasn't very convincing.

"What are these dreadful chains you bear?"

Roy projected directly to the audience, knowing this was an important line. "I wear the chain I forged in life. I made it link by link, yard by yard, and wore it of my own free will. You wear such a chain yourself. It is longer and heavier than it was seven Christmases ago. You have labored on it since my death!"

Percival scowled as he said his next line: "Jacob, please, speak comfort to me." An odd place to add a scowl.

Despite Roy's rough line delivery, the tension onstage crackled like a tesla coil. The wiry, energetic Marley bounced around the bedchamber, while the thin, gray Scrooge shot daggers from his eyes. Teena doubted that siblings often played the roles of Scrooge and Marley. Decades of history — of arguments, jokes, memories, and unsaid feelings — bled into their performances. It was riveting stuff.

She wanted to stay in the wings and watch it all unfold…but moreover, she wanted to speak with Roy ASAP. If he had information about who could be Percival's possible killer, she needed to know.

However, each second whizzed past with all the weight of a freight train. She was wasting time. Percival's life hung in the balance. She couldn't justify waiting around for this scene to end — she had to keep moving.

Perhaps Evelyn could be her next stop. She was likely in the green room, funneling homemade treats down people's throats. She didn't go on until Christmas Present, which was still a ways off.

It struck Teena:

Christmas Present. Even with her ongoing covert investigation, she would still have to perform.

It seemed silly to have to go through the motions of delivering lines and moving from scene to scene. But the killer couldn't know anyone was on to them. Thus, Teena had to perform as if nothing was amiss.

Even though pretty much everything was amiss.

She sighed. That wasn't going to be easy.

But she didn't have time to dawdle any longer. She slipped behind the set and tiptoed back the way she had come. As she slunk, the scene in Scrooge's bedchamber marched steadily onward.

"But you always were a good man of business, Jacob."

"Business?! Humankind was my business!"

"What mean you?"

"The common welfare was my business. Charity, mercy, forbearance, and benevolence… All were my business!"

Teena popped out the other side of the set and made her way to the green room. Since only two actors were currently onstage, the place was full and lively. Or maybe antsy was the right word. Chaotic? Spirited? All of the above.

After the current scene with Marley was the Ghost of Christmas Past's intro, which then led to Christmas Past itself. The cast was gearing up for the back-to-back scenes of Scrooge's old school and Mr. Fezziwig's Christmas party, both of which were heavy on the ensemble.

Victor Stassi stood up from a makeup desk with a flourish. "Time to shine!" he said. He wore a yellow tunic with a silver sash. And he seemed to shimmer. Teena looked closer. Was that…?

Yes. For opening night, he had added glitter to his mustache. The Ghost of Christmas Past was traditionally played as a being of pure light, but Victor was really pulling out all the stops. Either he truly cared about embodying the role, or he wanted to draw as much attention to his famous facial hair as possible.

He strode across the green room toward the backstage door. He would be going on in a few minutes' time, after the conclusion of the Marley scene. He said to the entire room, loudly and proudly, "Wish me double luck!"

In unison, the cast replied, "Break both legs!" They all laughed — it seemed to be a recent inside joke Teena had missed while she was playing Sherlock backstage.

Teena flicked her eyes over every inch of the green room. She didn't see Evelyn's bun of graying hair. Of course, it was crowded, so she could just be overlooking her —

"Hey!" Corrine stepped into her line of sight. She wore her Belle costume, and her face was positively plastered with makeup in an attempt to make her look at most college-aged. But at the moment, her face was scrunched up with concern and a hint of frustration. "Where've you been?"

"I, uhh…" Teena had no idea what to say. She knew she couldn't bring Corrine into the loop, but she hadn't prepped a cover story yet.

"Is everything okay?" Corrine's nose twitched as she practically smelled that something was off…but she couldn't quite put a finger on what.

"Oh yeah! Totally. Everything's great." Teena knew she was going overboard with her nonchalance, but she couldn't turn back now. She tried to look casual as she waved off her friend's concern.

But Corrine never liked being waved off. Her brows pointed skyward. "So if everything's great, where've you been? We always hang out in the green room during performances. That's kind of my favorite part of all this. *And* now I have to learn how to be the Ghost of Christmas Yet to Come, and I was hoping you'd help."

Teena's blasé façade melted immediately. "Oh, sweetie, I'm so sorry." She could see the anxiety in Corrine's clenched jaw, and she felt horrible for leaving her out to dry. "I just—"

The door to the green room opened, and Bernie shuffled in. All at once, the actors stopped what they were doing and swiveled to stare at him. It was almost an exact recreation of his entrance at the party last night, except this was even more jarring. The green room was the actors' domain, their realm. Bernie walking into it was like an elephant tramping through a butterfly garden.

"H-Hey, y'all," he said.

Once again, the kids welcomed him. Colton lit up and called out, "Bernardo! Hi hi hi hi!" The Cratchit children crowded around his legs, chattering over one another, lobbing questions at him, and basically treating him like a visiting rock star.

"How's it goin', kids? Hi, hey, cool, yeah…" As he placated the kids, he looked around the room. Finally, his gaze settled on Teena. Probably thinking he was being very subtle and 007-like, he bugged out his eyes and gestured with his head to the lobby. But, of course, everyone in the room saw exactly what he was doing.

Corrine turned back to Teena, somehow even more concerned and frustrated than before. "What's going on with Bernie?"

Teena sighed — she clearly couldn't lie and say everything was peachy. "Trust me. Okay?"

A tidal wave of "buts" and "whys" built up on Corrine's lips. Teena knew it took every ounce of self-control for her to hold them back and say, "Okay."

Teena seized her opportunity and peeled away from Corrine. She promised herself she'd tell her friend everything…once everything was settled and taken care of.

She hooked an arm around Bernie's and began to haul him toward the door, back the way he had just come from. The kids whined and moaned and begged her to let him stay.

"It's alright, kiddos," he said over his shoulder. "I'll be—" But Teena dragged him out the door, through the little hallway, and into the empty lobby.

From behind the auditorium doors, Teena could hear the muffled voices of Percival and Roy wrapping up their scene:

"Can't they all come at once and have it over with?"

"For your sake, Ebenezer, take care that you remember what has passed between us…"

She pulled Bernie back to their little corner of the lobby under the huge wreath and poinsettias, where they would be out of the way if someone exited the auditorium.

"Bernie!" she snapped. "What are you doing?"

He was shocked at her tone. "Just, uhh… Well, I…"

She took a breath and tamped down her irritation. Being snippy with her only ally wasn't going to help. "Bernie, we can't draw attention to ourselves. You've never come into the green room before—the killer might get suspicious we're onto them."

"Right right right." Bernie nodded like a broken bobblehead. He seemed nervous, shaken by something. "But you said to reconvene when we have more inf'rmation."

"Alright, good." She braced herself. Whatever he was about to say had put him noticeably on edge. "You have an update?"

"Mhmmmmm." He rubbed a hand over his unshaven face, clearly stalling.

"Is it bad?"

He said, "No no no no!" But then he immediately caved. "Well, I mean, yeah, it's not good."

Teena found herself wanting to stall too. She readjusted the holly crown on her head. All the sneaking and tiptoeing she'd been doing had knocked it askew. She finally said, "Okay, tell me. Rip the Band-Aid off."

"So," Bernie started, "I called my brother at the police department—his name's Tanner, r'member? I told him somethin' bad might be happenin' up here at the theatre. But we haffta keep it quiet, or the bad thing might happen right away. He said he understood. He told a couple of other guys he trusts to keep it on the downlow, and they started to drive up here."

"Started to…?"

He grimaced. "Yeah. You know the road that goes up Mt. Tennant? The road that leads up here? You know how it's the *only* road that leads up here?"

"Yeah…" She didn't like where this was going.

"Well, at three places on the road, some pipes blew. Or burst or broke or somethin', I don't really know the right word. Point is, a buncha water's on the road. I'm talkin' a *flood*. And it's the coldest night of the year. Way b'low freezing."

Teena blanched. "The road is iced?!"

He clenched his jaw and nodded once.

She had no words — her mouth gaped open and closed a few times of its own accord.

The scenic road that zigzagged its way up Mt. Tennant was beautiful. The trees and boulders made her feel like she was in a fantasy setting.

But that was when the road was safe. When ice entered the equation, the lovely, winding road became an impassable deathtrap. A handful of accidents occurred each year, but not many were too serious. Everyone knew not to mess with the road when it was slick.

She thought back to her drive up Mountain earlier that evening.

Bright orange work cones.

Placed periodically.

All the way up.

Someone had tampered with the water pipes. They'd planned it out. No one could come help them, at least not for a while. And no one could leave either.

No wonder Bernie was so shaken.

"So..." She gulped. "Your brother isn't coming."

"Tanner said he and his friends are gonna try to make their way up the road, but it's twisty and dangerous right now. It'll be slow-goin' for them."

Teena sized up her friend. His eyes were as round as eggs. Earlier, he had readily believed her story about the diagram, but he had to have harbored at least a few inklings of doubt—any sane person would. But now, he was one hundred percent convinced. There was no denying that someone had purposely made the mountain road impassible.

Either that, or three major water pipes had *conveniently* burst along the *only* road that led to the place where someone was *coincidentally* planning to kill Percival Jennings.

Yeah right.

Bernie asked, "You said the killer's gonna strike during the very last scene, right?"

She saw what he was getting at. "Yeah. Did your brother say how long it'll take him to get up here?"

"About an hour and a half. How much time is left in the show?"

"About an hour and a half."

Meaning, if Teena and Bernie failed to find out who the killer was, they couldn't count on the cavalry rolling in to save Percival.

Bernie exhaled. "Crap."

"Yeah. Crap."

They stood there for a moment, shellshocked. Teena was just a biology teacher and amateur theatre nerd. She didn't belong in a full-fledged murder plot.

And yet, she didn't really have a choice. The cops weren't coming. It was either her and Bernie or no one. She couldn't bring herself to sit back while someone's life might be in jeopardy.

Just then, Victor Stassi's loud, charismatic voice echoed from within the auditorium. The Ghost of Christmas Past had arrived. For some reason, Victor seemed to be doing a Scottish accent, which Simeon definitely hadn't directed him to do.

"Okay." Teena cleared her throat. She summoned her teacher's ability to sound self-assured and authoritative even when she wasn't sure what she was doing. "This doesn't really change things, if you think about it. We're on the clock. Each scene brings Percival closer to getting stabbed."

"Right. We can't let that happen." Bernie's tone shifted too. Whether some of her confidence had rubbed off on him, or he was pretending to be confident for her sake, she appreciated it.

"I'll get back to snooping around the cast."

"And I'll keep watch ou' here, make sure no one's bein' sneaky. And I'll watch the parkin' lot too, see if someone tries to escape."

Teena remembered how anxious and jumpy he'd been only a few minutes ago. And his trembling hands. And the thick scar on his bald head he'd covered up.

"Hey," she said, "you don't have to do this if you don't want. It could be dangerous."

A wry smile grew on his face. "No way. I'm not lettin' you have all the fun by y'rself. 'Sides, I kinda feel like I'm in my favorite Christmas movie."

Teena was confused by that last comment.

He saw her face and clarified: "Y'know, *Die Hard*."

She chuckled. "It's totally a Christmas movie, isn't it?"

"I literally don't get how people say it isn't."

"Okay, Detective Bernie." She put some steel into her voice, like John McClane. "As we were. Remember, keep a low profile."

He saluted. "Aye-aye."

Once again, they parted ways.

9.

As Teena returned to the green room, she heard Victor and Percival delivering their lines onstage. Victor's lawyerly charm lent itself naturally to the radiant, effervescent Ghost of Christmas Past, while Percival always sounded like he had just been woken up from a nap. It was excellent casting.

"What brings you here, spirit?"

"Your welfare, of course."

"I can't think of anything more conducive to my welfare than a night of uninterrupted sleep."

"Your salvation, then!"

The ghost's intro scene was nearly complete. Next was Scrooge's boyhood school, then young-adult Scrooge's place of employment. Teena ran through the script and cast in her mind. Was there anyone in those scenes she wanted to talk to before they were trapped onstage?

The school scene was mostly comprised of child ensemble members. But after that was Corrine as Belle and Markus as young Scrooge…

A moment from earlier in the night flashed in her memory. It hadn't struck her as odd before, but now, everything was different. Every little glance, gesture, or comment could be put under a microscope and interpreted as suspicious.

Just before the start of the show, Percival had spoken with Markus. The old man had said something with a sneering tone, but then Markus simply smiled, shook his head, and walked away. What had been so important that Percival had pulled Markus aside, literally as the cast was walking to their places? What couldn't have waited?

Teena decided she wanted to find out. It may have something to do with Percival's pending murder. Was that paranoid thinking? Most definitely. But she couldn't afford not to be paranoid.

She picked up the pace. On show nights, actors tended to get to their places about half a scene early, especially responsible people like Markus. He would be heading backstage any minute, and she'd lose her opportunity to talk to him without a dozen other ensemble members squished in the wings nearby.

But when she scurried into the green room, she saw she was too late. Most of the actors were migrating toward the door leading backstage, Markus among them. He was dressed in similar clothes that the crotchety old Scrooge wore: a long coat, a top hat, and a fancy waistcoat.

Teena picked her way through the crowd. When she passed Corrine, she gave her friend a pat and said, "Break a leg." She wanted to walk Corrine to her spot, as she had for the opening scene, but she pushed on to Markus.

"Hey, Markus." She tapped her former student on the shoulder.

He stopped and turned his permanent smile toward her. "Oh, hey, Miss F." They stood in the onslaught of actors like stones in the middle of a rushing river. He looked around, slightly confused. "What can I do for you?"

"I…" She hadn't mapped out the conversation beforehand. "Can I ask you something really quick?"

"Well, I should get to my place."

"It'll just be a second." She gently tugged him out of the current, realizing she was doing the exact same thing Percival had done to him right before the first scene.

When they were a few feet away from the rest of the actors, she asked, "How are you doing?"

He chuckled good-naturedly, but his smile was tinged with frustration. "I'm good, Miss F. But I should be on my way. Can we chat after the show?"

She was losing him. Diving right in looked like the best strategy for the moment. "I saw Percival badgering you earlier tonight. And honestly, I've seen him badgering you a lot. I just want to make sure you're alright."

For a second—just a split second—Markus's smile flickered. He glanced around and saw his fellow Christmas Past-ers were all gone. He muttered, "I should get to my place. Sorry, Miss F." He turned on his heel and sped out of the green room.

Teena was left standing there by herself. It seemed she'd hit a nerve. Or, rather, Percival had hit a nerve. She made a mental note to follow-up with Markus when his scenes were over.

Once the actors had completed their mass exodus, the room was quiet again. For the most part, only the eight Cratchits remained—pretty much everyone else was required to act as background characters in the Christmas Past section. The kids were scattered around the room, some playing on their phones, some quietly chatting to one another, the adrenaline of opening night having largely worn off. Jimmy flipped through a magazine while relaxing by the costume racks. Evelyn sat on one of the raggedy couches in the middle of the room, reading her script and going over her lines one last time.

Teena surveyed the Cratchits again…and her gaze stayed on Evelyn. Even after thirteen years as Mrs. Cratchit, Evelyn was still going over her lines on a show night. That was odd… Right? After all, she was the church choir director. She could probably sight-read music and memorize lyrics in a snap. With more than a decade of Cratchit experience under her belt, Evelyn hardly needed to be flipping through her script.

Unless she was trying to look innocent and busy.

Or she was just studious. A good actress who would rather be overprepared than under.

Or *OR* she was establishing an alibi.

Or she was just flipping through her script. Nothing more and nothing less.

Being a detective seemed to come with an unhealthy dose of mistrust.

Teena massaged her temples. A monster headache was brewing, all thanks to the constant theorizing she'd been doing for the past…

She sighed when she realized it'd only been about a half-hour since she'd discovered the knife and diagram in the air duct. It felt like she'd been on the case for at least a week, interviewing suspects, poring through motives, and tacking clues onto a big board with a lot of string and Post-It notes.

But no. It'd only been the length of a *New Girl* episode.

Time sure crawls when you're investigating a potential murder.

As she stood by the door leading backstage — between the two air vents, one of which housed a knife—Teena studied Evelyn. She wore an apron, black ladies' shoes, and a plaid dress. Her graying hair was up in a bun. A playful smile rested on her lips, as always. Her sharp eyes flicked across Mrs. Cratchit's lines in the script on her lap…

And just like that, a thought entered Teena's head. Jimmy Quinn didn't necessarily have a motive to kill Percival, other than his occasional hotheadedness.

But Teena remembered something Evelyn had said at rehearsal earlier in the week:

Once Percival was gone, she was in line to be the new Ebenezer Scrooge.

Teena leaned against the wall as she reexamined her conversation with Evelyn. The two had been sitting in the auditorium seats after Percival had called Teena "stunt casting." Teena was feeling low, and Evelyn had come to comfort her.

Over the course of their conversation, Evelyn had praised Teena for auditioning for a traditionally male role. She'd said something like, "Finally, another woman's going for it." And she'd expressed that she felt "stuck" as Mrs. Cratchit, a character with no first name and hardly ten lines. "Stuck" for thirteen long years.

Evelyn was better than that. She could handle a role with more meat. As First Baptist's choir director, she knew what went into an engaging performance. She dealt with large crowds every week. When she'd auditioned for Scrooge, Simeon had said she'd done a great job.

Compare that to Percival, who had been the show's leading man for thirty-five consecutive years. He'd had plenty of time in the spotlight. He was surly, unlikable, and difficult to work with. He didn't evolve at all from year to year, only doing the same old thing again and again. And most importantly, from Evelyn's perspective, he wasn't going anywhere. He showed no sign of wanting to step away from the role of Scrooge anytime soon.

And when Evelyn heard that Percival didn't have to audition anymore—hadn't auditioned for the past few years—she snapped. She concocted a plan to get rid of him during the final scene of to-night's performance. When she drove that wickedly serrated blade into Percival's back, eve-ryone would see what a good performer Evelyn Barrie was. For the first time, *she* would finally be in the spotlight. Not Percival. Not anyone else. *Her*.

At least... That was how it went in Teena's head.

She felt a little dizzy from all that speculation. And ultimately, that's what it was: pure conjec-ture. Little more than guesswork. Teena had taken a snippet of conversation between herself and a kind woman, and she'd spun it into a motive wor-thy of *Criminal Minds*.

But even though it felt a little soap-opera, it also felt believable. Could sweet old Mrs. Cratchit be plotting a murder?

Teena wouldn't go so far as to call it "likely," but it was in the ballpark.

She needed some way to test this theory. Sitting down next to Evelyn and flat-out asking her if she'd misplaced a slightly curved knife didn't seem like the best idea. Then again, mentioning something about the knife and gauging the woman's reaction could work. Despite Evelyn's talent, she wasn't a trained actress—if she was planning to stab Percival, and Teena started talking about the exact knife currently hidden in a nearby duct, it would be all over Evelyn's face.

Would "it" be guilt? Shock? Anger? Fear? Teena had no idea, but it would surely be unmistakable.

Teena felt butterflies in her stomach again. She silently told them this was neither the time nor the place, then cleared her throat and went for it before she could convince herself otherwise.

Speaking loudly yet casually, she said, "Does anyone hear that?"

She paused, allowing everyone in the green room to look at her. Using her peripheral vision, she locked in on Evelyn's face. She wanted to see every micro-expression the woman made.

After a sufficient beat of silence, she said, "I think there's something rattling in this duct. Sounds kind of like…metal and paper?"

Jimmy cocked his head to the side like a dog trying to hear the mailman down the block. The kids couldn't have cared less, and they went back to their dillydallying.

But Teena only had eyes for Evelyn. She focused as hard as she could on Mrs. Cratchit without being too obvious. This could be her big break in the case, the piece of behavioral evidence that linked Evelyn to the would-be murder weapon. The next few moments could wrap up this topsy-turvy night of impromptu detective work and breathless tiptoeing around the theatre.

However, Evelyn merely shrugged. "I don't hear anything, dear." And she went back to reading her script.

Her face was as relaxed as could be. Still smiling sweetly, but mildly disinterested. Untroubled. Completely normal.

Teena had learned nothing from this. Perhaps her theory about Evelyn being a vengeful starlet was nothing. Pure fantasy. One hundred percent paranoia.

Or was Evelyn a better actress than Teena had given her credit for?

Releasing a frustrated groan, Teena slunk across the green room. She was tired of thinking about her castmates as if they were suspects.

Evelyn had given her no reason to believe that she was anything but a kindly middle-aged choir director with a streak of ambition when it came to community theatre. Teena couldn't cross her off the list of possible suspects, but nor would she treat her like Roxie Hart. Innocent until proven guilty, right?

She was so mentally exhausted, she unconsciously broke one of her steadfast rules: She sat on the crumb-infested couch. While plopping down, a weary sigh escaped from her chest.

Evelyn glanced up again. "How are things, Teena dear?"

She smiled at Evelyn and answered truthfully: "I'm okay. Just thinking through some things."

"Ah." Evelyn leaned into the squishy old couch cushion and chuckled. "Aren't we all?"

"If you ever want to share, I'm here to listen. Well," Teena gestured to her green robe and holly crown, "until duty calls, of course."

Evelyn peered at the ceiling as she thought. "Just, uhh…" She too let a sigh slip from her lips. "To be honest, I'm just wondering how many more years I'll be in the show. It takes quite the commitment, you know, and…"

Her wrinkled fingers fiddled with the edges of the script pages, fanning them up and down. She seemed hesitant to finish her sentence.

Teena could see it on the tip of her tongue. It was something along the lines of, *"I don't know if Mrs. Cratchit is worth my time and effort."*

She sympathized with the woman. Evelyn was genuinely talented, and she felt trapped in a thankless, mostly arbitrary role. Teena forgot about her investigation for a moment and viewed Evelyn as a woman, castmate, and friend.

Remembering their conversation from a few nights ago, she offered her a similar word of encouragement. "Evelyn, this show would not be half as good without you in it." She set a hand on the woman's shoulder.

They sat like that for a moment or two, content in the stillness. Evelyn gently clasped Teena's hand with her own. "Thank you," she whispered.

Teena tried to think of more to say, other pieces of advice or reassurance that she could offer, but Evelyn seemed comforted by her simple presence. Sometimes less really is more.

Echoes of lines said onstage reverberated through the walls. If Teena's internal clock was accurate, the scene at Scrooge's boyhood school would be drawing to a close. Fezziwig's Christmas Eve party was up next on the docket.

And then Belle's breakup with Scrooge. Corrine's big scene. Teena felt she should be there, watching in the wings, supporting her friend. This was her first year in the role, and she was nervous enough — throw in her sudden casting as the Ghost of Christmas Yet to Come, and she had a certifiable case of theatre jitters.

Teena decided then and there: Regardless of her investigation, she was determined to be backstage to silently cheer on Corrine.

Evelyn gave Teena a soft smile and went back to reading.

The green room was in stasis, a sort of in-between state. Not empty, but not full. Not loud, but not totally quiet. Not busy, but not still. Teena enjoyed these moments of calm during a show. It felt like she was deep inside the hull of a ship as it sailed across choppy waters—she knew big things were happening just outside her field of vision, but she couldn't see them.

As Teena adjusted her seat on the couch, her eyes glanced over the open script on Evelyn's lap.

Wait. She noticed something odd: The pages weren't open to a scene that included Mrs. Cratchit.

Teena scooched closer for a better look. Yep—Evelyn was going over the Marley/Scrooge scene, with copious notes taken around Scrooge's lines.

So Evelyn had ambitions of playing old Ebenezer one day. Teena already knew this. But a new thought struck her.

The incriminating diagram had been drawn and written by hand. Maybe Evelyn's penmanship would match…?

She craned her neck, trying to get a good look without being too obvious. A ton of notes surrounded most of Scrooge's lines: self-directorial comments like "Whisper this to force the audience to listen" and "Remember schoolboy days while saying this." All good ideas, very character-driven, presumably from Evelyn herself and not Simeon.

But Teena was most interested in the handwriting. It was tight and straight, like a typewriter's font. It wasn't anything like the flowery writing a lot of Teena's eighth-grade girls used. No, this was the hand of a woman who'd taken notes during choir practices for decades.

Was it a match for the handwriting on the diagram? In that moment, staring at someone else's penmanship, Teena couldn't be sure. It was like trying to remember a song's melody and lyrics while listening to another. Everything got jumbled together.

She remembered thinking the diagram's handwriting was neat and sort of blocky. It was also written with a thick black Sharpie—Evelyn used a normal ballpoint pen. Was that significant? Again, Teena didn't know for sure.

A moment to think would be helpful.

As she stood from the couch, she said, "I'll let you get back to reading, Evelyn."

"Alrighty, dear." The woman's smile didn't waver.

Teena shook her head at herself. After all that, she didn't have much to go on: Evelyn may or may not have reacted to Teena's comment about something in the air duct, she may or may not be a vindictive star-to-be, and she may or may not have similar writing as that of the incriminating diagram.

Sherlock Holmes she was not.

She still couldn't think of that author's name. Even though Dickens also wrote a mystery or two, she was positive it wasn't him. It started with a D, though. For sure. Maybe. Drake? Dwayne? Drood? No, none of that was right. She bet Bernie would know the right name—he was way smarter than people gave him credit for.

It was a silly thing to be so hung up on…but it was precisely *because* it was silly that it bugged her so much. It was a trivia question most average joes would know off the top of their heads. And yet, Teena couldn't get the answer. That stupid author's name felt just out of reach, as if she was grazing it with the tips of her fingers. If she couldn't even remember a simple little factoid, how could she be expected to solve a real-life mystery?

Hopeless. She felt completely deflated, ineffective, and hopeless.

Across the green room, someone walked in the door from backstage: Roy Jennings, the ghost of Marley himself. Thanks to the hot stage lights, his thick layer of death-makeup streaked down his face. The dinky plastic chains around his shoulders jangled with each step.

His scene had ended a while ago—he must've been chatting with someone in the wings. Now, Teena wanted to talk to him as well. She needed to get a feel for Percival's potential enemies. Who better to supply that information than his brother?

"Hey, Roy!" She forced herself to smile casually, and she approached him for a chat.

Roy saw her and held up a finger to indicate he'd be with her in a second. He grabbed a paper towel from a table and began to dab away the sweaty makeup from his eyes. He then joined her by the door, between the two vents. Perfect—they could talk a little more freely with the huge ducts rumbling over their voices.

He heaved a sigh as he patted the towel against his face. "I don't know how you guys do this."

Teena said, "Who?"

"Actors! I'm a sweaty mess." He was careful not to mess with his makeup too much, or Simeon would yell at him. Marley's ghost needed to still be suitably scary-looking when everyone went out into the lobby after the show to sign autographs and take pictures.

She chuckled. "I'm not sure I'd call us *actors*. Just a bunch of theatre kids, really."

"Well, you're all more *actors* than I am. This is my first time being in anything like this. Ever. I think I'm this year's only adult rookie."

Teena hadn't realized that — being the sole first-timer who wasn't a child had to be somewhat intimidating. "You're doing great. For real."

"I appreciate that." He smiled, deepening his wrinkles and cracking whatever dry makeup was left on his face. "What'd you want to talk about?"

"I just wanted to say we're all glad you're here. In Tennant Park, I mean. Like I was saying before, the town really admires you for coming to live with Percival. How long's it been?"

"I moved in January first." He answered quickly, as if the fact was inscribed on his brain. "It's almost been a full year."

"Couldn't have been easy." She pressed ever so slightly, trying to get Roy talking about any enemies he may have encountered over the past year.

"Eh, well, coming out here took almost every penny I've got." He clicked his tongue. "I've been a vo-tech teacher for a long time. As you probably know, that means I'm about a million bucks short of being a millionaire. And moving to a small mountain town isn't cheap."

That surprised Teena. Since Percival was so wealthy, she'd assumed the entire Jennings clan was in the same money-flooded boat. "Did your brother not help you pay for the move? He's…well off."

Roy snorted a dry chuckle. "He's filthy rich! A bit more than 'well off.' He's also not the world's greatest sharer when it comes to his pocketbook. We have no other siblings, neither of us have kids, our parents are long gone, no cousins or in-laws or anything. That money is *alllllllll* his."

Teena felt this conversation was going well—way better than their previous chat at the makeup desks. Since Roy was being so candid and open, she felt comfortable asking more probing questions.

"You know, I've lived here seven years and known Percival this whole time…but I don't think I know where his money comes from."

Roy shrugged with an exasperated smile. "Stocks and bonds and other things that make my eyes cross. Don't ask me for more details, because I really don't know. Business was never my arena. He made some good investments when he was a young man. Mind you, he didn't share those investment tips with me, his little brother. Just went on and made 'em all by himself. And now, decades later, voila, he's the miser of Tennant Park. I can't tell you exactly how much he's got, only that he's rich enough to go swimming in his cash like Scrooge McDuck."

"Hmm." Teena thought for a moment. "So Percival didn't help you with the move?"

"Not a cent, nah." Roy got a new paper towel and went back to patting his sweaty forehead.

"That's..." She struggled to find the right word. "Rough."

"That's Percy."

Teena tried to steer the conversation the direction she wanted it to go. "Have you felt very welcome this past year? I mean, Percival doesn't have many fans. Is there anyone that's made you feel uncomfortable?"

He arched a brow. "Why do you ask?"

She'd been anticipating this question. "I just want to make sure you know you're welcome here. If someone I know is making you—or Percival—uncomfortable, maybe I could talk to them."

"Hmm..." Roy shifted from foot to foot and ruffled his hair as he thought.

She prompted further, "Maybe Percival has really ticked someone off this past year? I mean, as he's been grieving his wife, he may have pushed someone over the edge."

A harsh laugh exploded from Roy's throat. With his streaked makeup and bitter smile, he suddenly looked every inch the nightmarish demon. "His wife... I can't believe you bought that story."

It took Teena a few seconds to catch up with what Roy had just said. "What do you mean?"

Roy set his palms together as if he was praying and donned a mocking voice. "The story of poor old Percival Jennings, whose lovely wife Rebecca died on Christmas Day." He dropped the act and laughed again. "A story. Pure PR to try to cover his tail."

"Wait wait wait." Teena waved her hands like she was trying to flag down a taxi. She sputtered, "Why? What? Huh?"

Roy explained…with *relish*. "His wife didn't die. She left his sorry butt behind and ran off with another guy. She did leave him on Christmas, though — that part's true."

"No. Way." Teena's jaw hit the floor. She couldn't believe what she'd just heard. It was the gossip to topple all other gossip. News like this would rock Tennant Park to its core. How had no one found out about this?

Because the only two people who knew were the Jennings brothers, and Percival clearly didn't want anyone to know. Roy, on the other hand, had just freely told Teena all about it with great delight. Perhaps he was simply comfortable with Teena and felt he could trust her. Kinship among teachers, maybe?

Hold on. There would be one other person who knew the truth about Percival's wife.

His estate-planning attorney. The man Percival would need to go to in order to remove his recently-estranged wife from his will and make sure she didn't get a penny of his wealth. Victor "The Stache" Stassi.

Interesting. Teena didn't quite see how this fit together with Percival's planned murder, but it was all very interesting.

Roy jittered in his shoes. He wasn't quite done airing his brother's dirty laundry. "Wanna know who she ran off with?"

Teena snapped back to the present moment. She didn't love loitering in other people's misery, but at the same time, she didn't want to say no and end the rapport she'd established with Roy. "Uhh…"

Just then, the door flew open, and Simeon trundled in, his clipboard held close to his chest like a bad hand of poker he didn't want anyone to see. His frantic eyes scanned the entire green room before finally resting on Teena, who was only a few feet from him.

"Oh! Teena! There you are! I've been looking all over for you."

Teena wanted to mention that the very first place one would look for an actor who's not on-stage would be the green room…but she held her tongue. She may have gained some confidence over the course of the evening, but not *that* much.

She asked, "Is everything okay?"

"*No*, everything is not *okay!*" Simeon's dramatic delivery nearly convinced Teena he would make a good actor himself. "There are only a few more scenes in Christmas Past, and I just remembered… Your torch! The Ghost of Christmas Present's famous torch! It was broken earlier this week!"

"Oh yeah." Teena recalled Evelyn sitting on her foam-and-paper torch. When she was on duty as a teacher, she always made sure every little detail was taken care of, but in the theatre, she assumed someone else—namely Simeon—would take care of it all. She'd apparently been wrong.

"Yeah!" Simeon went on without taking a breath. "I need you to run downstairs to the prop room and grab something, anything, that could work in place of a torch."

Teena checked the clock on the wall. Her entrance as the Ghost of Christmas Present was right around the corner. "You mean now?"

"Yes, I mean now! *Run!*" With that, Simeon bustled backstage, leaving a cloud of anxiety in his wake.

Roy chuckled. "He's wound awfully tight."

But Teena didn't have time to dawdle. She'd intended to keep talking with Roy and hopefully glean more information about who might want to kill Percival. And she *really* wanted to watch Corrine's big scene from backstage. But the way things were looking, she would barely have time to dash to the prop room, grab a suitable torch replacement, and return backstage.

"Sorry, Roy, but I—"

"What are you waiting for?" He mimed shooting a starter pistol in the air. "Run like the wind!"

Off she dashed, moving her legs as quickly as her velvet robe allowed.

10.

Before she got too carried away, Teena paused just outside the green room, strained her ears, and listened. Voices emanated from the stage: Percival, Victor, and various ensemble actors. She tried to discern what they were saying so that she would know roughly how much time she had.

She picked up on Victor—the Ghost of Christmas Past—saying, "It's such a small thing, to make people feel so much gratitude and joy."

Percival then replied in his Scrooge-y way, "Small thing?!"

The ghost replied, "Is it not? After all, what exactly did this Mr. Fezziwig do? He simply spent a few pounds on a party. Does he deserve such praise as this?"

So Fezziwig's Christmas Eve party was nearly over. Then Belle's scene, then a brief interlude with Scrooge alone in his bedchamber, then Teena had to make her entrance.

She had very little time. About eight or nine minutes.

After peeking around the door and making sure the lobby was empty, she emerged and headed for the theatre's main entrance. The prop room was located at the bottom of a staircase near the front of the building.

She hurried past the folding tables and lovely décor Bernie had set up. But there was no sign of the man himself. As much as she wanted to see him and debrief what she'd learned, she couldn't spare the seconds.

With every step she took toward the theatre's front door, the air became more and more icy. The cold December night seemed to be invading, slipping through every crack and cranny the building had. Teena typically enjoyed brisk weather, misty breaths, and frost-blanketed rooftops…but not tonight. Not when the road was iced and help was a million miles away.

An image leapt into her mind before she could stop it: a car driving up Mountain, sliding on the sabotaged road, then flying off into the dangerous darkness.

She shook her head. Thinking about that wouldn't help. She found the staircase and began to walk down, down, down.

The so-called "prop room" was a mythical, mysterious place for everyone in the theatre, though it had no right to be. For all intents and purposes, it was a storage room. But it was even less glorified than that. It was more accurately a spare room where miscellaneous things were tossed and forgotten about: maintenance tools, brooms and mops, files and paperwork, and, yes, props and costumes.

Few people ventured down into the prop room, Teena included. Adults, because they didn't bother. Kids, because they were convinced it was haunted. Despite playing a ghost in the show, Teena didn't believe in them.

But she felt the specter of time looming over her all the same.

Time. She was running out of it. Time to save Percival. Time to be there for Corrine. Time to find a stupid replacement for her stupid torch.

Again, she shook her head to forcibly reorder her thoughts. She would need her wits about her to quickly navigate this place she'd never been before.

The staircase became increasingly cold and dark as she descended. The lack of an accessible light switch didn't exactly help the prop room's shadowy reputation. Same with the creaky floorboards, which probably hadn't been replaced since the theatre was built. Now that Teena thought of it, she didn't really know when this theatre had been constructed. It might be as old as Percival.

She reached the bottom of the stairs, blindly ran her hand along the wall, and—Aha!—found a switch. When she flicked it on, she found herself in a short hallway straight out of a horror movie: stained concrete walls, crusty carpet, flickering naked bulb dangling from the ceiling.

Yeesh. No wonder no sane adults ever came down here.

She headed for the only door in the hallway, threw it open, and turned on its light. Immediately, she wished she hadn't.

It was terrifying. Horrific. Disturbing!

Not because it was haunted. Because it was filled with ghastly, ungodly, unimaginable *clutter*. From wall to wall, carpet to ceiling, and corner to corner… Nothing but stacked, tossed, dumped, and discarded *stuff*. It set Teena's organized and orderly brain on fire. She nearly turned around and went back to the green room, torch or no torch. But she couldn't bring herself to explicitly disobey her director, so she waded into the mess.

Scattered in front of her, where they would be most accessible, were several open toolboxes. Wrenches, screwdrivers, and drill bits spilled out onto the floor, having been used and flung back absentmindedly. There was also a plastic grocery bag filled with other random tools that didn't fit in the boxes. Since Bernie was the only discernable employee of the theatre, Teena assumed this mess was his doing—she'd have to talk with him about the benefits of organization. But that was a battle for another day. She walked on.

Over there was a mass of boxes with labels like "office supplies" and "printer paper." Next to that was a filing cabinet overflowing with old, yellowed playbills from shows long since performed. And then there were buckets of bleach, detergent, and carpet soap…all of which was covered in a thick layer of brown dust.

Teena made herself as thin as possible and sidled past a leaning tower of milk crates filled with wigs. That was a good sign—she was getting closer to the props and costumes. She turned a corner around a plastic garbage bin filled with brooms.

And she nearly screamed.

Now she understood why so many kids thought this room was haunted.

Mannequins. Too many mannequins. Who on Earth needed this many mannequins? They weren't even dressed in costumes and standing up for display. They were nude and strewn on the floor, like drunken partyers after a long night.

The things one finds in the basement of a community theatre.

Teena did her best not to look at the mannequins as she slid by, lest she inspire their eldritch wrath.

As she passed a line of several clothes racks, she could practically smell the decades on them. Most of the theatre's costumes were rented from other venues or shops, but it had accumulated a few outfits of its own over the years. She couldn't help but pause for just a second or two and thumb through the racks. While *A Christmas Carol* was by far Tennant Park's biggest attraction each year, it wasn't the only show performed in this theatre. She saw costumes for *Tom Sawyer, Life With Father, The Odd Couple, Green Grow the Lilacs, The Emperor's New Clothes…* The staples of many a small-town community theatre.

Oddly, she didn't think she'd ever attended a performance at this theatre. Life was always too busy, she always had an excuse. It struck her as hypocritical that she expected people to attend a show that *she* was in, but she didn't go to any other shows. She made a mental commitment to support the theatre and attend performances throughout the year, especially those in which any of her students were performing.

Along the back wall of the prop room, she finally found the props. They sat in cardboard boxes, on shelves, and in haphazard piles. It looked like an exhibit from a time traveler's personal collection. There were items from the Old West, the modern era, fantasy realms, sci-fi worlds, and ancient China. As dusty and disorderly as these props were, they helped sum up part of what Teena loved about theatre in general: its ability to transport you to any place and any time.

But she could philosophize later. For now, she had to grab a makeshift torch and get out of there.

She scanned the shelves and boxes. What could work? More specifically, what wouldn't make Simeon burst a blood vessel?

One prop caught her eye: a tall, gnarled staff. It looked like something Gandalf would carry in the stage production of *The Hobbit*. She pictured the jolly Ghost of Christmas Present wandering around London, dressed in a lavish green robe, sporting a holly-wreath crown, and wielding Gandalf's walking staff. She wasn't super into *Lord of the Rings*, but even she knew that was a cool look. It also fit with the ghost's wise, wizened persona.

If Simeon didn't like it, he would have to deal. Besides, she was probably out of time. She had to head back and get to her place backstage. If she booked it, she might be able to catch the tail-end of Corrine's big scene.

She journeyed back the way she had come — now that she had a gnarled fantasy staff, she felt like she was trekking through a kingdom of clutter rather than a simple messy room. That somehow made it better and kept her from breaking down and organizing everything right then and there. It also gave her the courage to walk by the manne-quins one more time.

She neared the front of the room, stepped over the random tools, and headed for the door. But before she could flick off the light switch, something caught her eye. Something she'd missed before among all the clutter and dust.

Lying on the floor next to the grocery bag of tools was a rolled-up nylon cylinder. She didn't do a ton of fancy cooking or hardcore maintenance, but she recognized it as a roll bag that held several knives.

On the surface of the nylon was a light dusting of makeup. She almost dismissed it as fine white dust, but she'd know stage makeup anywhere. Plus, most of the dust in this room was brown and chunky.

She knew she should be hurrying up the stairs and to her place…but her gut told her to take a closer look at that nylon bag.

With her heart hammering, she crept toward the bag and nudged it with her toe. Instantly, she rolled her eyes at herself. It wasn't going to bite her or explode. It was just a bag. Harmless.

So why did a chill race down her spine?

She knelt beside it. Now that she was only a few feet away, she was positive: That was stage makeup dabbed on the bag. It was wiped all in the same direction, as if someone with makeup on their hand had unrolled it.

Should she touch it? There could be finger-prints on it. *Could* there be fingerprints on nylon? Her fingers hovered over the roll as she debated.

Oh well. She'd already touched the knife in the air vent.

She unrolled the nylon bag. It stretched out on the floor, holding five knives of different sizes.

Each blade was uniquely shaped and serrated to cut different materials.

But there was an empty slot in the middle of the roll. One knife was missing.

A small slip of paper stuffed into the bag showed black-and-white photos of the knives that came in the set. The lost blade was short and serrated, with a slight curve at the end.

Just like the one in the green room duct.

Her breathing became very shallow.

So now she knew where the murder weapon had come from. Someone had ventured all the way down here —among the costumes and props and brooms and mops and files and paperwork—and taken a knife for the purpose of killing someone. The place was so disorganized, Bernie would never notice.

Who, though? Who had taken the knife?

Someone who wore stage makeup, yes. But that was everyone in the cast. Truly everyone.

All at once, she had to get out of that room. She felt an ominous chill in the air, like the fog that shrouded Marley's ghost. It wasn't just the winter weather—the knowledge that she was kneeling right where the killer had knelt put her on edge. She rolled up the bag and jetted through the door, hitting the light switch on the way out.

She sped down the short hallway leading to the stairs…and barely remembered to turn off that light too. For some reason, seeing the slot from which the knife had been taken really spooked her.

It was all calculated. Planned out. With each piece of physical evidence she found, she further built the picture of a premeditated killing. This wasn't going to be a crime of passion or a spur-of-the-moment thing. Someone had snuck downstairs and purposely stolen a weapon. No, whoever the would-be murderer was, they'd been thinking about it for a while.

Hence the chill in Teena's spine and her sudden urge to flee the prop room. Her gut told her to get back to where there were witnesses.

As she galloped up the stairs, she heard voices from the auditorium. She gasped—after finding the roll bag of knives, she'd somehow forgotten about the ongoing play. She perked up her ears to listen.

Markus, as young Scrooge, was saying, "I have grown wiser and more astute, but I haven't changed my feelings toward you."

Corrine replied, "Oh, Ebenezer, our promise to one another is an old one…"

Teena felt a lump of coal in her stomach for two reasons: She was missing Corrine's scene, and she was due onstage in a matter of minutes.

When she reached the top of the staircase, a gust of arctic wind poofed up her robe around her thighs.

"Oh! Hiya!"

The theatre's front door was open, and Bernie had just walked in. He wore his puffy coat and had his cap pulled down over his ears. He must've been patrolling the parking lot, just as he'd said he would be.

Teena caught a glance of the outside world as the door swung shut. The sky was pitch black, which allowed the twinkling lights to shine even brighter. She inhaled a whiff of pine and fresh night air, her favorite smell combination. The parking lot was full of cars.

Bernie shot a finger-gun at her. "Cool cane."

She looked down at the walking staff in her hands. Oh yeah. She'd forgotten she was carrying that too.

He saw her hectic expression and immediately became concerned. "Is ev'rything okay?"

A lot of people were asking that tonight.

"Yeah yeah yeah," she answered over her shoulder as she moved toward the green room. "I just need to get to my place."

"Have you found anyth—?"

"I'm sorry, Bernie, I really have to go!" She left him behind in a panic unique to theatre performers. She felt like she was standing on a railroad track while a locomotive barreled toward her, with *A Christmas Carol* being the locomotive. If she missed her cue, the show would chug onward one way or another, and she would be flattened.

She dashed through the theatre. Through the hallways. Through the green room. Through through through.

She didn't even take stock of who was in the green room, as she'd done constantly that night. Someone could have been standing on the couch waving a big sign that said "I'm planning to stab Percival Jennings in the back" and she wouldn't have noticed. She only ran, making a beeline for the door that led backstage.

Her feet thudded on the floor, which was met with a chorus of shushes from everyone backstage. Going from a flat-out sprint to a fast walk wasn't easy—she couldn't slow her momentum all at once, but she did her best, practically leaving skid marks in her wake. As she made her way to her place, the stagehands and loitering cast members scrambled out of her path. She imagined she was quite a sight: panting and frantic, her holly crown askew, brandishing a tall walking stick that had never been used in this production before. Yeah, she would get out of her way too.

Onstage, the big breakup scene was winding down. Corrine stood next to a bench, upon which sat Markus. He stared off into the audience, pretending to be unaffected by the sadness of being left by the woman he loved. She, on the other hand, embraced the emotion, putting the back of her hand against her forehead and swaying with grief.

She said to Markus, "May you be happy in the life you have chosen, Ebenezer Scrooge!" Then, as if she'd been underwater for ten minutes and had just come up for air, she gulped a heavy sigh and stormed offstage sobbing.

It wasn't the most "realistic" acting in the world, but it was undeniably gripping. The people in the audience felt every ounce of her character's emotion, and wasn't that the goal?

Teena stopped in the wings of backstage-right, where Corrine had just stormed. She stilled her frantic nerves and tried to look as if she'd been there for Corrine's entire scene. She put on a huge smile as her friend approached.

"I know you just ran in," Corrine whispered as old Scrooge and the ghost continued the scene onstage.

Teena deflated. "I'm sorry, Corrine. I've been—"

"It's okay." Corrine cracked a small smile. "I know you, and if something is important enough to distract *you* of all people from a *play*, it must be pretty friggin' important. I wish you'd tell me about it..." She ground her teeth a little, then forcibly banished her frustration. "But I know you will when you can."

Teena hadn't realized how much keeping this whole situation from Corrine had been weighing on her. Though she loved and trusted Corrine, she knew it was the right decision to let as few people into the loop as possible. But it was hard for her to ditch Corrine, because she knew exactly how much it hurt to be ditched.

Now, though, Teena felt lighter. Her friend and ally was *still* her friend and ally. Just those few words of reassurance from Corrine worked wonders for her self-esteem.

"Thank you," she exhaled.

Corrine had reached her daily limit of sincerity. Her small smile turned wry. "What's with the wizard staff?"

"Uhh," Teena shrugged, "long story short, I'm using it instead of that foam torch." She shot a glance over Corrine's shoulder to check out the progress onstage. She still had a few extra moments, so she asked, "How do you think your scene went?"

"Good, I guess." Corrine took off her Belle bonnet and tousled her hair. "I'm mainly glad it's over to be honest."

"Oh?" Teena hoped Corrine wasn't souring on the play overall. She loved doing it with her, and if Corrine didn't want to audition next year...

"Yeah, it's super awkward playing Markus's girlfriend." Corrine shuddered. "I mean, nothing happens between us, but it's just...weird. I'm definitely not taking Belle again if they offer it to me next year."

Teena beamed. She hoped she and Corrine would be in this show for the rest of their time in Tennant Park.

A thought struck her and torpedoed her mood.

If she didn't find and stop Percival's killer, the whole theatre would probably be closed. At least for a while. And when it reopened, its only patrons would be those weirdos who wanted to go on murder tours.

She shoved that thought to the back of her mind. As if she wasn't under enough pressure.

"Spirit!" Percival's dramatic voice resounded throughout the theatre, drawing Teena's attention. "Remove me from this place!"

Victor replied in a spirited tone: "As I told you, these are shadows of the things that have been. That they are what they are, do not blame me."

"I beg you, take me away from here! I can bear no more. Leave me!"

Percival planted himself centerstage and set his face in his hands. Victor backed away slowly, waving his fingers like he was sprinkling salt on a dish. Teena assumed that was supposed to simulate the ghost fading away. Once Victor was offstage and out of the audience's sight, he began scrubbing glitter from his mustache so that he could change back into his Fred costume.

Teena squeezed Corrine's arm. "Okay. I'm off."

"Break a leg." Corrine gave her a sassy hip-bump and headed to the green room.

Suddenly, backstage sprang to life. The stagehands scrambled back and forth as they once again transformed the stage into Scrooge's bedchamber.

Sandbags and ropes zipped through the air as the Christmas Past backdrop disappeared into the ceiling. The wall, fireplace, bed, and easy chair were dragged back onstage.

Amid the chaos, Teena got to her place off stage-right. Simeon emerged from his position under the EXIT sign and came to stand next to her.

He eyed the gnarled staff. "Is that from *The Hobbit*?"

Teena slowly nodded, preparing for another meltdown.

Instead, Simeon grinned. "I like it. Very fantastical. Wish I'd thought of it!"

All the while, Percival stood as still as a statue in the middle of the stage, his head lowered. The world morphed around him, transforming from his boyhood past to his dreary present. It was another of Simeon's impressive creative touches— though he probably wished it would happen smoother and quicker. The scene change ended up taking about a full minute, with Percival just standing there and stagehands clomping all over the place. Still, A for effort.

Finally, Percival raised his face from his hands and looked around, "realizing" he was back in his bedchamber. He grumbled, "Humbug!" though he said it with an undertone of sorrow and self-pity. Teena couldn't deny that he was a good actor, despite being a cranky pain in the keister.

Simeon patted her shoulder. "Ready?"

Teena gaped, realizing she was truly moments away from stepping onstage. She'd dashed all the way up from the basement, terrified of missing her cue. Now that she'd actually made it on time, her heart-pounding panic began to fade away…

…and was replaced by a sort of seasick nervousness. She was about to perform. On a stage. In front of people. Even though she'd been in theatre for much of her life, she never got used to it.

Tired of waiting for an answer, Simeon nodded. "Okie dokie, then." He slunk back into the EXIT sign's red glow, among the ropes and sandbags.

Onstage, the lights dimmed, like a flame dwindling to a small ember. Percival looked around his bedchamber, confused and on edge. He made large movements to draw the audience's attention away from the wings, which gave Teena a few moments to sneak to her spot behind the fireplace.

Percival crossed his arms and huffed. "No more of this. I demand no more!"

All was quiet and stock-still for a heartbeat. Two heartbeats. Three.

Then the lights turned on full blast. The remote-control fireplace roared to life, and the sound of jolly laughter filled the auditorium.

"Come!" The laughter was accompanied by a full, lively voice. It sounded both enormous and intimate, youthful and wise. "Come forth and know me better, man!"

Teena stepped around the fireplace, sweeping the tall staff around the stage with a grand flourish. Her robe flowed behind her like a queen's cape, and her crown of holly was set just right, not crooked at all.

The Ghost of Christmas Present had arrived.

11.

At the appearance of a new ghost, Percival scuttled backward. He clutched his chest and looked Teena up and down. Twisting his face into a probing sneer, he said, "Who are you, then?"

First impressions can be tough, and it was time for the ghost to make hers.

Teena faced the audience, her arms spread open. She wanted everyone to feel like she was trustworthy. After the grief of Christmas Past, and before the terror of Christmas Yet to Come, her job was to radiate warmth and joviality. Later, when she had to impart some hard truths upon Scrooge, her kind demeanor would sell the idea that it was all for his own good. In short, her strategy was to channel Santa Claus.

The theatre was small and low-tech — and low-budget — enough for the actors to not use microphones. They had to project their voices to the back row, which was a pretty big obstacle for Teena. She took a deep breath and answered Scrooge while still facing the audience.

"Why, I am the Ghost of Christmas Present! My realm is today. Christmas Day!" She let loose another boisterous chuckle. For a moment, she wondered if the mailman she'd weirded out earlier that day was in the audience. At least then he'd know why she was laughing alone in her house like the Joker.

As she looked out at the auditorium, a sea of silhouettes stared back at her. The bright stage lights made it difficult to see past the first few rows, and even then, they were mostly hidden in darkness. It was a strange experience — performing for a huge group of people she couldn't really see. It was almost like performing for no one.

But she could feel them. She may not have been able to see the people in rows of seats, but she sensed them, like a cloud full of rain hanging over town. She could feel their breathing, their gazes, their collective attention. It was terrifying and exhilarating all at once.

Percival said, "I don't believe I've ever seen the likes of you in all my life, spirit."

Teena spun on her heel to approach Percival. "No?" she boomed cheerily. "You've never walked forth with any of my elder siblings born in these later years?"

"I don't believe I have. Have you many siblings?"

"Only eighteen hundred!" The audience laughed along with her.

Percival approached her and joked, "Quite a large family to provide for!" Already, Scrooge was becoming comfortable with the ghost. The dynamics of the scene were right on track so far.

For the first time that night, Teena was face-to-face with Percival Jennings. The man she'd been hyper-fixated on. The man whose world she'd been dissecting. The man she'd been trying to save…yet hadn't directly spoken to all day.

She had known Percival for years and interacted with him countless times, but now, he looked somehow different. In her eyes, he wasn't quite the intimidating, untouchable miser of Tennant Park anymore. Standing there in his stage makeup and Dickensian pajamas, he looked older. Smaller. Weaker. Susceptible to a knife attack. Very much touchable.

Just then, Percival cleared his throat and bugged out his eyes at her. He seemed pretty annoyed with her, and not just in character as Scrooge.

She startled. It was her turn to say a line, and the silence had gone on for about five seconds, which was an eternity in stage-time. She'd gotten lost in thought, thinking about murder.

Quickly getting back in the swing of the scene, she held out her elbow to Percival. "Take hold, Mr. Ebenezer Scrooge!"

Percival obeyed, grabbing onto her forearm. "Where are we going, spirit?"

"You shall see!" She held her walking staff above her head, and the lights dimmed. Once again, the black-clad stagehands sprang into action, changing the scenery around them. Sandbags dropped from the ceiling as the London street and cityscape reappeared.

In the darkness, Teena shook her head to clear it. She suddenly found herself in a position where she had to make a radical shift in her state of mind. For the past hour, she'd been trying to solve a future murder — finding clues, asking questions, and deciphering motives. It was literally life-or-death stuff.

But now, she had to remember her lines. She had to follow the blocking Simeon had given them. She had to go through the motions of these scenes and pretend to be an old-timey ghost. Performing in a play seemed so trivial compared to saving Percival's life.

That thought stung a little. She had never once in all her life referred to theatre as "trivial." It was one of the most important things in the world to her.

Before she could get lost in thought again, the lights brightened, revealing a bright and cheery Christmas morning. The ensemble actors milled about the cobblestoned street, laughing and chattering and hollering and singing and haggling and babbling and having a grand ole time. It was a perfect picture of festive merriment.

"Behold, the beauty of Christmas morning!" Teena displayed the scene to Percival, who acted as if they had magically materialized in the middle of the street.

A line of carolers stood in front of a shop window and began to harmonize: "I saw three ships come sailing in on Christmas Day, on Christmas Day. I saw three ships come sailing in on Christmas Day in the morning…"

Teena and Percival meandered through the crowd. She jigged along with the music, while he glowered and flinched against all human contact.

But she gulped when she realized the next bit of dialogue involved her torch…which was now crumpled up in a trashcan somewhere. She could only hope Percival was able to amend his lines on the fly.

As she walked down the street, she waved her walking stick over those who passed by.

Percival glared at the staff, then said his line: "Is there a peculiar flavor in what you sprinkle from your…" He hesitated. The ending word was supposed to be "torch," but he instead said, "Shepherd's rod?"

Relieved, Teena went on with the dialogue. "There is indeed. 'Tis my own."

"Would it apply to any kind of dinner on this day?"

"To any kindly given." She slowed, then stopped and looked him right in the eye. "To a poor one most."

He scoffed. "Why to a poor one most?"

"Because it needs it most," she answered.

The carolers finished their song: "Then let us all rejoice amain, on Christmas Day, on Christmas Day. Then let us all rejoice amain, on Christmas Day in the morning."

Having survived her first few bouts of dialogue, Teena released a breath. Now that she was actually onstage, the nervous thrills bubbled in her stomach more than ever…and it mingled with the ever-present anxiety in the back of her mind that with every moment, Percival's death got closer.

But her animal brain pushed that aside. She didn't see a knife-wielding maniac at that moment, but she *did* see a big group of people staring at her, so she felt stage-fright more than mortal danger. It was a weird sensation.

She knew that public speaking was one of the world's most common fears, and she understood why, but she wasn't really scared of it. Not exactly. It wasn't speaking she was scared of, but the idea that people might not like what she was saying. Might not like *her*.

Every day at school, Teena spoke to big groups of people. But theatre was different. Pretending to be a character made her feel both liberated and vulnerable: She had an excuse to act like a different person and do things she herself would never really do…but she was also opening herself up to criticism and ridicule. It was the strange contradiction of theatre. Freeing yet terrifying.

Again, her mind was wandering. That wasn't usual for her, but this night was the opposite of usual. She fortunately caught herself and said her next line in a timely fashion.

"Follow me, Mr. Scrooge. Shall we pay this kindly household a visit?"

"This house?"

They moved to the front of the stage and pantomimed looking at something while the stagehands changed the set. The scraping and creaking forced them to project their voices even louder than normal.

"Why yes!" she bellowed. "It's Christmas here too, believe it or not. This is the home of your loyal clerk, Bob Cratchit."

Behind them, the house's interior took shape: the cabinets, beds, oven, and large table. Six of the eight Cratchit actors also tiptoed onto the stage and to their spots — Bob Cratchit and Tiny Tim would enter later, with Colton on Jimmy's massively muscular shoulder.

"Bob Cratchit?" Percival asked. "I cannot think why I should come to his home."

"That is exactly why we are here." Teena swept her staff toward the completed scenery.

The Cratchit home was abuzz with Christmas-y energy. Evelyn, as Mrs. Cratchit, worked to prepare the goose for dinner. The younger kids sang a carol and ran circles around the stage, while the elder children helped set dishware on the table.

Teena and Percival moved to stage-right, where they would observe the Cratchit household. The next few minutes belonged solely to the family, with Scrooge and the ghost being mere spectators.

A thought tickled Teena's mind. Earlier, she had lamented that she'd missed the only moment in the whole show when Percival would be off-stage: when he was changing his costume before encountering Marley's ghost. She had considered using that time to warn him of his possible impending murder, though he almost certainly wouldn't believe her. But she had talked to Jimmy during that moment instead. She'd prioritized learning the killer's identity over getting Percival to safety.

Now, a new opportunity presented itself. For these next few minutes, Scrooge and the ghost would not be missed if they slipped offstage.

Teena quickly ran through the scenario: She could pull Percival into the wings of backstage-right, she'd tell him to be on guard, and they'd return to their spots. No harm done. It would likely take less than a minute, and the scene among the Cratchits would still be going on. The audience wouldn't even notice. Simeon might, and Teena would get a firm talking-to after the show, but that would be worth it if she could warn Percival.

Because Teena had to start being honest with herself. The show was past its midpoint, and Percival was slated to be attacked during the final scene. As much as her confidence had grown during the evening, she couldn't deny the fact that she had no solid idea of who Percival's would-be killer was. Being a hero and playing detective sounded great, but if she failed and Percival died, and she hadn't even tried to tell him it was coming, she would never sleep soundly again. That would haunt her for the rest of her life.

She only had a second or two to decide her next course of action, because the Cratchit scene was starting.

Evelyn heaved a sigh and wiped the back of a hand across her forehead. She said to Andy, who played Peter Cratchit, "Wherever could your precious father be, eh? And your brother, Tiny Tim?"

Andy jittered where he stood, almost too excited to form a coherent sentence. This was his stage debut, and he was clearly over-the-moon about it. He said, "I think he be walking from the church, coming from church, with Tim, Tiny Tim as well!" He'd gotten a few words jumbled up, but his smile was so big and radiant, several people in the audience couldn't help but *aww*.

While the audience was distracted, Teena grabbed Percival's elbow and yanked him off-stage. Despite his hard demeanor, he was pretty easy to push around.

As they scuttled offstage, Percival's face rocketed through a series of emotions: puzzled, angry, concerned, angry, snooty, and, finally, angry. Once they were in the wing off stage-right, out of sight of the audience, he shook out of Teena's grasp.

"What the heck are you doing?!" At least he had the good sense to whisper crossly instead of yelling and blustering about, like he usually did.

Teena tried to talk to him, but he wouldn't let her get a word in edgewise.

"Dangshootcrapdarndangit, woman! Do you know you just dragged me away from a scene? A very *important* scene. Scrooge needs to watch the Cratchits in their own home. He needs to see them as people for the first time in his life. That's the spark of empathy that builds into his eventual redemption, you nincompoop!"

She was taken aback for a moment. Despite his boorish insults, his analysis of the scene was surprisingly insightful.

Then again, he'd played the role for more than three decades: a fact that he was bound to bring up at any time.

"Percival," she butted in, "I need to—"

"In thirty-four years, this has never happened. Crap on a cracker! I can't believe it." He crossed his arms, looking more and more like Scrooge and less and less like his real self.

"Just listen—"

"I don't have to listen to a thing you say." He turned from her and began to storm back onstage.

But Teena caught his nightgown's long sleeve. "If you go out now, it'll definitely look like this wasn't planned. You'll have walked off, then walked right back on. The audience will be confused. Wait until the Cratchits are done with their conversation."

Percival stopped in his tracks. The last thing he wanted was for people to think less of his performance. Seemingly, that was the only attribute of his anyone actually liked.

"Roger Marius would never have put up with this," he grumbled. "I can't believe it. In the middle of a scene…"

She stepped directly into his line of sight so that he couldn't ignore her. "Percival, have you noticed anything off tonight? Anything that might have put you on edge?"

He laughed harshly. "You mean other than *this*? No. Nothing." He paused. "Actually…"

Teena leaned in. "What? What is it?"

"No one sent any flowers for my thirty-fifth annual performance. And the interview I gave for the *Telegraph* didn't run today." He *tsk-tsk*'d. "This town is full of philistines and ingrates, for sure."

Teena rolled her eyes. She wanted to ask, "*Then why don't you leave?*" But she got to the point.

"I think you're in danger tonight. Someone is coming after you. Hard. With a knife—"

"Oh *please*." Percival screwed his face up into the most incredulous grimace she'd ever seen.

She went on the defensive. "I know that sounds crazy."

"Crazy? It sounds stupid!" He waved her off like she was a pesky mosquito he was trying to squash. "You expect me to believe that platter of bullcrap? In all my years..."

"Fine," she said. "Don't believe me. That's okay, you don't technically have to. But keep an eye open. There's no harm in staying on your guard."

He shot her a squinted glare...then he gasped. "Ohhhhh, I see what's going on." He chuckled like a calculus professor teaching first-grade math. "Yeah yeah yeah, I see."

Teena had been prepared to keep on defending herself, but Percival's sudden shift in tone caught her off-guard. "You do?"

"Yes." He set his jaw. "You're trying to throw me off. Tarnish my thirty-fifth year."

"*What?!*"

"I can see right through you, missy. I'm no fool." He reared up, a cobra about to strike. "The pea-brained people of this town have been jealous of me for years. My money, my cars, and my talent too. Someone put you up to this, to try to get in my head. Well, let me tell you." He extended a knobby finger and poked her sternum with each word: "It. Won't. Work!"

Teena took a few steps back from him. She wasn't used to feeling angry, but he was well on his way to getting her there. A few bubbles of lava churned just below her lungs, enough to make her face feel hot. But she could push it down.

She glanced at the stage to try to get a sense of where the scene was and how much time she had left.

Bob Cratchit and Tiny Tim had entered. All six children were playing while Bob and the Missus chatted.

"And did little Tim behave himself in church?" Evelyn asked, in her sincere-Mrs.-Cratchit way.

Jimmy adjusted his tiny little glasses as he nodded. "He did. As good as gold, and better…"

Teena still had a few minutes before she and Percival would need to return to the stage. She turned back to the fuming old man. Since he was being stubborn and difficult anyway, Teena figured she could push a little harder and try to get some information she was still missing.

Before she could second-guess herself, she quickly asked, "What were you talking to Markus Daniels about right before the show started?"

Percival's mouth opened and closed a few times, as if he was literally at a loss for words. He eventually said, "What do you care? Have you been snooping on me all night? How dare you stick your nose into my business!"

She rubbed her temples. "Good grief." Her monster headache was making a comeback.

"That's just typical." He looked ready to spit in disgust. "You get a man's part, and you think you can go around doing whatever you want."

Teena rocked back as if blown by a stiff breeze. Just like the other day, when he had called her a piece of "stunt casting," she felt extremely visible. Her weight, her color, her past, even her name. But instead of becoming withdrawn and timid, she turned angry.

The lava inside her spread all over—through her fingers and toes, behind her eyes, and up her throat. She felt ready to breathe fire.

She couldn't believe he could be so rude and cruel to someone's face. It was a foreign concept to her. She'd spent her entire life being agreeable, wanting everyone to like her, treating others with kindness and respect. And yet, here was a wealthy man who walked all over everyone like they were dirt. He didn't even try to be kind or agreeable, like it had never occurred to him.

Evelyn had called him an ogre. Jimmy constantly clashed with him. Roy definitely wasn't a fan. Simeon, Markus, Corrine… No one would be sad to see him go. If Tennant Park woke up tomorrow without Percival Jennings, would that be so bad?

Was he worth all this trouble? Was he worth saving?

It was a dark thought, but Teena couldn't deny it passed through her mind for a second.

She wanted to strike back. To hurt him in a way that got under his skin, just like he did to her.

And so she did.

"I know your wife didn't die. She left you."

Her words hung in the air like poisonous gas. She almost surprised herself with her ruthlessness, the way she'd gone straight for the jugular. That was very unlike her. But she'd done it. She stared at him, waiting for his reaction.

Percival didn't stagger backward, or fly into a rage, or gasp or cry or say anything at all. He was completely frozen. Shellshocked by what she'd said.

After a few heartbeats, he thawed and began to speak. Or, rather, he tried to. "Y-You c-can't-t, I-I-I, you s-s-see…" His stutter had reemerged, meaning he was tremendously agitated.

Teena wanted to feel good about that. She'd taken him down a peg, and he'd likely stay down there for the rest of the evening. His performance as Scrooge would be thrown off, his worst fear actualized. She'd gotten to him in a way that impacted the core of his being, made him feel sullied, less than.

She'd won. She should feel victorious.

Instead, she just felt dirty. Harsh. Cold.

She felt like Percival Jennings. It wasn't a good feeling.

"Sh-Sh-She…" Percival forced his mouth to cooperate. "Sh-She didn't *leave*." He glared at Teena again, but his eyes were sad. "She's c-coming back. Really."

Without another word, he turned and waddled back onstage. Teena really had no choice but to follow him. They took their spots on stage-right, slightly behind the rest of the scene, watching it transpire. The Cratchits had all taken their places at the family dinner table, their fake food spread out before them.

Colton, as Tiny Tim, said, "God bless us, everyone!"

The audience cooed and fawned over him.

It turned out that Percival had walked out at the exact right moment. He cleared his throat and said his next line: "I-I had no idea Cratchit had a crippled son." His stutter wasn't too bad, but his voice was noticeably unsteady. He stood slightly hunched, as if wearing a heavy knapsack, looking smaller and weaker than ever. In the context of the scene, it worked really well.

But Teena knew it was because of her. She hated it.

Getting back in the mindset of the play, she clenched her vocal cords in order to create her big spirit voice. "I wonder why you did not know this." She laced her tone with sympathy and gentle admonition.

For the most part, she wasn't acting. She really felt sorry for Percival. If his brother could be believed—and he seemed to be telling the truth—Percival's wife Rebecca had walked out on him. On Christmas Day, no less. The one person on Earth who'd tolerated him for years upon years had called it quits. She'd had enough of the old man.

It seemed Percival couldn't accept that. He was convinced that Rebecca would come to her senses and crawl back to him. There would be a happy ending. His story couldn't end with the woman he loved thinking he was a terrible person. Everyone else in town could think he was scum, and that would be alright by him…but he couldn't wrap his mind around the fact that his own wife didn't like him either.

Teena found it all so tragic. Very Scrooge-like. She didn't excuse his cruelty or forgive him, but she definitely felt sympathy for him. For the first time ever.

As she and Percival went on reciting their lines, she found herself thinking about the next scene. It was one of her very favorites in the whole show. And it applied to Percival more than he would likely want to admit.

Indeed, before she knew it, the Cratchit scene was over. Teena and Percival stayed put while stagehands quickly rearranged the set to depict a new house.

Victor and a handful of ensemble actors scurried onstage to populate the scene. Victor was once again Scrooge's nephew Fred, though a lot of glitter remained in his facial hair. The actors held drinks and pantomimed chatting merrily.

Percival said, "Why are we at my nephew's home?"

"To listen and learn," Teena responded.

Victor launched into the scene, projecting to the back row. "He called Christmas a humbug. He believed it so!"

An ensemble actress said, "Shame for him, shame!"

"He's really a comical old fellow," Victor went on, "and not so pleasant as he might be. However, his offenses carry their own punishment."

"Well, I have no pity for him," said another.

"Oh, but I have!" Victor stepped to the front of the stage—it was time for him to give a heartfelt monologue, which meant everyone in the audience needed a good view of him. "Who suffers by his ill whims? Himself, always. Here, he takes it into his head to dislike us, and he won't come and dine with us. What's the consequence? He loses some pleasant moments, which could do him no harm. I mean to give him the same chance every year, whether he likes it or not…"

The scene continued. Teena glanced sideways to gage Percival's reaction. He simply watched, his face long and drawn like a bloodhound's.

Teena loved this scene because it is the biggest chip in Ebenezer Scrooge's bitter armor. One could call it his turning point, what really leads to his redemption.

He has the opportunity to hear what people say about him when he's not around. The text doesn't really describe what he *thinks* people think of him, but he would probably want his peers to be afraid of him or to envy his money.

None of that is the case. They think he's a joke, a sad sack of bones who would rather wallow in misery than take his happiness into his own hands. Either they pity him, which would be a huge hit to his pride, or they flat-out hate his guts. And it rocks Scrooge to his core.

That's true for most people. They go about life thinking of themselves a certain way—more often than not, they view themselves as the hero of the story, or at least in the right. But when others genuinely see them as a villain, their illusions are shattered. If they're wrong about themselves, what else are they wrong about?

That's what happens to Scrooge, and that's what happened to Percival when Rebecca left him. His wife, the woman who was supposed to be his partner in life, was sick of him. She viewed him differently than he viewed himself. And he couldn't take it. It sounded like he had persuaded himself to believe that she was coming back.

Scrooge, on the other hand, heeded what other people said about him. When he didn't like what they said, he gave them something positive to talk about. His soul was saved. Happily ever after.

Teena didn't know if Percival would go down that same path. He didn't seem like the type of person who valued introspection and self-improvement. She didn't know if he would ever change from Scrooge the miser to Scrooge the redeemed.

But he definitely wouldn't if he died tonight. He needed a chance to turn his life around. If the horrible Ebenezer Scrooge deserved a shot at salvation, then everyone did.

Even Percival Jennings.

Teena blinked heavily. She'd zoned out again. She looked around to regain her footing in the present moment. The conversation between Fred and his Christmas guests was winding down.

Percival turned to Teena. In his fragile voice, he said, "I would normally take offense at such tasteless banter and laughter at my expense. However, in view of the general gaiety of the occasion, I am inclined to overlook it."

For the past thirty-four years, he had said that line with a sense of arrogance and superiority, his nose in the air. Now, he sounded defeated. Lowly. Lying to himself about his own superiority.

Teena set a kind hand on his shoulder. With her eyes, she apologized for her anger earlier backstage. She didn't know if he got the message, but she hoped so.

She planned to apologize to him properly after the show. He, on the other hand, would never apologize to her or show any sort of remorse for his attitude — at least not with his heart in its current state — and that was exactly why she wanted to. She refused to be like him.

"That is very noble of you, Mr. Scrooge," she said.

The set darkened. Teena led Percival forward as the set was dismantled and shuffled offstage. A single spotlight shone down on the two of them, as if they were lost in a void outside of the physical world.

"My time draws near," Teena said, projecting over the sounds of the scene change. "I must leave you."

"Spirit, no!" Percival perked up, regaining some of his vigor. Perhaps it was because he knew she'd soon be out of his hair. "I have learned so much from the present."

"Then I can only imagine how much you shall learn from the future." She began to back away from Percival, drifting into the darkness. "I leave you in the hands of the Ghost of Christmas Yet to Come."

Percival stared out into the audience, fearfully quaking in his nightgown. "Th-The f-future?" His stammer didn't sound fake.

"Go forth," Teena said, extending her staff one last time, "and know her better, man!" She unleashed a final jolly laugh and disappeared offstage.

And just like that, her debut as the Ghost of Christmas Present was over. She stood in the darkness of the wings and exhaled slowly. The locomotive of *A Christmas Carol* rolled onward even after she stepped off. The role she so admired and had learned front-to-back was complete.

What a whirlwind.

Now.

Back to murder.

12.

Teena felt something tugging slightly on her hair. When she reached up, she realized her crown of holly had fallen to the side, only hanging on by a few intrepid hairs. She adjusted it to its proper position and reassessed where she was at.

All that remained in the show was the Christmas Yet to Come segment and the short epilogue of Scrooge's redemption. She truly was running out of time before Percival's attack. After all this scrambling around and amateur "investigating," she really didn't have much to go on. The identity of Percival's killer was as much a mystery as ever.

A voice from across backstage said to her, "Good job, Teena." It was Simeon, holding out a thumbs-up while his eyes were glued to his clipboard. She doubted the faint red glow he'd been standing in all evening was very good for his eyesight, but she wasn't his mom. If his perception of color was wonky tomorrow morning, that was his own doing. She had other worries.

At that moment, a clap of thunder shook the auditorium. Strobe lights that simulated lightning flashed across the stage. Audience members jerked in their seats, scared by the sudden noise and erratic lights.

Teena couldn't help but hang around a little bit longer. She craned her neck to get a good view of the stage. Corrine's entrance as the Ghost of Christmas Yet to Come was something she just had to see.

Percival stood centerstage, his arms wrapped around his chest as if he was cold. He glanced back and forth, up and down, wondering if he was alone in the dark void in which the Ghost of Christmas Present had left him.

And then, a figure stepped out of the shadows and into Percival's spotlight, looming menacingly behind him. The figure was dressed in a black robe and hood, so it seemingly appeared out of thin air. Again, members of the audience jerked with shock and a touch of fear.

Percival, however, didn't see the new ghost. He continued to look around, oblivious of the threat right behind him. A few children in the audience called out to him: "Look out! It's behind you! Turn around!"

Finally, after letting the audience stew in its dread for a few moments longer, the hooded figure set a skeletal hand on Percival's shoulder. He yelped and spun to face the ghost.

He breathlessly said, "I take it that I am in the presence of the Ghost of Christmas Yet to Come?"

The figure slowly nodded.

Teena beamed from ear to ear—she would know her friend's movements and stature anywhere. Even swaddled in a black robe and with a hood pulled over her face, the figure was unmistakably Coach Corrine. She was practically drowning in the huge robe, which had been fitted for the much-taller-and-wider Don Schrader. Fortunately, the bony gloves fit just fine.

Percival continued with his next line: "You are to show me shadows of the things that have not happened, but will happen in the time before us. Is that not so, spirit?"

Again, Corrine nodded without a word.

During rehearsals, Teena had wondered if this scene would work without any of the bells and whistles Simeon had used for Marley's ghost. No fog machines, very little sound effects, only one spotlight… It sounded too sparse for such an impactful character's intro. But Simeon had envisioned a stripped-down approach, where the Ghost of Christmas Yet to Come came into being as easily as a shadow. He said the horror would come from the simplicity, as if the ghost could emerge from any corner, not just the obviously spooky ones.

And Simeon had been right. The scene was working perfectly.

Teena wanted to keep watching the show — wanted to ditch all her cares, plop herself down in the green room, chat with her castmates, eat one of Evelyn's homemade goodies, congratulate Corrine when she finished her turn as the ghost, do the curtain call, sign autographs and take pictures with guests in the lobby, then go out to Crawful o' Waffles for an after-show scramble — but she couldn't. She had to get moving.

There was one more person she wanted to speak with, someone she'd tried to get a bead on earlier in the evening but who'd been pulled away by the riptide of the show: Markus Daniels.

He would likely be in the green room, so that was Teena's next destination. She hefted her walking stick so that it wouldn't scrape or bump against the floor, and she made her way across the backstage area in that direction.

As she walked, she heard the scene continue onstage:

"Spirit… I must say, I fear you more than any specter I have yet encountered. Will you not speak to me?"

No response. Corrine was nailing all of the ghost's lines so far.

Percival spoke again: "Very well. Lead on! The night is passing fast, and it is precious time to me. Lead on, spirit. I shall follow."

Stagehands and sandbags flew into action as a backdrop descended from the ceiling and the void was transformed back into the London street. While Scrooge ventured into the unknown future, Teena returned to the familiar green room.

The place was fairly sparse—Christmas Yet to Come involved a pretty big chunk of the ensemble. Jimmy and Evelyn were busy rounding up their stage children. The Cratchits had rushed offstage after Christmas Present to all change into mourning clothes… Well, all except Colton, who played Tiny Tim. He got to stay in his regular costume, since he was the one the family was mourning.

Neither Jimmy nor Evelyn had really signed up to be babysitters or costume-change facilitators, but since they were the kids' stage parents, they were also their de facto guardians from call time until curtain call. And, as Teena could attest, getting kids to do anything on time was a struggle, much less getting them all changed. As Teena watched Jimmy and Evelyn chase down the children and make sure they were ready to go, she silently saluted them.

She spied Haley Schrader standing by the air vent that housed the knife. The girl was fiddling with the buckles on her old-timey shoes, clearly ready to go backstage and killing time until her "siblings" were ready too.

Teena smiled. Just as she'd thought earlier: Responsible actors tended to get to their places about half a scene early. Haley had a long tenure on the stage ahead of her, if she wanted and worked at it.

She and her father were quite a sight at rehearsals. They couldn't have been more different. Don was tall and robust, looking like he could walk right through a brick wall without meaning to. He wasn't unkind, but he mostly kept to himself, clearly uncomfortable in group settings. Haley was dainty, energetic, and the very definition of a social butterfly. She could make friends with the brick wall her father had just walked through.

Maybe the biggest difference between father and daughter was their levels of enthusiasm for *A Christmas Carol*. Haley loved everything about the theatrical process — the rehearsals and long nights, the memorization of lines and blocking, the costumes and makeup, the mayhem and magic. Everything. She lit up whenever she walked into the auditorium, eager to engage with the artform.

Conversely, Don couldn't give two rips about theatre. He was only cast as the Ghost of Christmas Yet to Come because the production had needed one more body, and Haley had volun-told him for the role. He'd shrugged in acceptance, likely figuring he was dropping her off and picking her up anyway and he might as well hang around.

The fact that he didn't care about the show but went through the whole rigmarole anyway impressed Teena — it really demonstrated how much he cared for his daughter.

Or…

A theory prickled the back of Teena's mind. Don Schrader had no discernable reason for being in *A Christmas Carol*. He could've said no when Simeon offered him the part Haley had put him up for. Maybe…

Maybe maybe maybe.

Was it possible he had joined the production for the sole purpose of attacking Percival? Could Don be the would-be killer?

It was just crazy enough to be plausible. Don had been conveniently absent all night. He was "sick." What had Simeon said? Pink eye? A likely story!

What if Don was just pretending to be sick so that no one would suspect him? And then, during the final scene, he would pop out of nowhere and stab Percival in the back. The perfect crime.

Haley didn't seem to have the slightest trace of ailment. Teena was no expert, but she knew pink eye was extremely contagious. Was she in on it? Had Don roped her into his murderous conspiracy and made her an accomplice?

Teena had to know more. She inched toward Haley, trying to look casual.

"Hey, Haley?" she said.

Haley looked up from her shoes, eyes wide and bubbly. She was clearly excited to get back on-stage, even though she was supposed to look heartbroken that her little brother was dead. "Hi, Miss F.!"

"I, uhh…" Teena wasn't sure how to go about this. "How's your dad doing? I heard he's sick."

"I mean," Haley shrugged, "I haven't seen him for a few hours. He felt pretty sucky when I left our house to come here."

"That's a bummer. I'm sure he was excited to do the show with you."

Haley laughed. It wasn't a dry, bitter chuckle like an adult might have done—it was full and genuine. "Not at all! He doesn't really like doing this stuff. But he does it anyway. I think that's pretty cool."

"Well, I'm sure he'd rather be here than at home with the flu." Teena eyed Haley closely.

But the girl didn't hesitate. "My mom said it's something called pink eye, not the flu. I don't really know what that is, but I do know eyes are supposed to be white, so if it's pink, it's probably not good."

"Did you see your dad before leaving?"

"From across our living room, yeah."

"What were some of his symptoms?" Teena had unconsciously dropped her casual tone and launched into full-on interrogation mode.

Haley shied away slightly from the direct questions. "Umm… He said his eye was really itchy. And he had a Kleenex pushed up under it, like he was crying. But it didn't look like tears."

"Was the discharge colored?"

Finally, Haley huffed and clenched her jaw. "Miss F., I know you're a science teacher, but it's really weird that you want to know all of this. Like, the color of the goop coming out of my dad's eye? Seriously?"

Teena suddenly realized what she was doing. Her galloping mind screeched to a halt. "Yeah…" she muttered. "Yeah, it is really weird." She chortled, and thankfully, Haley laughed along with her. "Sorry, Haley. Forget I asked anything."

Already, Haley was back to her happy self. She said, "Okie dokie," and went back to studying her shoes.

As soon as Teena stepped away, Jimmy and Evelyn bustled toward backstage, with the other Cratchit kids in tow. Jimmy urged, "C'mon, Haley! We needed to get to our places five minutes ago! Geez, we better not be late…"

The Cratchit family streamed through the door leading backstage. And just like that, the green room was much quieter and stiller.

Teena rubbed her temples. It was all she could do to keep from pulling her own hair out. Had she honestly suspected Don Schrader of faking pink eye so that he could hide out until the time came to kill Percival? *And* had she just grilled his eighth-grade daughter to try to catch him in his lie?

Ridiculous. No, more than ridiculous—stupid. That was an absolutely stupid theory. If she had any other leads to go on, she wouldn't need to resort to accusing men who were only guilty of having pink eye. But she had no other leads. After a whole evening of investigating, she still had no idea who was planning to kill Percival Jennings in…

She glanced at the clock.

Soon. She still had no idea who was planning to kill Percival Jennings *soon*.

She was spiraling. As the night went on, she was getting more paranoid and more desperate. But as hard as she tried, she was more clown than crimefighter.

Sherlock Holmes would be spinning in his grave…if he weren't fictional.

The creator of Holmes was *definitely* not resting in peace. Teena still couldn't remember his name. She was half-prepared to mentally accept that Charles Dickens was the author of Sherlock Holmes, even though she knew it wasn't true. At least then she'd be able to pluck that burr from her mind and stop thinking about it.

Teena had read a few Holmes stories in high school English class, and while she'd enjoyed them, the author clearly hadn't made much of an impact on her. The old-timey style of writing left her cold and unable to engage very much with the characters or emotions.

That being said, a few of the plots had stuck in her memory. She really liked it when the detective explained what had led him to the correct conclusion of the mystery, especially when it was clever. She remembered one story where Holmes deduced what had happened based on the dirt on someone's knees. She liked another where Holmes knew who the killer was based on something that *didn't* happen—if memory served, a dog didn't bark in the middle of the night, meaning the killer was well-known by the household. And in another story, he knew someone was in disguise based on their clothes and makeup.

When Holmes laid it all out, it sounded so easy, as if the evidence had left a trail of breadcrumbs for him to follow. *He* didn't figure things out—the clues *told* him the solution, and he listened. Teena would give anything to have Holmes's ability to see things plainly, to turn chaos into order.

Because she was running out of time, and the clues were telling her jack-squat.

She spied Markus across the green room, dressed as a common townsperson. He only had to play young Scrooge for two scenes, and he filled the rest of his time in the ensemble. He sat at one of the makeup desks, his back to the rest of the room.

Teena sighed and walked toward him. She hoped this panned out. Markus was the last person on her list of castmates to talk to. If he didn't give her a key puzzle piece, she was flat out of luck.

She passed the table of props and leaned her tall, gnarled staff against it. She didn't know if they would perform the show again tomorrow—AKA if the whole theatre would be a crime scene and the production would be shut down—but if they did, she would know where she'd left her trusty staff.

As Teena got closer to the makeup desks, she saw that Markus was hunched over a textbook. Senior-level biology. Or maybe freshman-college-level. She felt bad storming in on his studying, but she did so all the same.

"Hi there, Markus," she said quietly, easing into the conversation.

Markus turned to face her, his permanent smile as dazzling as ever. "Hey, Miss F. Great show tonight so far, right?"

"Definitely." Teena usually relished small talk, but the clock on the wall was unforgiving. When she strained her ears, she could hear actors onstage talking about looting the dead Scrooge's home. Christmas Yet to Come was about a third of the way complete.

She sat at the desk next to Markus. For the first time in hours, she caught a glimpse of herself in a mirror. The vanity lights, which were supposed to make her look flattering, accentuated the bags under her eyes and the lines of worry that creased her forehead. The night's investigation had weighed on her more physically than she'd even known. Corrine's instant concern now made more sense.

"Listen, I need to ask you…" She scooted her chair a bit closer.

Markus set a finger in his textbook and shut it. He could sense her seriousness, and he matched his tone to hers. "Yeah? What is it?"

She cleared her throat. Markus looked at her with implicitly trusting eyes—just a few days ago, he had called her the best teacher he'd ever had. The last thing she wanted to do was wreck his image of her, so despite the looming deadline, she forced herself to tread carefully.

Well, come to think of it, that was the *second*-to-last thing she wanted to do. The *very* last thing she wanted to do was uncover some detail that confirmed Markus Daniels was the would-be killer of Percival Jennings. That would be heart-wrenching…but if that was where the clues led, she wouldn't be able to ignore it.

Once again, her mind had wandered. Markus was still staring at her. She got back on track.

She said, "I know Percival has been giving you a hard time over these weeks. He's not an easy person to deal with."

"Yeah, well…" Markus shrugged with golly-gee-aw-shucks charm. "I can't control what he does. Only how I react."

"I have to ask." She lowered her voice further. "What did Percival say to you right before the show began tonight?"

A shadow passed over Markus's smile. It didn't waver, but it blackened a little. He didn't say anything.

She pressed. "I've seen him goading you, but I don't know what he's been saying. Nothing pleasant, I can imagine."

Markus settled back in his chair. Realizing this wasn't going to be a quick and simple conversation, he took his finger out of the textbook and pushed it away.

"Please understand, Markus." She placed a hand on her heart, meaning every word. "I only want to make sure you're okay."

He gulped and shifted his eyes back and forth. He and Teena hadn't talked one-on-one since eighth grade. When one of his test grades slipped or he messed up on a lab, she would give him patient direction after class. Teena knew he wouldn't even consider opening up to her now without that prior bond.

"This is my first year as young Scrooge." As he spoke, he fidgeted with a pile of Q-tips that was sitting on the desk. "I was in the ensemble for two years. My sophomore and junior years. Those were fun. So I'd never worked directly with Percival before. This year, I've been around him way more. He doesn't like me. At all."

"What kind of stuff does he say to you?"

He bobbled his shoulders. "The usual mean old man things. 'Young actors were better in my day.

Kids are so soft and dumb now. Spend more time outside and less on your phones.' Stuff like that. I'm the only male actor my age in the cast, so I guess he has to take it all out on me."

Teena nearly laughed. Clearly, Percival didn't know Markus in the slightest. The young man was extremely smart, he worked very hard, he was a pretty good actor, and he was courteous to every-one he met. Every one of Percival's insults missed the mark.

"He's just a grouch, Markus. I know his words can hurt, believe me…" She paused. Winced. Reeled herself back in. "But he doesn't know what he's talking about. He's lashing out because he has nothing else."

Markus nodded. "Yeah, I get that feeling. But that's not the kind of stuff that gets to me."

He hesitated, and Teena let him rest in the beat of silence. She wanted to say, "*What? What gets to you? Tell me tell me tell me, I have a mystery to solve.*" But she held her tongue. This clearly wasn't easy for him to talk about, and pressuring him wouldn't help.

"What stings the most," he said, his fingers fidgeting more and more, "is when he really digs into my family's money."

Teena groaned internally. Knowing Percival, she should've seen this coming. Back when Markus was in middle school, Teena had been aware he didn't come from money. He qualified for free and reduced lunches, he couldn't afford to go on extracurricular trips or do fun things on the weekends, and his clothes and supplies weren't the nicest. He had every excuse to be coarse, bitter, and mean to the people around him. But on the contrary, he was kind, charming, and studious. He wasn't a genius, but he worked hard to get good grades. Teena had seen and acknowledged his good heart, and it was with pride that she watched him over the next four years grow even more mature. He was a good guy.

So of course, Percival had chosen to mock him for his lack of wealth.

Markus's permanent smile turned sad as he talked. "During rehearsals, between scenes, he would poke and prod at me. My clothes, my car, the fact that I have three jobs. You know, all that kind of stuff."

"That's..." Teena refrained from expressing her full, uncensored opinion on Percival Jennings. "That's cruel. I'm sorry." She felt her newfound sympathy for the man evaporating.

"It's, I mean..." Markus accidentally snapped one of the Q-tips. "I can't control what he does. Only how I react." This time, he whispered the mantra hollowly.

Again, she waited for Markus to fill the silence when he was ready.

"Earlier this week, at Crawful o' Waffles, where I'm a server—" He nodded in remembrance. "Oh yeah, you were there! I told you I was going to apply for CU Boulder, majoring in biology."

Teena had known this was big news. No one in Markus's immediate family had ever gone to college. The fact that he was shooting for his dream school was significant, not to mention something to be celebrated.

"Then Mr. Jennings came in and sat at a table across the dining room. He must've overheard someone nearby talking about me, because when I came up to take his order, he really laid into me. 'Oh, you must be flailing in this town, if you're looking to move so far away. You think you're smart enough to go to a school that big? You're so prideful for ditching your hometown.' And on and on."

Teena bit the inside of her cheek. "How do you put up with crap like that?"

"I control how I react. I keep smiling. I don't let him see that it hurts." A genuine glimmer returned to Markus's smile, though it was still tinged with sadness. "I'm not meaning to ditch Tennant Park. I really love my friends here."

"Of course you're not."

"It's hard enough to leave home without him bashing it over my head."

"I can imagine." Teena couldn't help but glance at the clock. She knew pushing Markus would only make him clam up, but the seconds were ticking by quickly.

But he continued of his own accord. "Tonight, as we were all heading to our places to start the show… He pulled me aside and offered to pay for my first two years of college if I dropped out of the show right then."

Teena nearly fell from her seat. She hadn't really known what she'd expected him to say, but it certainly wasn't *that*. "Two years at CU Boulder? In exchange for you dropping out?" As despicable as it was for Percival to offer such a cruel ultimatum, Teena had to admit: If she was in Markus's shoes, she probably would have taken the money.

Markus nodded. "Yeah. Ditching the show. Abandoning my responsibilities. Letting down everyone here. Letting him get to me. Letting him *win*."

Teena gaped. Well, when he put it like that, the money sounded way less appealing.

She asked, "But why? Why would he make you that offer?"

"He wanted to get me to crack… And I almost did. I almost took the cash. It would help so much. But…" With a swipe of his arm, he brushed away all the Q-tips. "That's not how I want to do things."

They both sat there in the quiet green room for a beat. Then two. He eventually grabbed his textbook and went back to reading, and Teena realized their conversation was over. Markus had answered her question, and he now looked emotionally and physically drained. But his smile was still there.

Teena stood. "Thanks for talking to me, Markus. I appreciate it."

He nodded without looking up from his book, but it didn't look like he was reading. She could practically see the gears whirring in his head.

She stepped away from the makeup desks, her own mind racing.

Was Markus thinking about what was going to happen next? Could he be capable of stabbing Percival out of anger and vengeance? Maybe he thought that, by killing the old man, he could get a hold of his money as well?

His mantra echoed in her memory: *"I can't control what he does. Only how I react."* Getting rid of Percival Jennings for good would certainly be a reaction.

But Teena simply couldn't imagine Markus Daniels killing anyone. It wasn't in his nature. Yes, people do insane things when they're desperate, but Markus was kind and thoughtful. He wasn't a murderer.

Unless he'd been pushed one time too many. Anyone was capable of snapping.

But she still had one more pressing question: Why did Percival try to bribe Markus to drop out of the show? According to Markus, the old man had been trying to break him, to force him to compromise himself. But that didn't quite ring true to Teena. Sure, that might be part of it, but Percival took great pride in this production. Sabotaging the play on opening night would be a huge deal to him. Something else had to be going on.

She heard a commotion coming from backstage. Or, rather, many commotions. A set change was happening. Next was the climactic graveyard scene where Scrooge confronted his own headstone.

A chill raced through Teena's bones. Christmas Yet to Come was nearly complete. Only a few scenes separated Percival from his death. Only a few minutes.

She jerked where she stood, as if her feet didn't know where to go. Should she run onstage and stop the production right now? Should she try to chisel away at the icy road so that help could reach them? Should she go talk to someone else, try to get more information?

But she couldn't think of anyone else. She'd run out of suspects. She had learned a lot and pieced together many motives, but ultimately, the clues weren't telling her anything.

She needed to talk it out. Hear her words and see them floating in the air. Maybe they would drift into something cohesive, and the answer would fall at her feet.

Yeah right.

Regardless, she booked it out of the green room, toward the lobby. She needed to talk to Bernie.

13.

As Teena walked down the hallway, her mind flipped through her list of possible suspects. In fact, she pictured them in a police lineup like she'd seen in movies.

Jimmy Quinn: hotheaded, felt like Percival was rubbing his wealth in his face, didn't like the old man in general, strong enough to stab someone and kill them.

Evelyn Barrie: ambitious, felt slighted and unseen by the theatre community, saw Percival as her main obstacle to a leading role, able to hide in plain sight.

Markus Daniels: intelligent, practically above suspicion, insulted and badgered by Percival, possibly knowledgeable enough about biology to stab someone to death in one blow.

Don Schrader: missing in action, lied about pink eye, has led a double life as one of the country's most infamous serial killers —

No no no. She had to stop dragging poor Don Schrader into her paranoid theories. The only thing he was guilty of was having pink eye.

But it would be such a sweet relief if it was that easy. *"Oh, it turns out Percival's would-be killer isn't a regular person I've known for years and been in plays with. It's a crazed maniac who escaped from an asylum down the road. Yep, normal, everyday people aren't capable of premeditated murder. Life is good."*

If only.

Teena stormed into the lobby, not bothering to tiptoe anymore. With every passing second, she lost another drop of patience and probably gained another gray hair.

There was Bernie, pacing back and forth in front of the auditorium doors. He was wringing his hands, looking like a man in the waiting room of a hospital. He turned toward her and lit up. "Teena!" He beckoned her over to their wreath-and-poinsettia-laden corner, but Teena didn't have time for that. She walked right up to him, already speaking.

"We're running out of time, Bernie. I don't think I can pull this off after all." Saying the words out loud made her heart sink, but she had to be realistic. In all likelihood, she wasn't going to figure out who Percival's killer was.

Bernie checked his watch. "Mhmm, we're almost at the last scene of the show, that's true. But you can do this." His words were more confident than his frenzied expression. He gulped and re-capped what he'd been up to. "I've been watchin' the parking lot and walking all 'round the interior of the theatre. There were people goin' to the bathroom and takin' phone calls and things like that. But no one sneakin' by, lookin' like a killer. If there was, I'da seen 'em."

Teena shook her head in defeat. "Then we have nothing. No clues to go on."

"Not nothin'. Never nothin'." Bernie set his jaw, determined to look determined. It may have been an act, but he almost convinced her not to give up hope. He twiddled his fingers like he was directing a backing-up car. "Tell me what you've foun' out since we last talked. What've you learned, Detective Fakhoury?"

"Umm…" Teena rubbed her temples. She had to get her brain into gear, but it felt like it was floating in molasses. "I talked to Evelyn and Markus. They both have very real grudges against Percival, but they just don't seem like killers. I talked to Roy too, Percival's brother. And then…" She snapped, remembering her trek downstairs. "Oh! I found where the knife came from!"

"The murder knife?"

"Yeah, it came from the prop room."

Bernie creased his brow. "Prop room?"

"Remember you saw me coming up the stairs?" As she talked, she waved her hands around, hoping that would jostle loose any pertinent information. "You were walking in from outside. I was down in the prop room, where there's a bunch of tools and brooms and filing cabinets and mannequins."

"Oh, I getcha. I call that the broom room. But yeah, there are props and tools in there too. And mannequins." He shivered at the thought.

She went on. "Anyway, I found a roll bag with a bunch of knives. One was missing, and its slot matched the knife I found in the duct."

"Wait." Bernie removed his wool cap and scratched his bald head. Then he rubbed the thick scar that bisected his scalp. Then he tapped his foot. Then he itched his unshaven stubble. When he'd said "Wait," he'd apparently meant it.

"Bernie," she hissed, "what are you thinking?"

"Can you d'scribe the knife for me? The murder knife, I mean."

Teena closed her eyes and pictured the weapon she'd found what felt like a lifetime ago. She had only seen it once, but its gleam and heft were seared into her memory. "It was kind of stubby, I mean short, and it was serrated, like it had teeth. And it curved at the end of the blade, but only a little. Not like a hook. A slight curve." She was rambling. Panic had nearly settled in.

Bernie itched his stubble again, and she just about screamed. But as he scratched, he spoke. "I know the stuff in the broom room pr'tty well. And I know that roll bag. There are a tonna other knives in there that'd be better for stabbin' a guy. Teena…" His eyes narrowed. "If I r'member right, and if you're d'scribing that blade right… I think that's a rope knife."

She wasn't following. "What do you mean?"

"I mean it's made for cuttin' rope." He pantomimed a demonstration. "When you use it, you saw back an' forth—that's the serration, y'see?—and then you pull upward and out—that's what the curve's for."

Teena set her hands on her hips as she thought. As far as she knew, all knives were more or less equal. She hadn't thought to describe the blade she'd found to Bernie. But of course, she should've—he was way smarter than people gave him credit for. "So you can't kill someone with that knife?"

"Well, you *can*. But there'd be five other knives in the bag that would be better for the job. If the killer went down there lookin' for a knife, and they chose *that* one, their goal isn't stabbin'."

Teena opened her mouth to respond…but she had no words. She couldn't believe it. What Bernie had just said changed her entire perspective of the evening. The person who'd taken the knife *wasn't* going to stab Percival? How did that even make sense?

"How does that even make sense?" She threw up her hands in exasperation. And exhaustion. And exhortation as well, while she was at it. She could use a little divine intervention at the moment.

Bernie grimaced. "Your guess is as good as—"

A trill of delight came from inside the auditorium. Someone was extremely happy. Percival's voice followed: "I'm alive! Hooray! I don't know what to do with myself. I feel light as a feather. I'm happy as an angel! I'm as merry as a schoolboy!"

Scrooge had returned to his bedchamber on Christmas morning. His time with the three spirits was over. The play was drawing to its jubilant conclusion. Everyone was going to get their happily-ever-afters—Scrooge, the Cratchits, the charity-seekers, everyone. Happy endings for all involved.

Except Percival Jennings. One way or another, he would be killed. Because Teena had failed to identify his killer.

Her heart was racing, and she felt faint. She suddenly reached out and grabbed Bernie's hand—partly out of kinship, mostly because his tremors masked her own.

"Should I stop the show?" she asked. Her voice had never sounded so small and uncertain. She felt the weight of a person's life on her shoulders, and it was staggering.

Bernie looked her deep in the eyes. "I know you'll do the right thing. If you don' think you can figure out who the killer is, yeah, stop the show. But I think you'll crack the case."

She squeaked, "In only a couple of minutes?!"

With a smirk, he said, "Plenty a' time."

There they stood, hand in hand. Finally, Bernie let go and gestured toward the green room entrance.

"I'll hold down the fort ou' here. You've gotta get movin'. Places, people! That's what they say in movies, at least." He chuckled.

From inside the auditorium, Teena could hear Scrooge chatting merrily with a boy on the street:

"Do you know whether they've sold the prize turkey that was hanging in the window?"

"What, the one as big as me?"

"What a delightful boy! Yes, the one as big as you!"

She really had to be going. With her feet moving under their own direction, she shuffled back toward the green room.

Her mind simultaneously felt like it was stuffed to the brim and rapidly emptying. She'd learned so much this evening, but she simply didn't know if she'd learned the *right* things.

This would be the time when Sherlock Holmes laid out all his evidence, presented his findings, and accurately named the culprit.

So. What did she know?

The knife was intended to cut rope, not flesh. As far as Teena was concerned, this changed everything. She'd formed her list of primary suspects based on their proximity to Percival, assuming they needed to be close to him in order to drive the knife into his body. But it turned out that wasn't the case.

Then what was the knife for?

All the play's backdrops were held up with thick rope. Maybe the killer was planning to cut down one of those as a distraction, during which they would…do something.

Hardly a master plan.

Teena was so lost in thought, she hadn't realized she'd walked into the green room until she stubbed her toe on one of the couch legs. She hopped back and cringed in pain—thankfully, no one was around to see. The place was empty. Everyone was already backstage, prepared to go onstage for the big triumphant finale. The last scene.

She headed toward the door that led backstage, but something caught her eye. The vent to the air duct was slightly ajar. She peeked inside and found nothing but dust. The serrated knife and hand-drawn diagram were gone.

It was happening.

A wave of nausea flowed upward from her gut to her head, as if the floor had dropped out from under her. She hurried backstage.

At that point, she decided: She had to stop the show. Run out into the middle the stage, waving her arms, shouting, crying, foaming at the mouth, anything to prevent the final scene from happening. It felt like giving up—she'd been working all night to find the killer's identity so that she wouldn't have to stop the show, but she saw no other option.

Now, the killer would slink into the shadows and try to take out Percival later, likely without anyone there to save the day. The killer would learn from tonight, tweak their mistakes, and succeed next time. Percival would die…but not today.

A hollow victory, but a victory nonetheless.

Then why did she feel so defeated?

Her breath was shallow, as if a thousand rubber bands were strapped around her lungs. Most of the cast members were waiting in the wings, ready to go on when the scene called for it. Teena joined them, feeling numb. A few people talked to her, but they sounded underwater, and she didn't respond.

Onstage, the scene was set for the finale: Church bells rang as if announcing Christ's second coming. Pigeons cooed and flapped their wings in tandem. Carolers of all ages and statures stood along the cobblestoned streets, smiles stretching across their faces as they filled the air with their joyous notes.

Percival and Victor, who was dressed as Fred, were reconciling, laughing, and embracing. It was a sweet moment that the audience was eating up. One by one, the rest of the ensemble began trickling into the scene, adding to the joyous ambience. Soon, the Cratchits would come in. Scrooge would have a brief interaction with them. Then, they would walk to the front of the stage, Scrooge carrying Tiny Tim on his shoulder. Tiny Tim would say, "God bless us." Scrooge would reply, "God bless us, everyone!" Scrooge would stand directly on top of an invisible X on the floor, and he would be killed.

She should be barreling onstage right at that moment to stop the show.

But she wasn't.

Why wasn't she?

Because Bernie thought she could solve it. And *she* thought she could solve it. That was the only explanation.

She muttered to herself, "Okay then, Holmes. Get on it."

The wings were nearly empty. Most of the actors were onstage, milling around the Dickensian London street, chattering and singing and having a grand ole time. Only a few precious minutes remained.

What was she missing?!

She rubbed her eyes with the heels of her palms, then stared up at the ceiling, hoping the answer would be scrawled up there. But no. Just the basic steel beams and curtain riggings of a low-level community theatre.

She called to mind the diagram. The single sheet of notebook paper she'd seen once a hundred years ago. She scrutinized it in her memory.

The names.

The handwriting.

The X.

And then she saw it. Up there in the ceiling. The key to understanding what the diagram really meant.

The sandbags. Several of them hung from the ceiling, acting as counterweights for the various backdrops. They were held up by ropes, all of which were anchored backstage.

The ensemble carolers began their song: "We wish you a merry Christmas, and a happy new year! Glad tidings we bring, to you and your kin..." Teena's pulse thudded in time with the rhythm. *THUMP-thump-thump THUMP-thump-thump THUMP-thump-thump...*

"Hey, Teena!" Someone was hissing her name. Corrine, dressed in the scary black robe. She and Victor, who had quick-changed back into the Ghost of Christmas Past, were beckoning her onstage. It was time for the three spirits to join the scene, looming in the background and approving of Scrooge's moral redemption. Teena remembered praising this directorial decision just last night, but now, she hated it. She was busy preventing a murder! She didn't have time to be a background character.

She *really* didn't have time. Once the three spirits showed up, it was a matter of seconds before

Scrooge and the Cratchits made their way to the front of the stage. Sixty seconds, at most.

As if in a daze, Teena reluctantly stepped out from backstage, joining Corrine and Victor in the ensemble. Her eyes were locked upward, studying the sandbags. She stumbled over a few of her cast-mates' dresses and other props, but she didn't care. Corrine whispered something to her in a concerned tone, but Teena didn't hear.

She had found it. *The* sandbag. It dangled directly over Scrooge's final placement onstage. That was what the big bold X on the diagram signified.

Someone was going to cut the rope holding that heavy bag aloft. It was going to fall and land right on the old man's head. Teena wasn't a forensic specialist, but she was pretty sure the weight of the sandbag would at least break Percival's neck. It would almost certainly be fatal for a frail, elderly man.

But who? Who could be the person cutting the rope? Everyone was onstage…

Almost everyone.

All at once, Teena's heart stopped racing. Her feeling of faintness vanished. She stood straighter and felt bolder.

Because she knew.

She *knew*.

The one person she'd immediately dismissed as a suspect because he wouldn't be onstage in the last scene. The only cast member backstage at that very moment.

Teena sprinted away suddenly, her holly crown barely staying on her head. Her fellow ensemble members glared at her sideways, and she faintly heard some confused muttering from the audience, but she truly couldn't care less. She ran faster than she'd ever run in her life.

She dashed backstage and headed for the wall of ropes and pulleys.

There, in the faint red glow of the EXIT sign, was a lanky figure. He was hunched over the ropes, sawing with all his might. His back was to Teena, and the lighting made everything a little murky, but she knew it was him.

She ran and yelled, "Roy! Stop!!!"

The figure froze. His shoulders sagged, like a kid who'd been caught sneaking into the cookie jar. He began to turn.

And then, the lights turned off.

All the lights in the entire theatre.

Everything went black. What little light there was backstage disappeared.

Teena skittered to a halt. She could barely see the hand in front of her face, and she didn't want to trip on something and break her jaw on the floor.

But wait. Not *all* the lights had gone out. The red EXIT sign was still on. It wasn't connected to the master light switch.

The master light switch that *someone had turned off.*

She could just barely make out the shape of the figure. Roy Jennings stood by the ropes and pulleys, holding the wickedly serrated knife, staring at her. In the faint red light, he was only a silhouette — she couldn't see his face, but she knew it was him.

They stared at each other for half a heartbeat.

Then the figure spun around and ran through the exit door, directly into the outside world. The door slammed shut before Teena could say a word.

By that point, both the audience in their seats and the actors onstage were murmuring about the unexpected blackout. The audience was curious, wondering what was about to happen next. But the cast was confused — they hadn't rehearsed this.

But Teena had other concerns. She had just solved *and* prevented a murder. She was *not* about to let the would-be killer simply run away.

She burst through the door like a linebacker, following Roy outside. The icy night sucked all the air out of her lungs and left her gasping. It had to be ten degrees at the absolute most. Having moved from Detroit, she was used to cold winters. But this was *cold.*

As she was forced to catch her breath, she surveyed her surroundings. The door had spat her out behind the theatre. It was dark back here, since all the festive lights and lampposts were out front by the trees and parking lot. She hurried around the side of the building, praying she didn't stumble on a rock or a stray root.

When she rounded the building and was finally able to see, she couldn't help but gasp.

It was snowing. An army of gentle but steady snowflakes drifted from the sky and settled onto the cars, asphalt, and tree limbs. With the illuminated evergreens, the smell of pine, and the beautiful snowfall, Teena felt like she had barged into the middle of a fairy tale.

Except for the fact that she was chasing an attempted murderer.

Speaking of which…

She spotted Roy's form zigzagging through the parking lot, his back still to her. He weaved between cars, up and down aisles, as if he was looking for something. What was he doing? Was he trying to find an escape vehicle? That was unlikely — she had a feeling he was responsible for the road being iced over, so he would know that escape was impossible. Or would he try to simply run down Mountain on his own two feet?

Again, she yelled out to him. "Roy, stop! I know what's happened! Stop running!"

But he wasn't headed for the road. Instead, he peeled toward the theatre's entrance…which was the last place Teena had expected him to run. The scene of his would-be crime? What was he up to?

Roy might have been on the older side, but he was fast. He rushed into the theatre and was even courteous enough to close the door behind him.

Teena, on the other hand, wasn't an Olympic athlete. She ran toward the theatre's entrance as quickly as she could. Her breath puffed out of her mouth like cigarette smoke, and the icy air burned the inside of her lungs. She usually loved that feeling, but right then, it hurt enough to slow her down.

It felt like she was in a nightmare — she pumped her arms and legs with all her might, but the theatre door remained the same distance away. The adrenaline of the past minute had begun to ebb. She reached out to the door's handle, straining, begging, stretching for dear life.

The metal handle was frosty in her grip as she yanked the door open. She lurched into the lobby and found…

No one. It was totally empty except for the décor and hot cocoa tables.

Where had Roy gone? Her instinct was the green room, and since he was a cast member too, she hoped he shared that instinct. For what felt like the millionth time that day, she headed for the green room.

But it was empty as well. She stood in the door's threshold, panting and seething.

Her hands curled into fists. She'd *had* him. Where was he?!

A sound arose from the auditorium. Static? A swarm of bees? No—it was applause. The audience was clapping.

Teena turned around and ran back the way she'd come. Through the hallway. Through the lobby. Through the auditorium doors.

On stage, the cast was taking its bows. The plastic snow had fallen. The live pigeons had flown. The actors had concluded their performances, and they were now soaking in their accolades. The audience clapped, cheered, and whistled.

Most notably, the lights were on. Everything was normal. Percival Jennings was alive and well, taking his bow centerstage.

Teena stood along the back wall, her blood still pumping. She set a hand on her chest to try to temper her galloping heart.

A voice came from right next to her: "Teena?" Bernie was standing in the back of the auditorium too. He said over the roaring applause, "The lights went off for a minute there. I thought that was it, that the old man was 'bout to be killed. But when the lights came back on, ev'rything was okay. The actors just went on with the curtain call. What's goin' on?"

She sputtered, "That's a good freakin' question! What are you doing in here?"

He shrugged meekly. "I thought you were gonna stop the show, and I was back here to step in an' help if I needed to."

"I thought you believed I would crack the case?"

Through a grimace, he said, "I was bein'…let's say optimistic."

She laughed dryly. "Well, I *did* crack the case. I know who was going to kill Percival."

"What?!" His yell was drowned out by the applause. "You do? Who?"

"Roy Jennings, his brother. I chased him outside and around the building, but I lost him."

Bernie looked at her with his eyebrows furrowed.

She looked confused right back at him. "What?"

"You mean that guy?" He pointed up at the stage.

Teena followed his finger across the auditorium, over the audience's heads, and onto the London street. There, taking a bow with the rest of the cast, was Roy Jennings.

She groaned and leaned against the wall behind her.

What was going on?

Act 3:
Encore

14.

"It was him, I'm telling you," Teena hissed to Bernie as they flowed into the lobby along with the rest of the audience. The general ambience was loud enough for her to speak freely, but she hissed all the same.

After the curtain call, the actors had filed offstage. Teena knew the plan was for them to wait a few minutes, then come out to the lobby to sign autographs, take photos, and mingle with the paying customers.

The hundreds of theatregoers were prattling amongst themselves, some raving about the show, some discussing where they were going to eat tomorrow. A few clutched their playbills, excited to get autographs from their favorite actors. A handful of people had bouquets of flowers.

But Teena barely noticed any of this. Again, she pled her case to Bernie. "It was Roy Jennings, I swear. I saw him cutting the rope that would've killed Percival. I *saw* him."

Bernie waved down her protest. "Hey, I believed you before, I believe you now."

But she was mainly trying to convince herself. She *had* seen Roy Jennings… Right?

Of course she had. With her own two eyes.

After Roy had run around the parking lot and into the theatre, he'd had plenty of time to zip backstage and join the curtain call without anyone noticing. Teena was a slow runner, and she'd checked the green room before coming into the auditorium and seeing him onstage. That had to have been what happened.

It had to be.

The lobby was already full. It seemed the hundred-year-old theatre hadn't been built to accommodate events that were actually popular. After the room had been empty and quiet all night, it was a jarring shift for Teena. Families took selfies in front of the decorations. Kids who had been freed from the confines of their auditorium seats began to run laps and chase each other all around. It was loud and chaotic, like the inside of a kettle making popcorn.

Teena settled on her next course of action. She said to Bernie, "The cast will be out here in just a couple of minutes to mix with the audience. I'll confront Roy."

He grimaced and said, "If I was him, I'd run while I have a chance. He migh' be long gone."

But she shook her head. "If he stuck around to take a bow, that means he's blending in, pretending nothing even happened. Plus, the road is probably still inaccessible. He's trapped up here, just like the rest of us."

As she said that, she glanced around at all the happy faces. It seemed they didn't know the road leading down Mt. Tennant was iced over. They didn't know they were stuck. She doubted they were going to take it well. But she didn't have time to worry about that right now.

Bernie nodded toward a throng of people clustered around the folding tables he and Teena had set up earlier in the week. "I'll be over there. I needta hand out that cocoa b'fore there's a riot."

She instinctively grabbed his forearm. "Keep an eye on me as I talk to him, okay?"

He tensed up. "You think he's gonna get violent?"

"I…" She answered truthfully. "I don't know."

Bernie nodded like a soldier about to charge into battle, then he held out a fist. Teena bumped it, and they parted ways through the dense crowd.

The largest decoration in the room was the poinsettia-dotted wreath she and Bernie had used as a meeting spot throughout the night. It was as good a place as any — she went and stood under it. Simeon's instructions had been for the cast to wait five minutes after the curtain call, then come out into the lobby. At least three minutes had passed.

While she waited for the rest of the cast to join her in the lobby, she had time to slow down and think things through. On what grounds did she think Roy Jennings was an attempted killer?

The events of the evening cycled through her mind like a PowerPoint presentation. All the conversations she'd had, all the details she'd picked up on, all the theories and clues… She quickly sifted through everything.

Roy was a vo-tech teacher. Had been for years, according to him. Teena had even bonded with him over their shared profession.

What was it he said he taught? She clamped her eyes shut and focused. Stars formed in her vision, she was clenching so hard.

Then she remembered. Construction and mechanics.

He had the knowledge to sabotage the pipes on the road leading up Mountain. He knew that was the best and most innocent-looking way to cut off any sort of police back-up. He also likely had the tools and knowhow to open air ducts.

Then there was the makeup on the bag of knives downstairs. True, everyone in the cast wore stage makeup, but it was undeniable that Roy wore the most. As Marley's ghost, he had white makeup caked all over his face and hands. It only made sense that he'd left some behind when he un-rolled the bag.

And of course, the only piece of evidence that should matter: *She had seen him cutting the rope.* She was a witness. Case closed.

But what was his motive? Yes, Roy was bitter and Percival was a D-bag, but why had Roy resorted to murder? That was the biggest piece of the puzzle, and it was missing.

An uptick in the noise level yanked Teena out of her thoughts.

The cast of *A Christmas Carol* paraded out of the green room. They smiled and waved at the crowd, beaming as if they had just completed a mission to Mars. They were justifiably proud of the show they'd put on, and now it was time to bask in the crowd's adoration.

Simeon trailed behind the cast, no longer clutching his clipboard. He looked like a frayed wire crackling with electricity. He had been inches from losing his cool all night long…but when he saw the lobby full of happy audience members, he instantly relaxed. People approached him to shake his hand and offer congratulations, and he looked ready to float straight to heaven.

The cast members spread out around the lobby, allowing people to walk past them for autographs or photos if they wanted. Friends and family congratulated the actors they had come to see. A lot of parents had brought flowers for their kids—

Andy's mom in particular gave him a bouquet bigger than his torso. Markus was popular among the teenaged girl demographic. Several people wanted to snap a picture with Percival, since he was the star of the show. Some kids in the audience went up to every member of the cast to get them to sign their playbills. It was a fun atmosphere, and Teena wished she could enjoy it. Instead, she only had eyes for Roy Jennings.

He was standing against a wall on the other side of the lobby, nodding politely as people told him how much they'd enjoyed the show. Teena steeled herself and began to maneuver her way over to him. There was barely enough room to take a step, so it was slow-going.

"Hi, Miss F.!" A few students from her biology class appeared in front of her.

She plastered on a smile—which wasn't too hard, since she was genuinely glad to see them. But she had places to be.

The students held out their playbills.

"Oh shoot," she muttered. "I'm sorry, I don't have a pen." She quickly sidestepped them. "See you after Christmas!"

Finally, she made it across the churning sea of people and planted herself next to Roy. He nodded to her, then returned his attention to the procession of audience members.

She nearly flipped her lid. She had caught him trying to murder his brother, then chased him around the building, then came to confront him…and he *nodded* at her?!

"Roy!" She clenched her jaw and glared up at him.

He jokingly matched her tone. "Teena!" He laughed and shoved her arm. "Hey, where were you in the curtain call? You deserved to take a bow!"

"You… I-I was…" Her mind short-circuited. Was he seriously trying to pretend nothing had happened? She snapped, "I saw you!"

"Saw me what?" His eyes sparkled, just as they always did.

"I saw you cutting that rope backstage. I chased you into the parking lot. You were trying to kill Percival!"

He jerked back in shock. "Whoa there! What?!"

"Don't lie to me. Don't you dare. You have a knife." She began patting his pockets forcefully, almost shoving him against the wall.

"Teena, I have no idea what you're talking about." He held up his hands in surrender as she kept searching the nooks and crannies of his costume, from his sleeves to his socks. A biting edge entered his voice. "What, do you want my wallet? My car keys? Or do you need a pen to sign autographs? I might have a few extra."

She wasn't interested in the keys or pens she felt in his pockets. She'd hoped to find the serrated knife hidden in a belt loop, or maybe the diagram crumpled up in his shoe. But no. He didn't have them. They weren't anywhere on his person.

"I saw you," she said again, but this time with far less vigor.

He sighed. "No you didn't, Teena. I wish I knew what you were talking about, so that I could help." He chuckled. "But you're speaking in tongues right now."

Had she seen him? Now that he mentioned it, she hadn't gotten a good look at the figure's face. It was dark backstage, and the low red light could've messed with her vision. And when they were outside, she had only seen the person's back. Maybe it wasn't Roy…

"Thanks for coming to the show." He shook a little old lady's hand, then another, then another. A retirement home had attended the production as a group, and it seemed all the ladies had a crush on Roy. They each wanted to take a picture with him, and one even asked if he was single. He laughed at their comments, bent down to talk with them, and generally oozed charm.

Was this the guy Teena had just accused of attempted murder? At the moment, she couldn't see it.

Roy twiddled his fingers in folksy flirtation as the ladies shuffled away. His laugh faded into a contented sigh. Then, out of the corner of his smile, he said, "You know, you're not acting like yourself right now, Teena. You're usually so agreeable."

A flame ignited in the pit of her stomach.

That did it.

Ever since her freshman year of high school, she'd backed down in disagreements. She'd been accommodating. She'd simply gotten by.

Not anymore. She wasn't going to let Roy off the hook that easily.

She sharpened her gaze and started examining him more closely. The fact that he was trying to get her to back off meant she was on the right track. She had to look past his charming smile and confident attitude.

Roy shirked back from her glare. "Teena, stop. You're making me uncom—"

She noticed the Marley makeup streaking down his face, especially around his hairline. "You're sweating, Roy. Because you and I just sprinted around this building five minutes ago."

He laughed off the accusation. "I'm sweaty all the time. Everyone knows that. What, you're going to come after me for having stage-fright? This is my first show!" His voice cracked. Just once. He was getting nervous.

"Your autographs. I've seen you sign five or six since I've been standing here."

"And?" He puffed out his chest like a proud peacock. "The crowd must have really connected with my performance."

"Neat and blocky. It matches the handwriting I saw on the diagram that outlined Percival's murder."

Roy snorted in shock, tripping over his own words. "Now hold on—"

"It *matches,*" she pressed. "And one of the pens in your pocket. I bet it's a thick black Sharpie. Just like the diagram!"

"Well then, where is this diagram? Show it to me, so we can compare."

They both knew Teena didn't have the sheet of paper. He'd hidden or likely destroyed it.

Teena moved on. She bent down and pointed at a line of chalky residue on the soles of his shoes. "Slush. Snow. You were outside!"

"So I got some fresh air! Geez Louise!" He clenched his jaw, no longer amused. The line of people flinched at his outburst—he quickly switched back to his megawatt smile, but the kids who had been waiting for his autograph skittered away. He leaned toward Teena and said, "As Victor Stassi would say, that's circumstantial evidence at best."

Teena shot back, "Victor's an estate-planning attorney, not a cheesy character on *Law & Order.*"

And just like that, the puzzle piece slid into place. She saw the whole picture laid out in front of her, and she was slightly embarrassed she hadn't figured it out sooner.

Victor. The Jennings estate. Percival's will.

"Crap on a cracker," she whispered.

"Huh?" Roy looked baffled by her use of Percival's favorite exclamation.

She looked him straight in the eye. "On Christmas Day last year, Percival's wife Rebecca left him. And on January first, just a few short days later, you moved in. You said yourself, it took every last penny to move here. Why would you do that for a brother who hates your guts?"

Roy began to interject, but she didn't give him the chance.

"Because with Rebecca gone," she shoved a finger in his face, "you assumed they'd have a messy divorce and Percival would write her out of his will. After all, she had humiliated him and broken his heart. Why *wouldn't* he cut her out of the will? Suddenly, you were next in line. You, his only living relative. If he died, you would get his wealth."

With every word, she grew more and more confident. And Roy's dashing smile twisted more and more into a scowl.

"Which means…you've been planning this for a year! I may not be a lawyer like Victor Stassi, but I know the word 'premeditated.' And it isn't good for you."

He drew back his shoulders, trying to look even taller than he already was. "I don't think you want to say anymore—"

She cut him off: "You don't have a dollar to your name. But you were talking to Jimmy at the church party last night about a big African safari you're going to take next year. Expecting an influx of cash, are we?"

Roy's eyes widened, and if his face wasn't already covered in white makeup, he would have gone pale. "Dammit," he hissed to himself.

As Jimmy had said: "*Rich people, man.*" They couldn't seem to stop themselves from bragging about their money, even when they didn't have it yet.

But Teena wasn't done. She wondered if this was how Sherlock Holmes felt when he gave his day-saving monologue, wherein he simultaneously solved the case and disemboweled the bad guy.

"You're a terrible actor, Roy. I mean, on the stage. You've convinced the whole world you're a good and decent person who *isn't* a murderer, so you must be an okay actor. But in terms of theatre, you suck. So then why would you audition to be part of a play?" She pointed toward the auditorium doors. "So that you could stage this little 'accident.' A rope snaps, a sandbag falls, and Percival dies. It looks totally accidental. Tragic, unfortunate, scary... But no one's very sad about it. They all shrug and move on without looking too closely. And you, his little brother, inherit all his money."

The lobby pulsed with energy all around them as the cast and audience members chatted and mingled. It was a kinetic environment, full of spirit and noise. But Teena and Roy were as still as statues, staring at one another. Neither dared move first, as if that would concede defeat.

Teena didn't breathe, but her nerves crackled. She was prepared to duck and run if Roy attacked her. She wanted to look for Bernie in the corner of her eye, but she didn't so much as flinch.

Finally, Roy clicked his tongue twice, making a *tsk-tsk* sound. His older brother had done the exact same thing earlier, but he likely wouldn't care for the comparison.

In a plain and level voice, he said to her, "You have no proof." He ambled away from her and stood on the other side of the lobby, where he instantly reactivated his charming persona. He continued posing for photos, signing playbills, and greeting people warmly as if he hadn't just effectively admitted to attempted murder.

She stared at him from across the room, as streams of people passed between them, but he didn't even look in her direction.

Two billows of emotion competed inside Teena's chest. The first was a swell of pride. She wanted to cheer at the top of her lungs, pump her fists in the air, and stomp around the room. Against all odds, she had figured it out. She'd pieced together the puzzle and concluded that Roy Jennings was the would-be killer. His frosty demeanor had all but confirmed it.

But at the same time, she was also very frustrated. As much as she hated to admit it, Roy was right: She had no concrete proof. Everything she'd just said to him was theoretical or, yes, circumstantial. If she couldn't nail him to the wall with evidence, he would walk away scot-free and try to off his brother on another day—a day when Teena wouldn't be there to stop him.

She needed indisputable proof. Evidence. A smoking gun.

Or, rather, a serrated rope knife.

That was it. She needed to find the murder weapon. Her career as a detective wasn't over just yet.

So where could the knife be? He didn't have it on his person now. He'd had it when she found him backstage, cutting the rope that would've bashed in Percival's head. They ran outside, then ran inside. Presumably, he zipped backstage and right into the spotlight for the curtain call—he didn't have time to hide it anywhere from the time he reentered the theatre to the time he was seen onstage.

Teena cycled through that series of events again and again in her mind, making sure she wasn't missing anything. She must have looked more-than-a-little crazy, standing by herself with her eyes slightly closed, clearly lost in thought. But it kept audience members at bay, allowing her to think without being interrupted.

Finally, she came to a conclusion she was confident in: Roy had the knife before he went outside. He didn't have it when he came inside.

Thus, he must have stashed it outside. Maybe he hid it somewhere specific, or maybe he simply threw it under a car or into the trees. Either way, it was outside the theatre. It had to be.

She had an idea for what to do next, and to execute it, she needed her partner.

If she didn't know better, she'd think the folding tables were handing out free Taylor Swift tickets, not paper cups of hot cocoa. People were swarming, reaching, snatching, chugging, and doing it all over again. Crumpled cups littered the surrounding floor, along with spilled cocoa and scattered powder. The neat-and-tidy section of Teena's brain nearly blew a fuse, but she bravely soldiered on, only picking up ten pieces of trash around the tables.

Poor Bernie looked like a Black Friday employee, filling cups from the drink dispensers as fast as his shaky hands allowed. Of course, it wasn't fast enough for the cocoa-crazed patrons. The temperature outside was below freezing, and they were surrounded by Christmas decorations — the festive itch in their appetites could only be scratched by Swiss Miss.

She got as close to his table as she could and said, "Bernie?" But her voice was drowned out by the throng of people. After a long evening of investigation and espionage, she wasn't about to let a group of cocoa enthusiasts stand in her way. She threw some elbows and made her way through the crowd. "Hey, Bernie!"

He snapped his head toward her. "Mhmm?"

"Can we talk?"

Before she was done forming the sentence, Bernie darted out from behind the table. The Black Friday employee had just quit during peak business hours. He set out the sleeve of paper cups, turned the drink dispensers toward the crowd, and said, "Self-service now avail'ble."

The people groaned at first, then perked up when they realized they could pour as much cocoa as they could drink.

He and Teena stepped aside for another team huddle. He asked, "How'd it go with him?"

"I've never accused someone of murder before." She sighed…then cracked a smirk. "It was kind of fun."

Bernie smiled too, but his was far more cautious. "I was watchin' both of you, t' make sure he didn' get violent. I've never understood th' phrase 'if looks could kill.' But now I do."

"So you believe me about him?"

"I've always believed you…" He paused. Thought. Nodded. "But yeah. I believe you."

"Good," she said as she got down to business, "because we're on the clock."

"Again?"

"Yep. We need to find the knife. That's the best way to prove it. When I chased him outside, he got rid of it. Hid it, tossed it, buried it, something. Right now, it's snowing. We'll go out and follow his trail of footprints. We'll look under every car he passed, look in the trees he ran by, look under the pine needles he passed. And hopefully, the knife will be there."

"Okay, yeah. I get what you're sayin'." But she could see in his eyes that he had an idea brewing of his own.

She spoke quickly, "We need to be fast. The snowfall is gentle, but it's steady. Soon enough, his footprints will be covered up, and the search will be a needle in a haystack. So we need to go *now*."

"Uh-huh. Good plan… Except for the 'we' part."

Confused, she said, "What do you mean?"

Bernie was already adjusting his wool cap, preparing to go out in the cold. "*I'll* follow his footprints and look for the knife. *You* stay in here and figure outta way to keep ev'ryone inside."

"Keep everyone inside?" She wasn't sure what he meant. "Why?"

"As soon as people leave, they'll walk 'round the parkin' lot, look at the lights, all that kinda stuff. And their footprints will mess up Roy's. It'll be a big mishmash of slush. So keep people in here 'til we find where he put the knife."

"Great thinking!" She hadn't thought of that. "Okay, we exited the theatre through the back door, behind the building. Some of my footprints will be mixed in with his, but his shoes are way bigger than mine, so they shouldn't be too hard to tell apart—"

Bernie cut her off with a smile. "I got this, don't worry. I can follow footprints and look for stuff, but I don't do good with people. That's your territory."

Teena returned his smile, then let out a nervous breath. "Okay, let's do this. Good luck. I hope you don't find any other mysteries while you're out there."

"Well, th' night is young."

They bumped fists again, then Bernie set off toward the theatre's front doors.

Teena decided right then and there: As soon as this was all over, she was going to retire from detective work. This crap was stressful.

15.

Teena stood in the crowded lobby and slowly turned in a circle. There had to be hundreds of people in the room, every single one of them jostling and chatting. It felt like she was in the middle of Grand Central Station. She saw folks of every sort: locals, out-of-towners, families, couples, men, women, children, teenagers…

How was she supposed to keep them all in the lobby? Fortunately, one of the favorite pastimes of small-town citizens is just hanging out. It didn't look like very many people had left already. Most were content to chitchat with friends and neighbors, stay in the warm building, and loiter around.

However, that would only last so long. Soon enough, dads would want to go home to watch the game, kids would get fussy, and grandmas would comment that it was past their bedtime. Restlessness would set in, and people would start to leave. Once the exodus started, Roy's footprints outside would be lost forever, and Teena and Bernie would lose any trail they might have to the murder weapon.

So. A plan. She needed a plan.

Teena flexed her fingers and bounced on her heels, as if moving her body would pump blood to her brain and pull an idea out of thin air.

No such luck.

She quickly scanned the room, hoping an idea would strike.

Every now and then, like a sprinkle on top of a cookie, stood someone in a Dickensian costume. It was an amusing sight: regular people dressed in sweaters, coats, jeans, dresses, and leggings, surrounding an actor in knickers and a top hat.

She spotted a cluster of people around Jimmy. A woman with positively enormous biceps had her arm looped through his. Five or six kids stood nearby, running the gamut of ages. Teena assumed these were the Quinns. She'd never met Jimmy's family during her years in the show. It turned out he had quite a lot of experience corralling children after all.

Each of the child actors was accompanied by their parents or guardians. Andy was poking around the Christmas décor, hoping as ever to do some more exploring. Haley was introducing her mom to a few of her new friends. Colton, who was being carried by his father, let loose a big yawn and set his head on Dad's shoulder. A lot of the littler kid actors already looked tired and ready to go home.

Percival stood off by himself. Or, rather, he was surrounded by strangers. Tons of audience members wanted to take a photo with him or congratulate him on a good show, but none were family. No friends had come to support him.

Most of the actors had amassed their own fan clubs of friends and family members. Markus had his mom and high school friends. Victor had scores of admirers from his billboards, as well as his close friends and co-workers. Evelyn had her husband, her brood of children, her friends from the church choir…

Bingo. An idea developed in her mind like a Polaroid picture.

Teena made her way through the crowd toward Evelyn. She didn't really have time to be subtle.

"Hey, Evelyn!" she said over the ambience.

"Hello, dear!" Evelyn's smile nearly touched her ears. Here, surrounded by her friends and family, she looked blissfully happy. "Wonderful show tonight! This is my hubbie—"

"It truly was wonderful, wasn't it?" Teena felt despicable for interrupting Evelyn's family introductions. She would love to meet the Barries…some other time. She went on, "This whole night is overflowing with Christmas spirit.

I don't want it to end! I was just thinking, I wish someone would lead us in a few carols."

Somehow defying the laws of physics, Evelyn's smile got even bigger. Stars glinted in her eyes. She may not be Scrooge, but this could be the next best thing. "That's a *spectacular* idea!" She turned to her choir friends. "I know it isn't Sunday, but how would we feel about spreading a little Christmas cheer right here and now?"

Without hesitation, the choir members agreed and began chittering about what carols they wanted to sing.

"How about 'Hark the Herald Angels Sing'?"

"'Silent Night' is the best carol!"

"No way, that's too slow. We should start with 'Joy to the World.'"

"I think 'Jingle Bells,' so everyone can sing along."

Teena saw a family headed for the exit, and her head nearly popped. She exploded, "All of them! Do all of them!"

The choir members started at her, thunderstruck.

She chuckled to cover her urgency. "I just really love Christmas carols. I want to hear one *right now*."

Evelyn, bless her soul, patted Teena's forearm. "Don't we all, dear. Don't we all!" She cleared her throat and made an invisible costume change into the First Baptist choir director.

"Ladies and gentlemen!" Her powerful voice projected over all the noise in the tightly-packed lobby. Instantly, everyone in the room turned to listen. She went on, "We all want to thank you for joining us tonight. You made it very special for us, just as we hope we made it very special for you. Now, I don't know about you, but I feel an abundance of Christmas spirit in the air! If you'll please join me — as well as the Tennant Park First Baptist Church choir, who sings every Sunday morning — in a few festive ditties…"

She faced the singers and held her arms aloft. The choir members stiffened under her direction, like soldiers after their drill sergeant walked in the room. She waved her left hand to help establish a beat: "'Carol of the Bells,' yes? And a-one, and a-two…"

The singers took a collective breath and slid into the music:

"Hark how the bells, sweet silver bells, all seem to say, throw cares away! Christmas is here, bringing good cheer, to young and old, meek and the bold…"

Teena was mesmerized. She'd never known that song had real lyrics — for some reason, she'd assumed it was all in Latin or something. But these singers were delivering the words with exact diction. And their timing was spot-on too. The song was very fast, and any hesitation or slip-up would throw off the whole effect, but they were nailing it.

Each singer had a beautiful voice and undeniable talent, but Evelyn's direction was the glue that held everything together. She stood up straight, waving her right hand like a feather drifting through the wind, while her left hand forcefully beat an unseen drum. She kept the rhythm perfectly, as if she'd done it a thousand times before. She was a professional through and through.

Teena felt terrible for even considering the idea that Evelyn could be a killer. And Jimmy and Markus. And Don Schrader, for that matter. When this whole escapade was over, she would explain and apologize to each of them.

The lobby was silent except for the expertly-sung carol. Despite the kinetic energy in the room, all the people were frozen, transfixed by the music. The rapid yet precise words were like a magic spell, one that everyone gladly surrendered to. They were all in a glossy, warm bubble, floating through the cold December night. It was a wonderful moment.

A moment Teena knew would end soon. She exhaled and allowed herself to relax, to stand, to think—to simply *be* without rushing from one thing to the next. It had been a long, *long* day. She'd been on the go for the past couple hours. Mental exhaustion was setting in. A layer of cotton had begun to wrap around her brain, making her thought process a little slower and a bit fuzzy.

So, as everyone enjoyed being cocooned in that warm bubble, Teena knew she had only a few minutes to figure things out. Because as soon as that bubble popped, the rat race would be on again.

While the choir sang in the background, Teena took a bird's-eye-view of the puzzle. When she did so, she realized it was missing a big piece. She'd thought Roy's motive for the attempted murder was the last piece she had to fit in, but no. There was one more. Something that, in all the chaos and confusion, she'd actually forgotten about.

Earlier, right when Teena was about to catch Roy in the act of dropping a heavy sandbag on his brother's head, someone had switched off the lights. Every light in the theatre was turned off at the same time, except for the EXIT sign, which wasn't connected to the master switch.

Meaning…

Someone had tried to help Roy get away with murder.

Someone in this room.

Teena attempted to rub away her headache, but it was a losing battle at that point. A thorn was lodged right between her eyes, and it probably wouldn't go away until she took a couple ibuprofen and went to sleep. And *that* wouldn't happen until this whole insane situation was wrapped up.

So. Who could it be?

First of all, it couldn't have been an actor. Every single one of them had been onstage at that moment, except for Roy himself, who was busy being an attempted murderer.

It also had to be someone who could access the master light switch: a location Teena wasn't even sure of.

Those points made Teena feel nauseous. Earlier, she'd eliminated all the stagehands from her list of suspects, saying they couldn't have hidden the knife in the green room without raising suspicion. And she'd been right about that—Roy had been the one who hid the knife.

But what about an accomplice? That could be *anyone*.

Her headache surged down to the base of her neck. She felt like she was starting at square one all over again.

Near the front of the building, a door creaked. Teena turned and saw Bernie slip in from outside. They locked eyes across the crowded lobby, and Teena's heart lifted slightly. Hopefully, he had found the discarded knife, and they could tie it to Roy, and he would burst into a frustrated confession right in front of everyone…

But Bernie's face was grim. And cold. And tired—he'd had a long day too. He shook his head. No knife.

Teena silently groaned, but she gave him a small nod, letting him know she would try to think of something else. He nodded in response, then gestured to the huge crowd listening to the singers and flashed a thumbs up.

Despite his show of support, Teena felt hopeless. If Roy hadn't tossed the knife outside, where had he put it? Maybe he'd stashed it somewhere inside, during his sprint from the front entrance to the curtain call: under a chair, behind a box, in a trashcan, or something like that.

But no, that didn't feel right. Roy wouldn't randomly throw his would-be murder weapon somewhere a person could accidentally stumble across it. He'd initially hidden it inside an air duct, which Teena had only found by chance.

Teena was certain—the knife was somewhere outside. It had to be. That was the only option.

She recalled another Sherlock Holmes tidbit from her English class. It was a pretty famous quote, along the lines of "when you've eliminated the impossible, whatever remains must be the truth."

Good ole Sherlock was a pro at finding things. He would find the knife in a matter of seconds, no doubt, then deduce the exact store from which it had been bought and what shoes the cashier was wearing. Nothing escaped him. He always uncovered the exact right clues at the exact right time.

Wait… Not always. Not the dog.

Teena focused. Her pulse picked up as she felt she was on the verge of a breakthrough.

Something was in her mind's peripheral vision, but she couldn't tell what it was yet. She forcibly ignored the carolers and let her train of thought keep chugging.

In that one Holmes story, the dog *hadn't* barked. That was how he knew who the culprit was.

The key wasn't what *did* happen.

It was what *didn't*.

Roy had been cutting the rope backstage, then he'd dashed out the back door. That was what happened.

What hadn't happened was any sort of intervention by Simeon. Simeon, who'd been standing by the ropes and pulleys all evening. Simeon, who'd been using the red light of the EXIT sign to read his notes. Simeon, who wasn't backstage at all when Roy was executing his plan.

Teena took a breath. She expected to feel her lungs shake, or her knees tremble, or her head spin. None of that happened. Just as before, when she'd pieced together that Roy was the killer, she felt good. When she had considered whether Jimmy, Evelyn, or any of the others could be the culprit, she'd been extremely conflicted, to the point of nearly fainting.

However, this theory felt right. She could practically see it all playing out before her:

Simeon had been standing by the wall of ropes. The show was near its end, and he was feeling relieved. Things had gone well, and by all measures, the production was a total success.

But, according to the people of Tennant Park, it wasn't Simeon Callahan who was responsible. It was the former director, Roger Marius. The decrepit old geezer who'd run off to Florida with a secret mistress last year.

The name Simeon Callahan wasn't capable of being forgotten…because no one knew it in the first place. As he had lamented to Teena and Corrine before the show, he'd poured his heart and soul into this production of *A Christmas Carol*, and in return, he'd gotten exactly diddly-squat. His show would never be put on the map. It would fade into obscurity, just like the thirty-four previous iterations. It would be as if he'd never even tried.

Then, a figure approached. It was Roy Jennings, holding a knife. Why did he have a weapon?

Roy froze. He hadn't anticipated Simeon being right where he was going to commit his crime. After a year of build-up, was it all going to be ruined?

Simeon considered calling out for help…but he hesitated. He had no idea what Roy was planning to do, but since he had a weapon in his hand and a murderous gleam in his eye, it was sure to be big. And splashy. And scandalous. He could see the headlines now: *"Curtains on A Christmas Carol." "A Dickens of a Murder Rocks Theatrical World." "Bah Hum-Bumped Off."*

That was sure to put his show on the map.

And so, Simeon stepped aside. He gave Roy a clear path to the ropes and an exit. And if the lights turned off during the dastardly deed, that would be one heck of a coincidence. Roy killed whoever he wanted to kill, Simeon technically had nothing to do with it, and the show would be famous. Everybody wins.

Teena knew this was all conjecture. Total speculation. But it fit perfectly. The puzzle was nearly complete. Only one final piece remained: Where was the knife?

Simeon knew the backdoor led outside, where Roy had direct access to the parking lot. He also figured that, after the death of a cast member, Roy might need to escape…so as he walked away from the wall of ropes, he slipped Roy the keys to his car.

Of course, Simeon didn't know the road down Mountain was inaccessible, but Roy did. When Roy ran away from Teena, he knew he needed to ditch the knife as soon as possible. He considered throwing it among the trees, or burying it in the dirt, or tossing it under a car…

Or maybe *in* a car. The best place to hide a needle would be in a haystack surrounded by other haystacks. No one would ever find the weapon in a car that was among a hundred other cars in a parking lot. So while Teena chased him, he zigzagged through the parking lot, looking for

Simeon's car. He found it, unlocked it with Simeon's key, tossed in the knife—and probably the diagram too—and ran inside the theatre.

That was how it all went down. Teena felt it in her bones. If she was right, three things would be true.

One: Roy's footprints in the snow outside would go by Simeon's car, which was a purple sedan.

Two: Inside Simeon's car would be the serrated knife and likely the damning diagram, drawn in Roy's hand.

Three: The car keys in Roy's pocket would belong to Simeon.

Just a few minutes ago, Teena had felt the keys in Roy's trousers pocket as she was patting him down for the knife. He'd even mockingly offered them to her: "*What, do you want my wallet? My car keys?*"

It hadn't struck her as odd in the moment, but now she wondered: Why would he be carrying his car keys in the pocket of his Marley costume?

Answer: Because they were Simeon's keys, given to him backstage.

It all fit.

"On, on they send. On without end, their joyful tone, to every home!"

A beat of silence.

Applause.

The conclusion of the carol snapped Teena out of her mental investigation. She looked around to see dozens upon dozens of people clapping and smiling, but no smile was bigger than Evelyn's. The woman looked on top of the world, as if an entire audience had just given her a standing ovation. And, since everyone in the lobby was standing, they technically had.

Once the musical notes in the air faded out, Teena felt a jolt of panic. She still needed to check if Roy's footprints led by Simeon's purple car in the parking lot, and if the audience mounted a mass exodus now, she wouldn't know for sure.

Evelyn, however, was just getting started. She said to her choir, "Are we feeling okay to keep going?" When they nodded enthusiastically, Evelyn addressed the whole lobby. "Sing along with us!"

After some whispered instructions and a few more hand waves from their musical director, the carolers launched into their next song: "Just hear those sleigh bells jingling, ring-ting-tingling too. Come on, it's lovely weather for a sleigh ride together with you!"

A good number of spectators joined in with the singing, bobbing back and forth. Many of them were families, and the kids were really getting into it. Many, however, shuffled on their tired feet, clearly ready to hit the road. Teena had to get moving.

As she walked toward the theatre's front doors where Bernie was lingering, she spotted Simeon. He stood chatting with some audience members, nursing a hot cocoa. He looked partly relieved, partly disappointed. From his perspective, no one had died, which was a double-edged sword: He hadn't contributed to someone's death, but his show wouldn't be famous. All in all, it could be better, could be worse.

Once Teena exposed the truth and he was indicted as an accomplice to attempted murder, his attitude would probably tilt toward "could be better."

16.

Bernie saw Teena coming toward him, and he walked to meet her. She must've had a determined look on her face, because when they stopped in front of each other, he grinned and said, "What next, detective?"

She couldn't help but return his smile. Excitement fizzed in her stomach, as if she'd chugged an entire bottle of champagne. They were inches away from the finish line—she could feel it. Just a few more boxes to tick.

"Head back outside to check on Roy's footprints."

"You wan' me to get frostbite, huh?"

"No, not at all! This is the last time, I promise."

He chuckled and shook his head. "I'm jus' givin' you a hard time. But I couldn' find a knife anywhere near his tracks. I looked, but…" He held out his empty hands.

"I know you did. Just check one more thing for me: Follow the tracks and see if they go by a purple sedan."

With a cocked brow, he said, "Purple?"

She grimaced. "I agree. But just check."

"What're you gettin' at?"

She opened her mouth, about to fill him in on all the outlandish theories and scenarios she'd cooked up in her head, but she thought twice. "I don't want to influence you. If those tracks really do go by the purple car, it'll confirm what I'm thinking. Besides, it's still snowing, so we need to move fast before the footprints are covered up."

"Aye-aye." He saluted and hopped back out the theatre's door, a dogged sleuth on the hunt. A burst of cold air made her squint, and she savored the piney scent.

Teena tried to tamp down on the sense of jittery anticipation she felt, but it continued to spread throughout her entire body. They were *so close*. After several hours of feeling like she was getting nowhere, they were a few pieces of information away from tying up the whole case with a big red bow. The meal had been cooked — all it needed was a few final garnishes, and it was ready to be served.

That made her stop and gulp. How was she going to present this to Roy and Simeon? Was she going to confront them head-on? It hadn't gone well with Roy the first time. Most of her evidence was, admittedly, conjecture. It would be helpful if they both confessed, but she didn't see that happening anytime soon.

Would they get aggressive? Roy had tried to kill his brother, so it was a distinct possibility. She couldn't imagine Simeon turning violent, but after the day she'd had, anything was possible. Could Bernie take them on, hold them down? She honestly had no idea.

She heard a door open and close, but it wasn't the main entrance. She turned and saw someone coming through the door that led from the green room. Percival had changed out of his Scrooge costume and into his regular clothes…which were actually very Scrooge-like. He hadn't wiped off his stage makeup, and his steps toward the exit were heavy but quick.

He was trying to slip away unnoticed. What was he up to? Did he know something? Percival loved being the star of the show—the fact that he was leaving a crowded lobby was highly suspicious.

Yesterday, Teena would've let him go. And two hours ago, she might have followed him quietly. But now, she yelled at him without hesitation.

"Where're you headed, Percival?"

The old man skittered to a halt, surprised at being detected. He turned, and when he saw it was Teena, his wrinkles deepened. "Leave me alone."

She wasn't about to let him go that easily. "You still have a lot of fans in the lobby."

"Oh please. Don't p-patronize me." Normally, he would have spat that remark at her like a venomous cobra. Instead, he said it softly as he stared at the floor.

She crossed her arms. His attitude was off. He knew something he wasn't letting on. "What are you playing at, Percival?"

"Just let me —"

"Why are you leaving?!" she rumbled with force.

His eyes snapped up to hers as he blurted, "N-No one's here for me!" The bags under his eyes were heavy, as if filled with sand. "There's no p-p-point in me hanging around."

Teena reeled herself back in, feeling embarrassed and ashamed. She had been flying so high on her detective skills, she'd completely misread the situation. Percival wasn't acting suspiciously — he was sad and lonely. He was self-conscious that he had no friends or family to meet him after the show, and he'd wanted to slip out before anyone noticed.

For the past several decades, his wife Rebecca had occasionally attended his performances…but not anymore. And she wasn't simply not there. She'd left him and run off with another man.

And he knew Teena knew this. Everyone else thought Rebecca was dead, so they might look at him with compassion. She knew the truth, so she looked at him with pity, which he clearly hated.

He clasped his hands in front of himself and began rubbing his fingers together. It was a nervous tic she'd never seen him do before. He must be more flustered than usual.

Teena had no love for Percival—not even after working her tail off to save his life—but she felt for him.

"Hang around a bit longer," she said gently. "Listen to the singers, have some cocoa…" She paused, then begrudgingly added, "Hang with me and Corrine, if you'd like."

He responded with a sharp snort. Apparently, he wasn't lonely enough to lower his standards of company.

"Besides," she went on, "I heard the road is a little dangerous right now. You might as well stay inside where it's warm."

"The road?" Percival arched a brow. He hadn't heard anything about Mountain being inaccessible—no one had. "R-Really?"

"Yeah, trust me. Or don't!" She gestured to the exit. "Drive partway down Mountain, see the flashing warning lights, and turn around and come right back here. Up to you."

Percival didn't say anything as he studied the carpet, clenched his jaw, and rubbed his fingers. "Okay," he finally grumbled. "Do you know if they have coffee?"

"Just cocoa, I'm pretty sure." She lightened her tone. "But it's gourmet."

He perked up. "Oh?"

"Nah." She giggled. "Store-bought powder. But close your eyes and I bet it tastes just as good."

Percival muttered under his breath…but the tiniest smile tugged at one corner of his mouth. He unclasped his hands and shuffled back into the crowded lobby, toward the cocoa table.

Now that his hands were exposed, Teena noticed something. A golden glimmer on one of his ring fingers. He'd been nervously rubbing a wedding band on his left hand.

That was unusual… Or was it? Over the past year—since Rebecca had left—Teena hadn't been in close proximity to him when he wasn't in his Scrooge costume. When she saw him in his normal clothes, it was always from afar, like at Crawful o' Waffles. He could've very well been wearing his wedding band for the past year without her noticing.

He was certainly committed to his wife, even if she wasn't committed to him. Teena wasn't one to pass judgments on someone else's marriage, but she found it interesting. Very, very interesting.

Earlier, Percival had told her that Rebecca would return to him someday: "She didn't leave. She's coming back." Whether or not that was actually true, he believed it with his whole heart. He seemed to have no choice but to believe it.

Which made Teena wonder…

She was no legal expert…

But what if…

No, that would be crazy. Delusional.

But what if Percival hadn't removed Rebecca from his will? Given his devotion to her, he likely hadn't signed off on a divorce or legal separation. If they were still technically married, and he hadn't gone through the intensive process of removing her from his will…

Then even if Roy had killed Percival, he wouldn't have inherited his wealth. It would've gone to Rebecca. After going through the trouble of murdering his own brother, Roy would have failed, because Percival couldn't accept the fact that his wife had left him.

She wanted to know if this theory held any water whatsoever. Only two people would know whether or not Percival had removed Rebecca from his will: Percival himself, and his estate-planning attorney, Victor "The Stache" Stassi. She doubted Percival would be open to more probing questions from her about his wife, so that left Victor.

Weaving through the lobby, she thought about what she could say to him. It would be against the law for him to tell her anything about his dealings with a client. But she had a plan.

Victor had a very big and expressive face — hence the countless billboards. If she asked him point-blank, she bet his face would flicker with honesty before he got it under control.

Hopefully.

She saw Victor hanging out with his friends. He had inched closer toward the green room door, indicating he was ready to change out of his costume and head home.

She had one shot at this.

Storming right up to him, she said, "Did Percival write Rebecca out of his will any time in the past year?"

He was caught totally off-guard, and he took half a step back as if she'd shoved him in the chest. His mouth automatically formed the word "No"…but then his rational mind caught up. "Teena," he chuckled, "I can't talk about that kind of thing. Attorney-client privilege, you know?"

It was too late, though. His impulse was to answer no. Odds were that Rebecca was still Percival Jennings's primary beneficiary. At least, that's what Teena was going with.

"Hey." A breathless voice came from behind her.

She turned to find Bernie panting and flushed as if he'd just finished a marathon. As they stepped away from the group of people, she said, "What's wrong? Are you okay?"

He caught his breath. "Oh yeah. I jus' walked in and was about to talk to you when you booked it across the room and o'er to that mustache guy. You looked on a mission. I hadta run to keep up!"

She laughed. "Yeah, I had an idea, and I guess I was a little excited to see if it panned out."

"And? Did it?"

"You first." She leaned in. "Did the footprints…?"

He cracked a triumphant smile. "Went righ' by a purple car. And there was a clumpa footprints by the doors, like the person stood there for a few seconds. I peeked through the win'ows an' saw a buncha copies of today's *Tennant Telegraph*, some em'ty Starbucks cups, and a headlamp like the ones runners use."

She grinned too. "That's Simeon's car alright."

"So what next?"

"Next…" She sized up the lobby. The loud, full, teeming lobby. "We nail him to the wall." In an instant, the occupants of the lobby transformed from random audience members into a full-fledged jury.

Bernie followed her gaze and picked up on what she meant. "I like it."

Teena led Bernie into the heart of the lobby. A whole new wave of nervous thrills bubbled in her gut, as if she was clicking up the first hill of a roller coaster that she wasn't sure she wanted to be on. The show may have been over, but she was about to give the most important performance of her life.

"And in case you didn't hear..." The impromptu choir was finishing up their third song. "Oh by golly, have a holly jolly Christmas this year!" They hit the last note with a flourish, posing back-to-back as if they were in a cheesy Andy Williams TV special. Evelyn had taught them well.

The crowd applauded. As the noise hit its peak and started to die down, that was when Teena interjected.

"Everyone, your attention please!" She barreled on before she could talk herself out of it. Or before her accommodating, don't-rock-the-boat instincts kicked in. "I have something to say. Please, everyone!"

The people closest to her turned to listen, mostly out of curiosity. But the majority of the audience members in the room continued chatting and shooting the breeze, not paying her any attention.

Bernie tapped her shoulder and offered a folding chair. He must've had one stashed nearby for miscellaneous use. He held out a hand, and she grabbed it as she boosted herself up onto the seat. She now stood a head taller than everyone in the room. Bernie stood directly beside her, like she was a judge and he was her bailiff.

"HEY!" She projected as loudly as she could. "Listen up! Everyone, I have something to say!"

One by one, the people in the lobby quieted down. Turned toward her. Listened. Most of the audience members were smiling, thinking this would be along the lines of the caroling that the last announcement had yielded.

But everyone in the cast looked at her with confusion — they'd never heard her use such a firm, bold tone of voice. Corrine's face contained a multitude of emotions: concern, fear, uncertainty…and a hint of pride. She could sense that something big was about to go down, and her best friend was going to be the one making it happen.

"Okay…" she muttered under her breath, then began: "During tonight's production, someone tried to kill Percival Jennings."

A chorus of shocked whispers swept throughout the lobby. Teena could hear some people asking one another if this was part of the show. She also caught a glimpse of Percival standing by himself — he was stunned, frozen, eyes wide.

She went on, "I know it sounds crazy. Believe me, I know. But it's very, very true. That person obviously failed in their murder attempt."

Bernie added, "Because of her!" He cocked a thumb up at Teena. "She stopped him!" Maybe he was less a bailiff and more of a hype-man.

"*We*, Bernie and I, have been working all night to find out the would-be killer's identity and stop that person." She pointed an accusatory finger across the lobby. "Roy Jennings."

More gasps. Even a few small shrieks. The mood of the room had shifted from confusion to dread. No one thought this was a performance anymore. The people standing next to Roy stepped sharply back from him, as if it was just announced that he had the Plague.

Roy, in contrast, didn't move a muscle. He leveled an icy glare straight at Teena.

"An' he had an accomplice," Bernie said.

"Someone turned out the lights during the show's curtain call, when Percival was meant to be killed," Teena explained. "This allowed Roy to slip away from the backstage area and hide the knife he was using to cut one of the stage's sandbags. The sandbag would have fallen onto Percival, breaking his neck or worse."

Percival was getting paler by the second. He had to lean against a wall to keep from totally collapsing.

Someone in the audience shouted, "Who?!" Several voices agreed, needing to know the identity of the accomplice.

Already, Simeon was shifting from foot to foot and sweating profusely.

Teena again pointed from her position above the crowd. "Simeon Callahan."

"Say *what* now? *Me?!*" Simeon clutched his chest, as if grabbing a pearl necklace. He clearly wasn't an actor. "This is just *preposterous*. I can't *believe* it. This is *utterly —*"

Roy finally spoke, cutting off Simeon's pathetic rambling. He used a low, frosty tone, forcing everyone to lean in to hear him. "You have no proof."

"Both of you," Teena said, "empty your pockets."

"Huh?" Simeon had no idea what Teena was getting at.

But Roy did. His glare dripped with poison. He raised his voice and turned hostile, hoping to distract everyone from Teena's demand. "This is stupid. I don't have to do anything. I have nothing to prove."

"Just empty your pockets," she pressed. "Couldn't be simpler. I'm no lawyer, but I don't think it's illegal for me to ask you to do that."

"No."

Bernie said to him, as if offering legal advice, "Y'know, not doing something so easy makes you look real fishy, pal."

Roy barked, "No one asked you, retard."

"HEY!" came an angry squeak. Colton stepped away from his dad's side, as if to confront Roy all by himself. "Don't talk to him like that, you jerk! That's Bernardo! He's an honorary Ninja Turtle!"

Andy also stepped up and yelled, "Yeah! And he's our friend!"

The rest of the Cratchit kids began to hurl their words at Roy in defense of Bernardo. Their parents and friends followed suit. Then the rest of the cast.

In a matter of moments, the entire lobby was shouting their support for Bernie.

Bernie looked twenty feet tall. He smiled and shot thumbs-ups at his little friends.

Meanwhile, Teena and Roy continued their staring contest. From her position standing on the chair, she could finally look down on the tall, lanky Roy. It felt good. She said, just loud enough for him to hear over the roar, "Turn. Out. Your. Pockets."

"*Fine!*" But it was Simeon, not Roy. As the director turned his pockets inside-out, the crowd simmered down, wanting to see what Teena was looking for. Inside Simeon's pants pockets were his wallet, a wrapped mint, his phone, and a few tissues. It was a bit anticlimactic for the audience, but not for Teena. She'd gotten exactly what she wanted.

She said, "Simeon, where are your car keys?"

"Well, they're..." And he finally understood where Teena was going with this. "Ohhhhh shoot."

Roy whipped his deadly scowl from Teena to Simeon. He didn't need to speak in order to convey his message: "*Don't you dare.*"

"Your turn, Roy," she said.

This time, the crowd shouted for him to empty his pockets. A dark realization settled on Roy's face: Teena was in charge here, not him.

Slowly, with malice in every twitch of his muscles, Roy reached into his pocket and pulled out what Teena was looking for: a set of car keys. He jingled them mockingly. "This what you want? Do you need a ride home that badly?"

"Simeon," Teena asked, "are those your keys?"

"I…"

"Don't answer," Roy growled.

From across the lobby, Jimmy said, "They are."

"Yep," Victor agreed. "I've seen him drive that car to and from rehearsals for weeks now. Those are his keys."

Several other voices from cast members corroborated this fact. Roy glared at each of them, but no one wavered or backed down.

Teena went back to addressing the entire room. "Simeon gave Roy those car keys, I assume for a quick getaway. He didn't know that Roy had sabotaged the only road leading to or from this theatre. He tinkered with a few pipes, causing them to burst and freeze the road solid."

The crowd reacted quickly, bellowing in outrage. They hadn't known they were trapped on top of a mountain on the coldest night of the year.

She went on. "When I found Roy in the act of cutting loose the sandbag that would kill Percival, he ran out the back door, circled the building, and found Simeon's car in the parking lot. He used those keys to hide the knife in the car, then ran back inside for the curtain call."

Bernie pointed at Roy, getting in on the accusatory action. "Your footprints lingered at that ugly purple car for a loooong time." His finger trembled in the air, but it clearly wasn't from fear. He was having the time of his life.

"And if we use that key," Teena said, "to unlock that ugly purple car—"

"Oh, come on," Simeon moaned, "it's a good color."

"—we will find a serrated, slightly curved rope knife with Roy Jennings's fingerprints on it."

The crowd *ooh*'d. They were enraptured.

Roy collected his thoughts for a beat. "I bet there would be a lot of fingerprints on this theoretical knife. Not just mine."

"Maybe." Teena shrugged. "Let's find out."

"Psst! Hey, Simeon!" Bernie whispered loudly to Simeon, again offering advice. "Just tell us what happened. Be plain an' honest, and this'll all be a lot easier for you."

Simeon's neck tightened. "Well, I—"

Roy bored holes into the director's skull with his eyes. "Don't. Speak."

Teena said, "Simeon, just tell the truth!"

"He has nothing to tell," Roy snarled without taking his gaze off the director.

"Come on, Simeon!" Markus called out. "Do the right thing!"

Evelyn also hollered, "Tell the truth!"

More and more shouts were lobbed at Simeon from the audience and cast members. Simeon held up his hands and hunkered down as if he was being pelted by snowballs. His eyes darted back and forth, and he ground his teeth together, using all his willpower to keep his confession bottled up. But finally…

"*Okay!*" he screamed. "Okay okay okay! What Teena said is true! I saw Roy with a knife backstage. I… I let him go. And I turned off the lights too."

"And *I* saw Roy trying to kill Percival." Teena couldn't help but smirk. "Putting two and two together, we get a pretty clear picture of what went down tonight. Or, what *almost* went down tonight."

Roy shook his head slowly, then quickly, then frantically. He sneered, "Well, *I* say you're both lying! How about that? You're hanging all of this on the fact that I have Simeon's car keys? That's laughably dumb. Circumstantial. A total coincidence!"

The younger Jennings had apparently shed his charming exterior and was content to show his true colors to all of Tennant Park for the first time. He had the aggressive energy of a leashed junkyard dog, and with his sweaty Marley makeup, he looked truly demonic. There was little doubt that no one in the crowd was on his side.

But he was right. Teena's only proof was circumstantial. A total coincidence. So she activated her backup plan. A final hail-Mary.

"Roy," she said plainly, calmly, looking down on him from up on her chair. "He didn't cut Rebecca out of his will. If you'd killed him, you would've gotten nothing."

The crowd settled into a confused silence. A few people muttered to each other, wondering what she was talking about.

Roy sputtered like an old engine and let out a big, unrestrained laugh. "Are you out of your mind? There's no way that's true. There's no way..."

His laugh tapered off as his mind raced. For the first time, he shot a glance at his older brother. The two locked eyes. Percival began to tremble, and he nervously rubbed his wedding band. Roy saw this, and his jaw fell open.

"There's no way," he bit, trying to speak his truth into existence.

Percival didn't respond...but his lack of response spoke volumes.

"You selfish prick!" Roy exploded and stomped across the lobby toward Percival. He elbowed aside anyone in his way. "You absolute twerp! You kept *her* at the top of your will and not *me*?! I'm your brother, your only frickin' living relative!"

He reached out his claw-like hands to strangle Percival. But Jimmy and his wife bounded over and wrapped their massive biceps around his torso. They were more than capable of holding back the elderly Roy, but that didn't stop him from yelling and swiping at his brother.

"I moved to this stupid little town to help you after she left! And what do you give me in return? *Nothing!*"

Teena didn't think it'd be worthwhile to point out that Roy had only moved in with Percival to kill him. As Roy squawked and screeched, Bernie helped Teena down from the chair, and they hurried across the lobby to Percival's side. The old man was hyperventilating, near the point of collapse. They each held one of his forearms and helped guide him to the folding chair.

But Roy still wasn't done. "If I had succeeded in killing you tonight, no one would have batted an eye. In fact, they would've been glad! No one can stand you! Not even Rebecca! She's in Florida right now, shacking up with Roger Marius, drinking margaritas as far away from you as possible!"

The room had gone silent except for Roy's crazed shouting. And soon, Roy too shut his mouth as he realized why.

He'd just confessed to attempted murder.

In front of a room full of witnesses.

It was over.

An eerie calm descended on the lobby, like the aftermath of a tornado. Debris and wreckage were everywhere, but the storm had passed.

Roy slumped in the Quinns' arms. All of his fight was gone. Simeon too put his face in his hands and wilted to the ground. He sat all alone — no one had to stand guard over him.

Just then, the theatre's front door creaked open. Dozens of eyes swiveled all at once to see who had just showed up.

Three men waddled inside, each wearing heavy-duty winter gear to contend with the icy December night: gloves, coats with hoods, thick pants, and boots. Fat snowflakes sat on their shoulders, and their boots were caked in dirt and slush. The apparent leader of the pack lowered his hood so he could get a good look at the lobby...but he clearly didn't know what exactly he was looking at.

"Umm..." The man cleared his throat. "Hi?"

"Eyyy!" A huge smile split Bernie's face, and he darted across the lobby to embrace the newcomer. "How's it goin', lil bro?"

Teena smiled. This had to be Bernie's brother Tanner from the Tennant Park Police Department. He and the other two men, who were also cops, must've trekked up the frozen road on foot.

"Uhh, good," Tanner said, hugging Bernie back. He again sized up the strange crowd in the theatre lobby. "I just feel like I'm late for a party. Didn't you say something bad was going down?"

"Aw, don't worry 'bout it." Bernie chuckled and waved off his brother's concern. "Detective Fakhoury here has it all figured out."

Teena sheepishly waved. "Hi. I guess that's me."

And just like that, it came to her.

She gasped and shouted, "Doyle! Conan Doyle! Sir Arthur Conan Doyle! Ha, yes!" She pumped a fist in the air…then realized everyone was staring at her. "Sorry, that's been bothering me all night."

17.

The night was calm. Tranquil, like the inside of a snow globe sitting on a shelf, not in any danger of being shaken. As Teena sat alone on the sidewalk outside the theatre, heavy snowflakes fluttered from the sky and landed on her knees. She could see their beautiful, intricate designs before they melted. If only she could capture and frame them all, so she could show them to her class next semester.

She was still wearing her velvet green robe. It was big and comfy, and she didn't feel like taking it off quite yet. She had ditched the holly crown, though—it never stayed on her head just right. The night air was freezing, but it was a nice change from the stifling interior of the theatre. She enjoyed the blast of air-conditioned heat on a cold night as much as the next person, but she'd been cooped up inside with a bunch of people for long enough. She needed to breathe in the pine needles and painfully cold air for a bit.

The white lights on the surrounding tree branches seemed to glow brighter in the cold. Teena took it all in: the ornaments, the tinsel, the overall design. Bernie really had done a great job decorating. He always did, but this year was top-notch.

In the distance, beyond the parking lot, orange work lights flashed from down the road. The city workers should be done clearing away the ice in a few minutes.

It had been an hour or two since Roy had screamed his confession and the three cops had arrived. Bernie and the rest of the lobby had tried to summarize the events for the cops as succinctly as possible...but everyone wanted to add their own details, so it ended up being a saga full of tangents and dead ends. Eventually, Tanner had gotten the gist. When he'd asked Roy and Simeon if it was all true, they'd agreed without protest. They were drained and defeated...and cornered. They had nowhere to run, so they were as cooperative as could be. When Simeon willingly unlocked his car for Tanner to have a look, there it was: the serrated rope knife, buried under a pile of Frappuccino-encrusted cups. The diagram was there too, crumpled up and tossed in among the clutter.

When Tanner had pulled out his cell phone to relay the situation to his superiors, everyone in the lobby suddenly remembered they had phones of their own. They'd immediately begun to text and call everyone they knew, giving updates, telling their loved ones they were okay, or bragging that they'd had a front-row seat to the craziest thing that had ever happened in Tennant Park.

Over time, more cops and city workers had arrived at the theatre on foot, supposedly to restore order and quell any unrest. But everything was peaceful on top of Mountain. Neither Roy nor Simeon were resisting their fates. No one had even gotten hurt, much less killed.

Thanks to Teena.

As she sat by herself in the cold, that realization kept dawning on her again and again. She'd saved Percival's life. She certainly couldn't have done it without Bernie…but she'd played detective and won. Never in her life had she ever imagined she would do something so big. So bold. So heroic.

She inhaled deeply through the nose. It burned, but it felt good. *She* felt good.

Roy's final revelation continued to echo in her mind: Rebecca Jennings had run off to Florida with Roger Marius. *She* was Roger's unknown mistress. That ought to keep the Tennant Park rumor mill running for the rest of time. Or at least a day. Gossip comes and goes quickly in small towns.

And just like that, she understood. The last loose end was tied up. The final question niggling in the back of her mind had an answer.

Why had Percival attempted to bribe Markus into dropping out? The show would have been sabotaged for sure. Everything would go haywire. Reviews would be terrible. People would be ticked at Markus, without a doubt, but most of the blame would be placed at the feet of the new director, Simeon Callahan. Cast members and theatregoers would grumble, "*This never happened under Roger.*"

Roger Marius, the former director whom Percival constantly praised. The man who had stolen Percival's wife.

If Markus had dropped out and the show had been ruined, Percival would've likely led a campaign to bring Roger back from his retirement in Florida.

Along with Rebecca.

Percival had known all along. He'd known his wife had run off with Roger. He must've hated Roger's guts, but he was playing the long game, drumming up nostalgia for the old director so that when Simeon failed, Roger would be brought back. And hopefully, Rebecca would come with him.

"*She's coming back,*" Percival had said. And he'd had a plan to make it happen.

Teena couldn't help but admit it was a solid plan. Devious. Cunning. And sad.

She sighed. Very sad.

Finally, at long last, the mountain road was deemed clear for driving. It was time for everyone to go home.

People trickled out of the theatre and dispersed across the parking lot, leaving crisscrossing trails of footprints behind them. Teena would never look at footprints in the snow the same way again…nor sandbags, purple cars, or *A Christmas Carol*. She chuckled at the thought. Very little had changed tonight, and yet everything had.

Two police cars drove into the parking lot. Neither had their lights flashing. They parked by the theatre's entrance like Ubers waiting to pick up their passengers. A moment later, Tanner, the two other cops, Simeon, and Roy exited the building. Simeon and Roy didn't need to be forcibly escorted or shoved into the cars — they walked of their own accord. Roy, who was typically so energetic and spry, looked much older than his actual age.

As the group walked by, Simeon glanced at Teena. Roy didn't. Teena didn't know what to do, so she waved. A sad smile crossed Simeon's face, and he waved back. Then the five of them got into the two cars, and they drove off.

From a legal standpoint, Teena had no idea what would realistically happen to Roy and Simeon. Prison? House arrest? Hefty fines? She really didn't know. What she knew for a fact was that their days of being welcome in Tennant Park were over. Regardless of their fates, they wouldn't be calling this town their home anymore.

It looked like Simeon would get his wish after all: This whole situation was likely going to be national news. His production of *A Christmas Carol* was going to be remembered for years to come.

The parking lot was now only about half full. Everyone was leaving pretty quickly. Exhaust puffed from car tailpipes, brake lights faded down the road, tires crunched over snow…

Someone sat on the sidewalk next to her. It was Corrine, bundled up in three or four coats. She shivered like a dead leaf on a branch, but she knew Teena liked the cold, so she was there. "Hey," she chattered.

"Hey," Teena said back with a smile.

"So." Corrine cocked a mischievous brow. "You were busy all night sleuthing and solving a murder?"

"Well, the murder hadn't happened yet. But in a nutshell, yeah."

"That's amazing." Corrine bumped Teena's shoulder with her own. "*You're* amazing. You saved a guy's life. Even if it was Percival's—"

"No." Teena gently pushed back. "Not 'even if.' I would want someone to do the same for me, whether or not they liked me. He deserves to live, because I deserve to live, and you deserve to live."

Corrine wrapped an arm around her friend. "And that's why you're the best of us, Miss F." She squeezed, then returned to her huddled cocoon of warmth. "I'm proud of you."

They sat in the quiet as more bodies filed past them. People spread out across the lot, unlocking their cars from far away so that they could jump right in and escape the cold. Occasionally, someone would whisper and look at Teena, but for the most part, everyone made a beeline directly for their cars. They'd had enough excitement for one night.

"But next time," Corrine said, grinning like an overly-competitive kid in a dodgeball game, "count me in."

Teena groaned. "There better not be a next time."

The remaining theatregoers walked out of the building in a clump. Among the crowd was a thin, gray man with thin, gray hair and thin, gray eyes. Percival Jennings. The man himself. He headed for his boxy, vintage car, which was parked in the middle of the lot. Teena hadn't noticed him slip out of the theatre—whether or not he'd done that on purpose, she didn't know.

He got into his car and drove off without giving Teena a glance, a nod, or any sort of acknowledgement. For some reason, she was okay with that. She hadn't done what she did for any kind of thanks or reward.

Another body joined her and Corrine on the sidewalk: Bernie. He buried his hands deep inside his puffy coat. "Geez, I thought I'd spent enough time ou' here followin' footprints." Every syllable was accompanied by a wisp of frost from his mouth.

"You definitely cracked the case, Detective Bernie," Teena said.

He cackled. "Noooooo way. *You* cracked the case, for sure."

She began to downplay herself…but instead, she grinned. "You know what? I did!"

The three of them chortled, their laughter echoing across the mountain. An owl hooted at them from inside the trees, complaining about the noise. Once their laughs faded, they basked in the sounds of a silent night: the chirping crickets, the hum of the electric lights, the air scraping ever-so-slightly across the pine needles. It was lovely.

Only a handful of cars were left in the parking lot. A man wearing a suit and tie exited the theatre, headed for an expensive-looking sedan. Teena recognized him as the head of the theatre's board. A few hours ago, Teena never would have done what she did next:

She yelled after him, "Hey, Mr. Board!"

The man spun around, shocked at being addressed.

"You're going to give Bernie a raise! Got it?"

Bernie gasped and yanked his wool cap down over his face, as if the man wouldn't see him sitting there.

"Uhh…" The man unlocked his car, opened the driver's door, and set one foot inside. "I don't see why not…" He clearly just wanted to get away. Having someone almost get murdered at your theatre was probably a nightmare scenario. He quickly cranked his car's engine and peeled out of the lot.

From under his cap, Bernie muttered, "I hope I don' see him tomorrow."

"You probably won't see *anyone* tomorrow," Corrine said. "I can't imagine the show will continue this year. I heard a crazy rumor about the director and the guy who plays Marley."

This hadn't occurred to Teena. The thirty-fifth annual production of *A Christmas Carol* was over. Her debut as the Ghost of Christmas Present had come and gone. She likely wouldn't see a lot of her castmates until next year's production…if she even auditioned. Would she return to the show?

It also occurred to her that she and Bernie would have to answer a ton of questions for the police tomorrow.

But that was the future. Her realm was the present.

"You know what I want to do right now?" she asked her friends. "I want to get a scramble at Crawful o' Waffles, then go home for a Christmas movie marathon. Care to join?"

Corrine smiled. "You get first pick."

She didn't even have to think. "*Muppet Christmas Carol.*"

"Followed by *It's a Wonderful Life?*" Corrine asked hopefully.

Teena looked to Bernie. "Finish us out strong."

He answered without hesitation too. "*Die Hard.*"

Teena hoisted herself to her feet. "Sounds perfect. Meet you two at Crawful?"

With that, Bernie locked up the theatre, and they all got in their cars. The gentle snowfall was past, leaving layers of white powder on the evergreen branches. It was so picturesque and fairy-tale-like, Teena almost didn't want to leave…but late-night breakfast was calling her name. The last three cars in the parking lot pulled out and left the theatre behind.

When she was halfway down Mountain, Teena realized she was still in her green robe. Everyone in the restaurant was bound to stare at her.

She let out a big, hearty laugh. Let them stare. She was comfortable, and that's what counted.

About the Author

Luke was raised on a steady diet of stories. You can find him with a book constantly in his hand. He is the author of full-length fiction as well as a handful of published short stories. He lives with his wife in Oklahoma City.

Other Titles by
Luke Swanson

Epicenter

Spectators of War

The Other Hamlet Brother

Note from Luke Swanson

Word-of-mouth is crucial for any author to succeed. If you enjoyed *Curtains on A Christmas Carol*, please leave a review online—anywhere you are able. Even if it's just a sentence or two. It would make all the difference and would be very much appreciated.

Thanks!
Luke Swanson

9 781685 133306